What readers are saying about
The Flying Burgowski:

"… a compelling novel that weaves together fantasy elements with the dark, absurd, and sweet aspects of a family's ordinary life. Alcoholism, divorce, and sibling relationships are touched on realistically and often hilariously; everything is seen through a young teen's point-of-view, and her relative innocence keeps the story from veering too far into adult territory for young readers (although adults will be moved too)."
—Miriam Angress, author of *How Water Speaks to Rock*, and other plays

"Gretchen Wing has a natural talent—a very distinctive voice, great timing and a good punch, creative imagery, and a super sense of humor. I absolutely loved the story…a sensitive and imaginative tale of one girl's struggle to deal with the junk she's been handed by life."
—Michelle Isenhoff, author of the *Divided Decade* trilogy, and the *Song of the Mountain* and *Taylor Davis* series

"Bought this book for my 13-year-old daughter, but both my husband and I gulped it down in a few days…Well written in a convincing teen's voice, and fun, despite the background of serious topics."
—Abigail Porter

"So great! The characters are quickly likable, not syrupy, and very relatable. The author authentically addresses topics all preteens, teens, and even adults can relate to. I loved the genuine relationship interactions between the characters in the book in the midst of the "fantasy" parts…Deals with topics of love, relationship hardship, friendship, and family dynamics in an authentic but PG-rated way. ..A definite recommend."
—Lindsey Webster

HEADWINDS

THE FLYING BURGOWSKI
BOOK TWO

Gretchen K. Wing

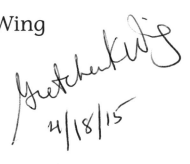

MADRONA
BRANCH
PRESS

HEADWINDS

MADRONA
BRANCH
PRESS

www.GretchenWing.com
info@GretchenWing.com

Book cover and interior design by
Robert Lanphear
www.lanpheardesign.com

Library of Congress Cataloging-in-Publication Data
Wing, Gretchen K.,
Headwinds/The Flying Burgowski
Gretchen K. Wing
ISBN: 978-0-9914213-1-2

Printed in the USA

*To Flyers everywhere—
whatever form they may take.*

ACKNOWLEDGEMENTS

My Lopez Writers, Suzanne Berry, Iris Graville, Kathy Holliday, Rita Larom, Ann Norman, Lorna Reese: Jocelyn's true mentors, if she only knew. And mine—but I do know.

Bonny Becker and her YA Fiction Workshop at the Northwest Institute for Literary Arts Residencies: thank you for the tough love.

Anah-Kate Drahn: yup, those are still your hands on the cover—my eternal thanks.

Virginia Herrick: thank you for being so much more than a copy editor.

Bob Lanphear, book designer: thank you for seeing me through the "this-is-SO-not-my-department" business.

CONTENTS

FOREWORD

Just so you know: this is a disaster story. Oh, not *that* kind of disaster. There's no volcano under Los Angeles, no tidal wave about to slam New York. If you're expecting that kind of story, go turn on your TV. Nothing blows up here, okay? Except my dad.

Most people think of a disaster as something bad that happens. But there's another way to think about it, I found out. A volcano couldn't destroy a town if people hadn't decided to build it there. Tsunamis drown people who choose to live by the ocean. Maybe they had great reasons, maybe they didn't know any better, but still: they put themselves there.

This is that kind of story.

Remember Icarus, the guy who crashed when he flew too close to the sun? He wasn't a real Flyer like me, but he was trying to soar. The lesson from that, Mrs. Mac told us, back in our Mythology unit, is, don't push your limits: you're a human, not a god. And I nodded with the rest of the class, thinking, *Yeah, Icarus got carried away by his power.*

Little did I know, back then, how easy that was.

Little did I know that a real Flyer's threat comes not from the sun, but from below. If I had paid more attention, I might have, you know, looked down while I was flying. Noticed the patterns, seen the threat. I might not have put myself smack in the path of the tsunami.

But when your heart is soaring, down is the last place you want to look.

CHAPTER ONE

RULE NUMBER ONE

I was stuck: the stupid equation wasn't working. I really wanted to call Savannah for help because she gets math faster than me, but she'd been so Queen Savannah lately that I had practically quit speaking to her. Michael was practicing guitar in his room; he could have helped. But if I asked he would say, "Okay...for doubles," which means that I would owe him a flight on a day of his choosing. And I was getting tired of flying with my brother. He makes WAY too much noise, whooping in my ear, which is stupid if you're trying not to be Seen. And taking off is tough. *You* try being fourteen and leaping off a rock with a sixteen year-old guy on your back. Hurts my knees. So no Michael either. And Dad's not great with math; he's more fisherman than store-keeper even though he had to sell his boat before I was born. Plus he hates being distracted when he's making dinner.

So I was doodling some cursive initials on the margins—never mind whose—when the back door slammed open and my More-Annoying-Than-Evil Stepmother rushed into the kitchen.

"Hey, can you help..." Then I noticed her face. Lorraine has a naturally sweet expression, which usually bugs me, but right then it was all tensed up.

"Bethany's in trouble," Lorraine blurted. Lorraine never blurts.

Dad turned his back on his frying onions. "Oh, great. What now?"

"It's okay, Ron, she's not hurt or anything," Lorraine said, patting his arm. "She's stuck up on the roof of Howe's Drugstore.

Reverend Paula was talking my ear off about an Easter display at the library, and, oh my goodness—I *saw* Beth up there, all hunkered down, and...I think Reverend Paula might have seen her too. And I don't see how she can come down without making it worse."

"Dammit," Dad said. That's about as bad as he ever swears. "On the *roof*? You mean she's just frozen up there like a weather vane or something?"

"Flatter than that," said Lorraine, her voice coming down to its normal breathiness. "She was sort of draping herself over the pointy part."

I visualized Mom lounging on the roof the way our cat, Tion, drapes over her shoulders. But it was cold and damp outside—jeez, it was February. This wasn't funny.

"And you think Reverend Paula saw her?"

"Well, maybe not. She didn't say anything, even though we were both facing the same way. But..."

"But what?" Dad demanded.

"...but I'm afraid," Lorraine's voice dropped even lower, "Mr. Howe might have."

This time Dad said some things I'm not comfortable writing here. Mr. Howe happens to be my mom's boss.

"Dad, stove," I warned him, and he rescued the onions before the smoke alarm noticed them.

"Should I go out there? What kind of damage control are you supposed to use when your witchy ex-wife exposes herself to her boss and the minister?"

I couldn't help it. I giggled. Totally inappropriate.

"Not that kind of exposing herself, all right? Jocelyn, we have a real problem here!"

"It's not funny," Lorraine added, all librarianish. "Reverend Paula left, but Mr. Howe's still out there. Just squinting up at the roof like he can't believe his eyes."

"Well, someone needs to go distract him then!" I snapped. *Duh, people—try using your brains instead of treating me like a baby.* "'Cause he'll go and get a flashlight. That's what I'd do. Oh, if he gets a flashlight on her, she'll be so—"

"I'm on it," Dad said, turning to grab his windbreaker from the back of the door.

"Ron, no, it has to look normal," Lorraine said. "Why would you be out there? Maybe if you called him…"

"That's lame," I said. Yeah, it was rude, but they were practically ignoring me! "I'll go. I'll run out there for…for valentines." Dad and Lorraine looked blank. "You know, for our class party this week. It makes sense!" *Yes! A mission to save my mom.* That familiar rush. I yanked my fleece off the hook.

"Wait, Jocelyn, hold up—what are you going to do? You can't just rush out there without a plan."

Hmm. Yeah. "I'll…I'll think of something to get him back inside the store. All Mom needs is a couple minutes to slide off the back, right?"

"And clean herself up," Lorraine nodded, like it was her idea.

"Yes—and I'll sneak around behind to see if she's scraped or anything, see if she can go right to work or if she needs to go home and call in sick."

"Okay," I agreed, because saying "No, you stay here, I want Dad to come" would be asking for it. "I'll talk to Mr. Howe about Tyler. I want to anyway." This was true. I got my fleece halfway on and slipped out the door before Dad could say more than "Joss…"

I ran. Only two blocks or so (we don't exactly have blocks in Dalby Village), but the dampness had turned to drizzle, covering my fleece with fine droplets as I scurried to the drugstore. Thank goodness it was nearly dark. If Mom would only stay put a little longer, not panic and fly off. Or fly straight at Mr. Howe and hope he would convince himself he dreamed it all. *Be cool, Mom.*

Yeah, right.

Howe's was staying open late for Valentine's Week. I hate that week. Everyone at school starts yakking about who's going to give valentines to whom, like we're all in second grade instead of ninth. And ever since my best friend Savannah started "going with" Tyler Howe, it's like I'm banished to Planet Immature with Louis and the rest of the losers. I mean, Louis is my buddy, but who would give a valentine to Louis? He is my only friend who knows I'm a Flyer, 'cause Savannah can't keep a secret for more than two seconds. I REALLY wanted to tell her at first, but now...damn. Savannah makes me feel like, who would give a valentine to me?

People were hurrying into Howe's, I guess to buy candy and cards and little talking M&M's dolls—amazing how that crap shows up even on Dalby Island, where most people eat whole-grain cereal. No one seemed to be looking at the roof ...

... except Mr. Howe. There he was in the parking lot, glasses in hand, rubbing his eyes as he peered into the twilight, muttering to himself. At least the roof was nice and dark, blending in with the sky. Because—*oh jeez*—was that my mom's foot, up on the crest of the roof? I guess she needed to hang it down there for balance, and now, with Mr. Howe watching, she was afraid to pull it back.

No flashlight, anyway. I bounded up to him. "Hey, Mr. Howe. Looking at the stars?" *No, dummy, it's raining.*

Mr. Howe turned his startled jump into a polite nod. "Hello, there..." He obviously didn't know my name. "Got a raccoon up there, or...hmm...I could have sworn...ah, these glasses are useless." Back to the roof went his eyes, his lips moving in soundless concentration.

Time to distract. "Yeah, that's cool. Um, Mr. Howe? I've been wanting to ask you. I'm Jocelyn Burgowski? Tyler's in my class?"

That got his attention. He turned his back on the roof (*yes!*)

and looked me full in the face. Which is kind of intimidating from someone as big as he is. Mr. Howe's even taller than Dad, and a whole lot larger. Now I could see where Tyler gets his size from. Since last year Tyler's grown so much people started calling him The Hulk, which he liked at first, till he noticed they weren't saying it in a nice way. Then Tyler went after the next person who called him that, threatened to kick his ass. I hate when people talk so comic book-y.

That's what I wanted to speak to Mr. Howe about. *Yeah, and the way Tyler feels up Savannah in the back of math class where Ms. Schneider can't see, and Savannah gets all giggly and I hiss at her to shut up, and she says, "Damn, I thought by now people would be mature enough to mind their own business."* Right, Joss, good topic.

"Um, I wanted to..."

Mr. Howe began swiveling toward the roof again, a man with more important things to do than chat with a kid.

"I wanted to invite you," I announced, and added, "sir." Some people like that; I've heard Dad use it on some of the puffed-up Seattle tourists who make a fuss in his store because he doesn't carry something called "gorgonzola."

He turned back around. "Invite? My goodness, Miss Jocelyn, that sounds intriguing." Tyler sure didn't inherit that old-fashioned politeness.

"We're having this, like, Career Day thing? At school? And we're supposed to invite someone who has a job that we find interesting to come and, you know, speak to the class..." I sounded lame even to myself.

But Mr. Howe bit. "Career Day, eh? Funny, Tyler never mentioned this. Well, I suppose he's never shown much interest in his old man's..." He looked at me sharply. "Now wait. Why not ask your dad? He's been running his store a lot longer than I've been running mine. But I'm flattered, of course."

"Yeah, um, I thought Dad's store would be boring," I mumbled. "'Cause he, like, just sells food and toilet paper and stuff, but your store is much more...you know. I like the cards." *Yeah, there you go.* "You really changed the place when you started selling all those cute cards and things that are, like, more normal than the homemade artsy stuff people sell around here, and I like how your store is like a piece of, like, the regular old world in the middle of Dalby Island." *Wow, where did that come from?* I mean, it's true that Howe's would fit right into McClenton, on the mainland where we lived with Mom last year. But I hate thinking about McClenton.

Mr. Howe was looking at me curiously, nose twitching like a giant bunny. I risked a quick glance over his head; Mom's foot had disappeared. "Now aren't you the little consumer analyst," he said, but it sounded like a compliment. "Do you know, that's just what we were shooting for when we opened: giving Dalbians the whole range of free enterprise choices, so they're not limited to hippie craft stores. No offense intended about the hippies." *Does he mean Lorraine? She has that type of hair.* "But to your invitation...well, yes, I would be glad to, if I can fit it into my schedule. I may have to ask..." his eyes widened suddenly, which was pretty intense because they're already big, like Tyler's. "That's right, it's a family affair, isn't it! I may have to ask your mother"—he gave a weird little bow, leaning in and breathing a long sniff through his nose like he was trying to absorb me —"if she can come in early that day. When is this event?"

As I chattered on about not being sure when exactly Career Day was (luckily it really existed, I hadn't just made it up on the spur of the moment), my brain was doing this: *What was up with that bow when he said "your mother?" Did he really see her? And how's Mom going to get in the store if we keep standing out here? Is there a back door she can slip through? What if Mr. Howe asks me straight out why my mom was on his roof?*

He didn't, of course. He kept his big face locked on mine, twitchy nose and all, took me inside so he could write my teacher's name on a sticky-note, and reassured the hottie behind the cash register, "Just a little longer, son, I'm sure Beth's on her way." I was dismissed. Where was Mom? There was nothing to do but say good-bye politely, turn, and go.

"Well, Beth," I heard Mr. Howe say behind me. "Is everything all right?" He didn't sound angry, or sarcastic, only concerned about his employee who was a good half-hour late.

"Sorreee!" My mom's voice sailed across the store, ultra-perky, which for her means ultra-fakey, but Mr. Howe wouldn't know that. "You would not be-leeeve what my cat just did, I didn't think I'd ever get her out of there…"

I didn't stick around to hear how Mom was using Tion as her excuse. I felt too…I don't know what to call it, but my insides were all squiggled up with adrenalin and exasperation, plus anger at being pushed into that situation, even if it had been my idea.

And yeah, I guess, a little bit of admiration for The Flying Burgowski Mother—my special name for her, since she kept our last name. Makes me feel closer, especially since Lorraine doesn't use Burgowski.

More than a little admiration. Flying to work… I would never try that. But it was kind of—no, it was REALLY cool.

Not to Dad, though. His fuse burned for three days, till Mom popped by for breakfast on Valentine's Day.

That's exactly what Mom does: she pops by. It's like rediscovering her Flyer self has handed her some kind of Freedom License that says you don't have to do what normal people do, like call first to see if you're invited in your ex-husband's home, or apologize for disrupting everyone's lives because you were so busy being Free that you forgot to be Careful.

Okay, gotta admit, I stole that Freedom License thing from Dad. It was part of his explosion—the middle part, I think.

We were eating our usual school day breakfasts: me, expired Corn Flakes from our store; Michael, leftover turkey casserole. Dad was drinking coffee and reading the sports pages; Lorraine was prepping the store for opening, behind the curtain where it attaches to our kitchen, before heading off to her library job.

Enter the Flying Burgowski Mother.

If she'd apologized first thing, that might have stopped the fuse right there, even though Dad's grumblings had been increasing with each day that she didn't show up to say sorry, or thanks.

Not Mom. She zipped in, without knocking, of course: "G'morning, sunshines! Who wants to be my valentine?"

Dad, super-icy: "Nice of you to drop by, Beth."

Mom: "Wow, what's up your butt?"

Dad (a.k.a. Mr. Frosty): "Do you even have the slightest idea what you almost got yourself into?"

Mom: "What are you talking about?"

Thinking about it later, I don't think she was deliberately trying to infuriate him like Michael does. I think in Mom's world, she had simply passed by that little difficulty of the drugstore roof, flew right over it, and moved on. Of course Dad didn't get that.

"You selfish little diva," he began, calmly enough, but Michael's face jerked up, and it looked pale. I guess he was old enough when my mom left us to remember the fights that caused that leaving, which I don't, much. "You nearly crapped in the nest, didn't you? Just had to *whoosh* off to work, huh? In the middle of the damn day when about a million damn people are right outside, including your BOSS? What do you think he would do if he saw you? Huh?" His voice rose. "Fired your ass for being a freak, Number One, and Number Two, called the damn media! 'Hey, wow, what great publicity, we have a flying witch right here on Dalby Island, and I'm the big smart dude who discovered her!' You think that internet video was the worst exposure you could get?"

"Oh, for goodness' sake, Ron," my mom said. She had those matching spots of color on her cheeks that Michael and I knew all too well. The curtain at the back of the kitchen twitched as Lorraine stuck her face in, then disappeared. At least it was too early for customers to be hearing this.

"Uh-uh, don't even start!" Dad roared. "We've had enough of your selfish, thoughtless, idiotic behavior, Bethany! You can't always do what you want, just because you can!" I think this is when he said the thing about the Freedom License.

Mom's eyes narrowed, her mouth made to say something, but Dad barreled past. "It's like you're *trying* to get caught. Is that it? Life isn't edgy enough for you on this quiet little isle? You have to make some trouble for yourself? Get yourself back on the internet?"

"Dad," Michael said.

"You and your special powers! What do you magic people think would happen if your special little talent got discovered? What would happen to all of us? Oprah'd be out here in a heartbeat, and all those scuzzy networks and newsrags, hounding us, hounding our neighbors, giving us cute little nicknames like the Flying Burgowskis..."

Luckily I had stopped eating my cereal or I would've choked. Only Mom and I knew about our secret name. It was shocking to hear it from the mouth of this red-faced, quivering firepit who used to be my laid-back dad.

"Dad," Michael repeated, a little louder. Mom leaned against the fridge. Her cheek-spots had faded and she looked tired.

"No, Michael, I'm not done," Dad boomed. "And I won't be done until Beth and Jocelyn accept Rule Number One—in this house, on this island, in this damn state or anywhere they are. Don't. Get. Seen. That's it. That's the whole rule. Think you guys can handle that?"

You guys?! My mouth went too dry with outrage to say anything. I'm *not the one with a flying video out there on the internet!*

Yeah, someone got Mom on video, flying, way back before I was born, and then stuck that clip on YouTube last year for anyone to see. *Dalby Island Ghost?* it's called. Far as we know, no one's paid any attention, but still—someone Saw her, and we still don't know who, and they could still be out there! So she's the one who needs Rule Number One tattooed on the inside of her eyelids. Not me!

*Well, except...*I flashed guiltily to last week, when Louis and I had been flying doubles over at Whittier's Bluff, and we ran into someone at the top of the cliff where we like to swoop. We pretended we'd been up in a tree and just jumped down, but the guy sure looked at us funny, and we were glad he wasn't someone we knew who would start asking questions.

But Dad didn't know about that, so he didn't have to bellow at me. At us. And Mom just stood there and took it.

"Dad!" Michael shouted. We all looked at him.

"Dude, that's enough. She gets it, okay?" His hair's pretty short these days, so you could see his eyes, dark and narrow. And what do you know, he had those cheek-spots like Mom's. Never noticed those before.

Dad was breathing hard from his performance. "Does she?" he grumped.

Mom straightened. "Yes, Ron, she does," she said, with just a little of that rasp in her voice that means emotion. "Rule Number One. Got it. Don't Get Seen. Yup. Think I can manage that. Sorry about the other day." We waited, but she wasn't making any excuses. That's not Mom's way, I'll say that for her.

"How 'bout you, Jocelyn?" Dad In Charge wasn't ready to let it go. "Can you commit to this rule? That means no using your...powers...in daylight, right?" Even two and a half months after learning that his daughter and ex-wife can fly, Dad still had trouble saying the word. "Except in really secluded locations which you've checked out ahead of time. And absolutely never anywhere near the village. And—"

"No whooping," I muttered. Michael shot me a filthy look.

"—no bending the rule by getting yourself in a situation where you 'have to' do it in order to get somewhere on time or something. You never *have to*...fly. The rest of us can't, remember? You can. But you don't have to."

Finally, silence. Mom sat down at the end of the table. I spooned in some cereal, but it was hard to swallow.

Everyone's face was just like a billboard, with one giant message and a smaller one written underneath. Dad's face said "Yup, Made My Point," and underneath: "doubt and worry." Michael: "Life Is So Damn Unfair." And: "you go, Mom." My mom's face has always been harder to read, but I thought I saw this: "Huh, Go Figure." But that was all.

I wonder what my face said. Because I was thinking, *Don't lump me in with her. I may not be all "mature" like Savannah, but when it comes to flying, I'm the grownup. And: yuh-huh—sometimes you do have to fly.*

CHAPTER TWO

HOW WAS YOUR DAY?

That delightful breakfast pretty much set the tone for the rest of Valentine's Day.

But maybe you're confused about Flyers.

We're magic, kind of. I know I'm not supposed to say "kind of" in writing, but this time it's true! It is a *kind of* magic. The kind that makes you fly—duh. But also the kind that you can't always summon when you want it. Or resist when you need to. I had some problems with the summoning part, back when I was adjusting to my new power. Mom's problem is the resisting—can you tell? Resisting stuff has always been an issue with her, and it's like flying is just another substance for her to abuse. Not me, though—I'm in control. So it was totally unfair of Dad to yell at both of us.

I know, okay? How can a grown woman fly across the village with the teensiest hope that no one will look above the nearest fir tree and see her freestyling along up there? (Mom flies like a swimmer. I prefer Superman-style.)

You'd be surprised. When I first started flying last summer, I was shocked at how much I could get away with. Even in a place full of bald eagles and herons and float-planes, people don't look up very often.

But still—flying to work? What was she thinking?

Life had been going pretty well up to that point. Yeah, Mom had tried to kill herself around Thanksgiving, back in McClenton, and don't think I'm some sort of monster for being able to come out and say it that way, okay? Of course it's hard to deal with, but it doesn't get any easier by pretending it didn't happen. Turns out that bottling up your flying powers for years, trying to be a normal wife and mom, can mess you up pretty bad. By the time she'd quit trying, she'd found other ways to fly, namely alcohol and pills. Anyway, Dad went and rescued his ex-wife, and she was so out of it she didn't even mind being rescued by the guy she had ditched when I was five. He brought her back here to Dalby Island, safe and sound, three hours (including the ferry ride) and a universe away from McClenton, Washington.

And then a kind of—no, a real miracle happened. Mom got better. She went back into therapy and joined AA for her addictions. She got a job, right after New Year's, that pays her insurance and everything, at Howe's Drugstore.

Hold up—my pillhead mom working in a *drug*store? But it's not like that. When Mr. Howe moved to Dalby a few years ago he turned the old pharmacy into sort of a card shop. Not trading cards and Pokémon, I mean the stuff with matching envelopes. Stationery. So Mom sells those, and candy, and wrapping paper, and for a few weeks it seemed to be calming her right down, like she'd started believing the sayings inside those stupid cards. *"I'm just here to say / That you make my day / Each and every way."* Hey, I bet I could get a job writing that stuff.

So why did Dad have to lay down the Flying Law? That was Michael's fault. My brother kept egging Mom on, and Mom doesn't stand up well to egging.

Okay, I did my share too. It was so cool, seeing my skinny little mom come to life again when she got herself back up into the air after all those years! Her therapist doesn't know about the flying, of course, but Mom says she encourages "getting back to the parts of myself which make me happy," and then I say, "C'mon, Mom, let's go fly together, you're the Flying Burgowski

Mother," and she does, and it's amazing, and then Michael goes, "Hey, yeah, me too," and I fly him piggyback like we've learned how to do, with Mom flying alongside, and of course it's SO awesome, being practically in a flock like that, that I want to keep doing it forever.

Not Mom, though. She'd rather fly alone. We first flew together around Christmas, then every day for a glorious two weeks. Then in January she dropped off—only a couple of flights a week. "I'm getting old and stiff, Joss. I'll cramp your style. You go on out there and fly on your own." Mom's, like, thirty-six.

"Nuh-uh, I like being in a flock with you!"

She laughed her scratchy laugh. Mom appreciates my descriptions. But she shook her head. "Not this time, babe." Or any time since a whole month ago. She made it look like she was practically retired.

And then she ends up stuck on the roof of Howe's Drugstore and gets us both screamed at.

The rest of the day went downhill from there, starting with Savannah's mom picking us up for school.

You try carpooling with someone you're not speaking to. Our teachers used to joke that Savannah Enderle and I were "joined at the hip," we were so close—kind of funny since we look so different, stick-person Joss and Wonder Woman Savannah, but that's how we were. Carpool, lunch, every single class, carpool again—then home to one of our houses, together. But these days Savannah leaves the front seat open so I get to sit there answering her mom's questions, while she sits in back with Michael, dropping hints about what she and Tyler do together. By the time we got to school, I felt like a nine-year-old.

Didn't help that first period is math. I don't hate math, okay? I mean, I'm not one of those dumb girls who "don't get it" and send Ms. Schneider into a lecture on You Girls Are Creating Your Own Negative Stereotypes. It's just not my favorite—all this right-or-wrong, black-or-white neatness. There's no wiggle room like there is with words.

Someone had passed out chocolate hearts and kids were stuffing them into their mouths before class started, because Ms. Schneider's one of the strict ones. Tyler had managed to gather a double handful, which he tried to stuff down the front of Savannah's shirt when she went to give him a perky little nose-kiss. She giggled her head off, up and down the music scale like she does. Made me want to throw up.

"Happy V.D., Hamburger," Nate Cowper said. Of course he was sitting with Tyler the Jerk. How can anyone like someone who likes someone like that?

"Get your feet off my chair," I snapped.

"Whoa, somebody took the Burger to McDonald's and got her an Unhappy Meal," Nate sighed, shaking his head. His hair's only blond in the summer; now it was kind of dark gold.

"There's no McDonald's on Dalby, idiot," was my lame reply. I hate that stupid Burger nickname. Tyler started it when he first moved here in fourth grade, and of course it stuck: Burgowski Burger, Hamburger, or just Burger for short. I sat down and turned my back.

But then Ms. Schneider started rattling through morning announcements and handing out our worksheets. The goat pen! I had forgotten we were starting the design today. We ninth graders had fund-raised to buy a pair of pregnant goats to take care of and study and write about. But before they arrived, we had to build their pen, which meant figuring out how much wood to buy. Boom: math, science, and Language Arts, all in one goaty package. As much as I hated McClenton High, that's how much I love my tiny little weird Dalby School.

Today, though, it found a way to get to me. Ms. Schneider put us in groups of three to work out our calculations, and she put me and Savannah together. Either she hadn't noticed us glaring at each other, or she thought this would fix it. And she threw poor old Molly in with us as a buffer.

"So, length times width…that's, like, fourteen times twenty-one, right?" Molly started her equation in her horrible handwriting. Savannah had slid her chair to the far end of our table, hanging her arms behind her so Tyler could draw on them.

"Nuh-uh, don't forget, the part which attaches to the shed is, like, five feet shorter, right? So we have to do two different length times width thingies," I explained.

Savannah examined her arm, where Tyler had drawn something that looked a lot like boobs. "I think, when the baby goats are born? We should name them Paris and Avril," she announced to the ceiling.

"Why?" asked Molly.

"Sophistication, dahling," Savannah said, batting her eyelashes. She's been wearing a ton of mascara lately. "Our goats gonna bring some class to da house, y'all, knawmean?" Suddenly she was all ghetto.

"Since when do you talk that way?" I said. "And those names aren't sophisticated, they're ridiculous."

"Oh, yeah, you would know, right? 'Cause you're so much more sophisticated than the rest of us."

"At least I don't have boobs on my arm."

"What, this?" Savannah extended her arm like an ice skater. "FYI, this is a picture of the tattoo Ty's gonna get. I would tell you where, but I'm not sure you're ready to hear that."

"Wow, you're sophisticated all right," I snarked. Behind us, Tyler and Nate were snorting, enjoying the show.

I reminded myself: she's been jealous ever since I got to live on the mainland last year. Even though I kept telling her how horrible McClenton was. Jealous, that's all. Then she tilted her head back so her hair was practically in Tyler's lap, closed her eyes and ignored me, and I wanted to slap her sophisticated face.

"Hey, you guys. Are we gonna do this problem?" Molly asked plaintively.

"Yeah," I said, shutting out Savannah. "What do we got so far?"

"Um...two hundred and ninety-four?" Molly looked up hopefully as Ms. Schneider breezed over.

"How you doing, girls? Let's see how you're working it."

Suddenly Savannah tossed her hair and leaned back to our table. "No, look, Molly, here's what you do," she said, like she was the teacher. She began zipping Molly through the problem, Molly nodding with grateful understanding. Not me. I was too busy feeling pissed. Ms. Schneider gave me a little half-smile and moved on to the boys behind us.

Some BFF. I started doodling cubes on my scratch paper, nice dark ones, while Molly and Savannah became the first in the class to summon Ms. Schneider and tell her exactly how much wood to buy. Ms. Schneider was in the middle of praising their Teamwork when someone kicked my chair.

I turned around, ready to throw my pencil at Tyler, and saw Nate's face...or rather, mine, which I guess he thought he was imitating. I do *not* pout my lip out when I'm mad, but that's what Nate was doing, and I had to clench my jaw to keep from smiling. Just because it looked so stupid.

"Mm, what's that smell?" his lips whispered. "Burger got burned."

Two parts of me felt suddenly warm. My face, duh, because someone else noticing is what really burns, right? The other warm part was down by my stomach. Something about the shape of Nate's lips when they made the word "burger"...

"Shut up, Cow-pie," I whispered back, clenching away.

He leaned across his table, looking up at me through his eyelashes. I bet he knows how long they are. "Here," he said, and stuck something down the back of my sweatshirt.

I scrabbled my fingers, trying to pull whatever-it-was from behind my bra strap. *Feels like…a piece of paper…and…*My stomach glowed. *It's one of those foil-wrapped hearts…from Nate!*

It was. Taped onto the back of some red construction paper. *Ohjeezohjeez.* Totally first-grade-y, but totally adorable. *Is this really happening? Nate Cowper?* I swept it into my lap so no one else would see.

Another kick to my chair. I leaned my chin in my hand before turning around so Nate wouldn't see how red I was.

Good thing. 'Cause I got even redder when he hissed at me, "Don't give it to her till lunch, okay?"

And that's when I pulled the valentine out of my lap, turned it over, and saw the sticky-note which said: "Give to Savannah, k?"

Maybe it only felt like everyone was looking at me. I snatched the thing back into my lap, but not before I caught Savannah's eye. She didn't need me to pass on that valentine. She already knew. And my BFF looked sorry for me.

My stomach squinched into a cold lump of humiliation. I walked as slowly as I could to Language Arts, studying the floor tiles.

And now…Mr. Evans. Wonderful.

I used to live for Language Arts. Okay, there was that horrible time living with Mom in McClenton, when I started ninth grade with Mrs.—yay, I've forgotten her name. But before that, here on Dalby, I had wonderful Mrs. Mac for eighth grade, who's doing really well with her chemo, by the way, and starting an amazing hat collection. She would write stuff on my papers like, "Considering blah blah blah, this makes a lot of sense!" as though you were having a conversation with her. I loved that, I loved her, and she loved me. She never said so, but she was always extra sarcastic with me, so I could tell. She was the one who convinced me what a terrific writer I was.

Amazing how fast I've gone from terrific to sucky. At least in Mr. Evans's opinion. In the three months I've been in his class, the nicest comment I've had on any margin was: "yes." More often it's something like, "Pare this down," as if my sentence was a potato. The worst one had come just yesterday, on my Emily Dickinson paper. I was really proud of it. In the conclusion I wrote, "Emily was a gentle flower whose petals were too easily crushed by the world." Mrs. Mac would have written, "☺!!!!" Mr. Evans's pen said, "You don't know the lady, so she's Miss Dickinson. And watch the purple prose." I thought that was a compliment, but when I showed it to Lorraine, she winced. Turns out you can actually make the word "purple" an insult.

So, Language Arts. Blech. At least Nate didn't have this class. *Oh jeez, Nate and Savannah.* Was she trying to lure him in by hanging out with Tyler, or did she enjoy torturing him? Did she have any clue how I felt, or did she enjoy torturing *me*? I sat as far away as I could.

"Morning, folks," Mr. Evans said briskly. He says everything briskly. He also hates it when we write too many –ly words like briskly. Briskly, briskly, briskly. Hah. "Shall we?"

No we shall not, my brain said, but I can't help it, I've been too well brought up not to sit up straight when a teacher says that.

"So now that we've bid a fond farewell to our poetic pals, it's time to focus on our Goat Unit. I've searched high and low for some good literature on goats, and you would not believe how inappropriate some of it can be." He paused for us to chuckle. I wasn't playing. "So what we're going to do instead is focus on the whole do-it-yourself thing, the whole back-to-nature, let's-build-our-own-goatpen-from-scratch-and-drink-fresh-goatmilk-with-our-homemade-cornbread movement, which is as American as that baseball and apple pie everyone's always talking about."

A moment of confused silence. "You mean hippies?" Greta ventured.

"Like Molly's parents?" someone added.

"Hey," said Molly, but she looked flattered.

"Yes and no," said Mr. Evans. He rested his hands on his muffin-top, enjoying his moment. *Why not just go ahead and assign us an essay so you can tell us how stupid we are?* "What you think of as hippies did not invent the whole back-to-the-land, flower-power idea. They simply rediscovered some writers and thinkers from over a hundred years earlier who had these radical notions. And I do mean radical."

"Like, that's *rad*, dude," Tyler said goofily. Goofily, goofily, goofily.

"Exactly. These were some radical dudes. You might, perhaps, have heard of them—I'm sure some of your parents have. Their names were Henry David Thoreau and Ralph Waldo Emerson. And..."

"Waldo?"

"Hey, Where's Waldo?"

"He's gone back to nature, maaaan."

He lost the class on that one for a few minutes. Served him right. But then he passed out some papers with that big "I Noticed" section he always has, and made us watch a dumb movie clip about a crazy teacher, and the stupid class went along like sheep. What did any of this have to do with Language Arts? Lorraine was going to wince again when I told her.

When we were Sharing our "I Noticeds," I noticed Mr. Evans looking at me like he expected me to Share. *Sorry, you'll have to pick on someone else.* I looked away.

Then he got all dramatic and wrote this word on the board: **TRANSCENDENTALISM.**

"Whoa. WAY too many syllables," Savannah said.

Molly asked, "Do you want us to write that down?"

"Not only do I want you to write it down, Molly, I want you to say it out loud. Repeat after me..." I kept my mouth shut. "I want you to know what it means. I want you to know who the Transcendentalists were, what they believed in, and how they put those beliefs into action and writing. I want you to see how they influenced our definition of our American selves. And when we're done, I want you to tell me about it in the essay to end all essays."

The class groaned, but it was a kind of let's-all-play-along groan. That did it. I raised my hand.

"Jocelyn?"

"Yeah, why don't you go ahead and give us our essay grades now so we don't have to waste our time writing 'em?"

Mr. Evans's bushy gray eyebrows popped up over his big black glasses, but he didn't say anything. I stared back grimly. Molly gave an uncertain giggle.

"C'mon, Joss," came Savannah's voice behind me. "Aren't you kind of looking forward to doing some college-level stuff? Poetry Projects are so freshman, right?" She sounded like her mom, all encouraging.

"We *are* freshmen," I muttered, aware that Savannah had maneuvered me into sounding immature again.

"That's enough, ladies," said Mr. Evans, and I'll give him credit for Noticing that we were having a much more serious fight than it probably sounded. "Jocelyn, let's discuss that essay after class. For now..."

I don't remember much about the reading he gave us. Something about a guy who climbed a tree in a windstorm to see what the tree felt like. Whatever. When your brain keeps repeating *Unfair, unfair, unfair*, there's not much room for anything else.

Suddenly everyone was packing up, so it must have been break time. We don't have bells at Dalby School, a fact I didn't realize was special until I got to McClenton High last fall and jumped a mile when the first bell went off.

"So my comments have been getting to you, is that it?" Mr.

Evans was hovering behind me, like he thought I might try to sneak out of the room. "I feared as much," he added.

Suddenly my eyes were burning and it became very important not to talk.

"Jocelyn, you have to understand something," Mr. Evans said, resting his pudgy corduroy butt on the edge of my table. "The comments I write to you, I would not write to…just anyone in the class. You're at a level where you are, let's say, ready to make the leap with your writing. So when I see you still dwelling in the land of the average, I'm going to tell you so. I'm going to push you until you are no longer satisfied with writing the same old way you have always written."

"I used to be a good writer," I managed, but my voice didn't sound right.

"A good fourteen-year-old writer, yes. Those comments I'm writing, they're for the next writer in you, the one who's a good bit older than fourteen. If I'm really hurting your feelings, fine, I'll back off. But what I'm attempting to say is, you should take my critique as a compliment to your potential. Do you feel like that makes sense?"

What I felt was more humiliated than ever, and hungry for the peanut butter cookies I'd packed. So I nodded, and he let me go, probably thinking, *Yup, handled that one skillfully, didn't I?* But I was thinking, *Yeah, I want to be taken seriously, but why does complimenting my potential have to feel so mean?*

Louis was waiting for me. He's a year behind me, still in Middle School, but we all have the same breaks, and he doesn't have a lot of friends to break with. Well, any friends, except me. I could never figure it out, he seems like exactly the kind of person you'd want as a friend, always noticing if something's wrong, always there for you, but for some reason he drives people nuts and they want to pick on him.

Or snap at him. I didn't mean to. But when he asked me where

I'd been and I told him about Mr. Evans's lecture, he finger-combed his bright red hair backward till it stood up. "Huh," he said.

"Huh what? Huh, Evans is a jerk?"

"No, that just made me think of something Mrs. Mac said yesterday. She was talking about..." he paused, his little blue eyes wide.

"What?"

"...about the difference between Critique and Criticism. She said one's positive and the other's negative, but it's kinda easy to lump 'em together if you're too sensitive."

"Oh, so I'm too sensitive? Wow, thanks."

Louis blushed. "No, I mean, I was just putting together what she said with what you said about Mr. Evans, and...I mean, I know you like Mrs. Mac, so I thought..."

"Yeah, I heard you. Whatever."

"Don't be mad," he pleaded, crinkling his eyes up like he was about to get hit, and suddenly I understood all those people who chose not to be friends with Louis Cleary. God, he was annoying—not understanding when his only friend was upset, then getting all flustered trying to make things better. What a baby. Even Nate was more mature than that. My stomach clenched again.

"Why would I be mad?" I shrugged, and snatched up my pack. The little foil-wrapped heart I was supposed to give Savannah fell out of the hole at the bottom and I stepped on it. Savannah didn't need another heart.

During PE was when the flying urge kicked in.

It's a hard feeling to explain, but I'll try to show my "potential," or whatever, and describe it. It starts with tiny engines revving up, right in the spot where your ribs drop off. A little whirring feeling. This can go on for hours without me noticing, but when stuff happens and I start feeling super stressed or super happy, it flares up like all the tiny pilots just stomped on their little throttles (or whatever you do to throttles). That makes my whole chest vibrate. If I ignore it too long, the energy starts buzzing down into my legs. Then, yeah, it can get a little scary. I came awfully close to flying not-on-purpose in McClenton, but it's all been good since I came back to Dalby.

Now—yikes. When I ditched Louis, I felt the flare below my ribs. PE nearly sent me down the runway.

We were doing soccer drills, which I am great at. Weaving through the little cones, stopping, backing up, passing to the next person—I missed that stuff. McClenton girls were too mean for me to join their team last fall. The grass smelled great, since the weather had turned strangely nice for February, like Valentine's Day really counted for something. *Hah.* The weak sun tried to warm my back, but it took the soccer ball to loosen the knot in my stomach. *Boof*—that's your lame valentine, Nate. *Boof*—that's Savannah's "oh-poor-Joss" expression. *Boof boof*—there goes Mr. Evans and his Critique. *Boof boof boof*—okay, I should probably apologize to Louis...

On my second go-round of the drill, I *boofed* a sweet pass to Molly, and I heard Tyler say, "Nice one, Burger," from the next line over. He was just making sure I could see he'd switched from my line to Savannah's like she probably told him to, and was standing behind her with his hands who knows where. She was mashing her butt into him in the way that gets school dances cancelled.

Whatever—him and his nasty tattoo. I rolled my arms in big circles, staying loose, and that's when I saw Nate. Halfway down the next line over, he was looking at Tyler and Savannah with an expression that made all the flying-fuel pour down into my legs. *Schoooom.* I sat my butt on the ground to keep from taking off right there. Then my line of teammates started yelling at me and I had to excuse myself to the bathroom.

Through social studies, science, and art, I sat on myself. Literally. This is what you do when you need, need, NEED to fly: you

cross one leg over the other—whichever leg is least twitchy—
and you push down on it with your elbow. Yup—just like when
you need to pee. It helps to pretend your arm is an iron stake
attaching you to the ground.

I nearly lost it in science, when the sperm diagrams in our
Goat Biology Unit got the immature kids giggling. I opened my
mouth to say, "Oh, act your age, not your shoe size," but Savannah said it first, and I saw Nate flash her another one of those
looks. *Wouldn't matter if I'd said it, he'd never look at me like that.*
His stupid valentine letter was still in my backpack, minus the
chocolate. *I have to give it to Savannah.* That thought made my
right foot quaver right off the ground.

So I sat on myself and waited for art class. No Nate. And Ms.
Vaughn was letting us have a party. Maybe I could work off my
flight-energy eating junk food.

I can get pretty excited about chips and soda and Oreos. Ever
since Lorraine moved in last fall, Dad's been super healthy, like
he's afraid she'll dump him if she finds out we used to get Pop-
Tarts for breakfast. So when I saw the wall of cookies and Dori-
tos lining the pottery shelf in the art room, I gave Savannah her
valentine before I started hating her again.

She didn't even open it. Just looked at me, sad and far away,
from Planet Mature Where Joss Does Not Live. "I'm sorry, okay?
For reals. Nate's crazy. He doesn't even know what love is."

I grabbed at a stool to keep myself grounded. *Oh, like you do?
You're only half a year older than me!* "Who cares?" I tried shrugging.
"Jeez, Savannah, it's not like everybody needs a guy to make
them feel good about themselves."

"Uh-huh." She unscrewed her Oreo and licked it.

"What's that supposed to mean?" I snapped. My arms were
tingling right down to my fingers.

She cast me a teensy glance, I guess to show No Hard Feelings. "Don't get me wrong, Joss. Ever since you came back to the

island, it's like, I don't know…like you were in a time capsule or something. And some of us kinda, like, moved on, I guess, while you were gone. But you don't have to be rude about it."

Moved on? I can FLY! What gives you the right to act so superior? Here I had been feeling guilty because, yeah, I haven't breathed a word about flying, not for eight months. It does kind of rip a hole in a friendship if one person gets supernatural powers and doesn't bother to tell the other person. And turns out she's been feeling sorry for me! I loaded my plate with treats in silence.

"So? You mad at me?" Savannah said, smiling, as we sat down with Greta and Heather.

"Wow, are you two finally gonna quit bitching at each other? That'd be nice," Heather said, stuffing Cheetos into her mouth.

"Yes," said Joss, and the two best friends hugged and cried and told each other they were sorry, and then they went home and the magic one showed the non-magic one how she could fly, and took her up in the air, and she was totally amazed and felt bad for calling her old friend immature, and they all lived happily ever after.

Or not. It might have happened like that. But my stomach was too tight to accept all that glorious junk food, and my engines were revving on high from Queen Savannah's expression. So I shrugged again.

Her smile disappeared. "Really, Joss?"

I kept the shrug going in my face while my legs quivered under the table. "I dunno."

Savannah said, "Well, excuse ME for trying to be sensitive about this situation."

"Oh jeez, here we go again," said Greta.

"Oh, you guys…" Heather started, looking distressed, but Savannah cut right through.

"Y'all see what I mean? You try to talk to her and…"

Then I really did get immature. "'Y'all'?" I mocked. "Now

she's going all ghetto again. Hey, wassup, Dawgs? We just be chillin' over here where e'rybody be actin' like Jocelyn's a baby, yo."

How did she always manage to turn me into a stupid little kid? *No wonder that valentine wasn't meant for me.* A wave of flying-steam pulsed through me so hard I felt my butt lift from my seat. I gripped the table and closed my eyes, forcing my body down, but I could still hear Savannah rolling her eyes.

Gotta get some distraction. "Ms. Vaughn?" I called. "Is it okay if I start my coil pot?"

Our art teacher straightened up from picking crushed chips off the floor. "Sure, go ahead! I'm glad to see that someone in the class is more tempted by art than by calories!"

She should have saved her enthusiasm. It wasn't artistic inspiration that dug my fingernails into the cold clay, rolling it so hard it broke and I had to redo the coil twice. And even when I got it going, laying over itself like bad thoughts going round and round, my pot still came out like crap. Like the whole day.

Yeah, I kept myself on the ground. But my arms ached from being iron stakes, and I felt shaken to think how close I'd come to losing control. *Wouldn't that show Savannah? I've "moved on" beyond your wildest dreams! And Nate's too. Oh, just get me home…*

I made it through carpool with Carolyn Enderle asking her usual How-was-your-day questions. In the backseat, Michael told Savannah about getting his driving permit, and she acted so impressed I could barely keep from saying, "Yeah, you're a real grown-up!" That, or flying out the window. But I managed, and walked across my yard with every muscle clenched.

"Hey," said Michael, stopping me at the door.

"What?" I needed to GET INTO THE SKY.

"So it's a really nice day."

"Yeah," I said. *Oh, jeez.* I knew what was coming.

"So…whaddya say? Take me up?"

"You have Drivers' Ed. Thought you were getting your permit today."

"Not for another forty-five minutes. We'd have time, if we went right now and quit talking about it."

I felt trapped. *Not doubles, not now. I can't handle it.* But I'd been putting Michael off so much lately, how could I tell him that this time I really meant it? "I'm too tired."

"What?" Of course he didn't believe me. "You're never too tired to fly. Come on, just for a few minutes."

"I just don't feel like it."

"I'll help you with your math."

"I don't need help," I lied. *Fly, fly, FLY.* "I said I was tired, okay? Why can't people leave me alone?" And with that I stomped into the house, and then I really was trapped.

Michael knew I was full of it, and he kept his door open, which he never does, just to keep tabs on me. So when I couldn't stand the chest-whirring anymore, when I couldn't concentrate enough to reread Harry Potter Book Six, when I finally gave in and tried to sneak out the back, it hadn't been quite forty-five minutes. And Michael, putting on his jacket and heading out to Drivers' Ed, gave me the nastiest stare as I grabbed the back door, like: *"Forget being Seen—I see you, little liar."*

That was the last rev my inner engines could take. I barely made it out of the kitchen.

CHAPTER THREE

CHILLED OUT

"GAAAAHHH!" I'm pretty sure that's the noise that ripped out of my throat when I dived straight up from the back steps and into the air.

Usually I have to take a running start. Well, usually I'm smart enough to walk to the edge of the woods where I have some cover, and not fly right out of my house where anyone coming into the Quik-Stop Convenience Store could see me from the other side. But USUALLY I'm not a human missile whose fuse has been burning since seven in the morning.

Oh, wow. Oh, wow. The air made way for my body like someone had dipped me in silky lotion. In that first burst of speed I was already over The Toad, the old giant rock-hump that was my very first launch-pad, way last summer. All my muscles celebrated. I wasn't just flying, I was *flying*.

Whoops, a pasture—I banked hard left. Lucky for me, Dalby Island is more woods than fields. Skimming the tops of the fir trees is easy, no one can see past the first row, and if they do catch a glimpse of me, well, I'm probably just a golden eagle—they're awfully big. So I was circling low in the February sun: big, slow loops like making a coil-pot.

I switched my brain to Silent mode so nothing would interfere with the feel of the air, oh, and the smell of it. The air smells a bit like lilies. Only Flyers know this—and, yeah, super smart librarians named Lorraine who do a lot of research—but in February, on Dalby, it also smelled like the first hint of spring, like earthworms, or those tiny shoots pushing their blind way through the dirt on those sped-up nature shows. I flew and I breathed.

But after about a gazillion circles, I started getting cold. And I guess that woke my brain up.

What if Savannah likes him back? it wanted to know. *What if she figures out Nate's the one she wants after all? What if that was her whole plan?* So much for Silent mode.

Nate Cowper. Not even all that hot, it's just those eyelashes…and yeah, his lips. A wave of shame pulsed through me as I remembered my excitement at that chocolate heart. *What an idiot.* But Savannah said last summer that he liked me. *Her way of being nice. Why would he pick me, anyway? Savannah's way prettier, Greta has all that beautiful, shiny, hair, not dull and brown like mine. Even Heather has those big ol' boobs.* But he was so cool when I got back from McClenton, he talked to me like a regular person for almost a week. *Yeah, and he makes you give a valentine to his buddy's girlfriend.* Now it was my brain doing the circles.

"Shoulda put a jacket on," I muttered, tucking my hands inside my sweatshirt sleeves. It was February, sun or no sun, and the chilly air flowed down my neck. The smart thing would be to fly home and wrap my hands around a cup of cocoa. *Nope,* my brain said: *Better idea. Let's fly out to the Spit.* Where Nate lives.

"This is ridiculous. I'm cold," I argued with myself. But I kept flying, following tree-clumps, hovering carefully before crossing a road to see whether a car was coming. Being a good little Flyer, like Daddy said. "What am I gonna do, fly by and peek in his window?" *'Course not, that'd be dumb. I'm just going to…go over there.* "What if he's outside?" *Then, duh, I'll fly home.*

Hmm, running out of trees. The sun was lowering, but there was still way too much bright sky. *Maybe just hover here at the edge of the beach and look across…*

Suddenly my breath stopped. *There he is!* A golden-headed figure, heading across the lawn toward the road. *Don't look up, don't look up*....No, false alarm. It's his dad.

A blush burned right through my cold cheeks. *I am the Flying Burgowski. I am NOT wasting my time getting my stomach scratched by a fir tree while spying on a stupid boy.* I turned and flew for home without bothering to check if someone was coming down Harbor Hill, and saw a car swerve sharply into the opposite lane. *Great, and now I'm getting Seen.* An extra burst of speed got me safely back above the woods, but my legs were quivering with cold.

Is this what happens to Mom? I wondered, heading for the village. She lets herself fly, and then loses control like a dog off the leash? *Well, she should fly with me. I hold onto my own leash, I am totally in con—*

Holy shih tzu. Savannah and Nate. Right there on the back steps of the marina store.

So much for control. I flailed hard to stop myself from flying over the gravelly lot where a bunch of boats are parked. And where Savannah apparently hangs out with boys she's not going out with.

Couldn't tell that from the way they were sitting. Thigh to thigh, at least that's what it looked like from two hundred feet away and a hundred feet up, through treetops. Did Nate have his arm around her? The light was bad, it was definitely getting late... I should just cut back over the trees and head home.

So of course that's what I did. NOT.

Savannah's hands were free, I could see them dancing in front of her like they do when she's excited about something, and I could hear her musical voice playing up and down, but I couldn't make out the words.

This isn't the first time I've caught my bestie out with my...with Nate Cowper. That flight last summer—Nate had almost Seen me in that orchard! It was Mom's favorite of my Flying stories. But nothing had happened, right? Nate liked *me*, Savannah had said, and she was going out with Tyler Howe, that big, nasty, pot-smoking... *Whoa.* Now Nate was standing up to face her. Were they having an argument? If only I could hear!

Thought you weren't going to spy on boys anymore, Magic Girl, my brain sneered. "Shut up," I whispered to myself. There was a clump of trees on the other side of the parking lot, a whole bunch closer, if I could just...

"No way!" cried Savannah, jumping up and grabbing Nate's hands. Yup, she definitely did that. And Nate started leaning forward, and I suddenly knew I did not want to see what was coming next. So I turned tail in the air and flew home as fast as I could.

Which was not real fast. It wasn't just the cold, though my whole body was vibrating in the air by this time. *You pathetic idiot, you actually thought that valentine was for you.*

I didn't crash, okay? Just kind of stumbled into the scratchy grass at the edge of the woods and staggered back to my house. It was nearly dark. And we were out of cocoa.

"Why don't I get some from Ron?" Lorraine asked, but she waited by the oven, her hands in mitts that looked like roosters. I guess when your stepdaughter pulls away from your "Oh, my goodness," and your attempts to rub her freezing shoulders, you don't go rushing into the next helpful thing.

"'Salright, I'll get it," I mumbled, and went to grab an afghan from the living room couch to drape over myself.

Lorraine hadn't needed to ask me where I'd been, of course. She knows way more about Flyers than I do, even more than Mom, and she can smell the lily-scent of flying on our skin. Or, in Mom's case, the sour lack-of-flying from all those years she tried not to. 'Course right now any moron could see I'd been out doing *some*thing in the February air.

I shuffled in my afghan across the kitchen to the store-curtain as Lorraine opened the oven. A hot wave of cornbread-smell followed me into the back of the store.

"Mmm!" Dad must have smelled it too. Perched on his stool, he turned from his newspaper to smile at me. "Ah, makes all those years of tuna casserole seem like a bad dream, huh?"

"Uh-huh." Tuna casserole was our little joke, a symbol of Dad's attempt to keep us feeling whole and well-fed and forgetting that our mom had ever walked out on us. I'm not being poetic, he really did make it once a week for about eight years. But I felt too numb to play along. "Can I get some cocoa?"

He looked at me more closely. "You look frozen. Have you been...?" His eyebrows lowered. "It's only just now turned dark, Jocelyn. I thought you promised you would not do that during daylight."

"It's okay," I grumbled, feeling like Michael. "I didn't, like, go anywhere." I found the cocoa on the little baking goods aisle and brought it over, avoiding his eyes.

Dad said something that sounded like "Hmph," and just in case I didn't get the message, he added, "Forget driving. *This* is what they should give permits for." But he was talking to himself, ringing up my cocoa and putting money from his pocket into the register. I was going to make a cup and take it back to my room and let the smell of dinner make him and Lorraine forget to ask me more questions. Then I'd do my homework and go to bed and get up next morning and do the whole thing over again, except the part about flying until you turn into an ice cube and your best friend...*yeah, we'll skip that part.* I hitched my afghan tighter, muttered, "Thanks," and was headed back to the curtain when the store's front door banged open.

"You have to promise you won't think I'm crazy," announced a high, nasal voice, "and then I'll tell you what I just saw."

"Hello, Reverend," Dad said politely. He stays neutral on Reverend Paula, when Lorraine says she wishes she weren't so pushy. That's the worst thing I've ever heard Lorraine say about anyone, but Dad says he figures ministers have to be that way. "What did you see?"

"So I'm driving down the Harbor Road hill, heading into town for some gas and my humble groceries, and I look up, and I see…"

I froze. Probably should've zipped on out of there, but I found myself as captivated as Dad.

"See what, Rev?" She was shaking her head as though whatever she had seen was stuck in there. Her tight gray curls didn't move; she must use a lot of hairspray.

"You haven't promised me yet," Rev. Paula said playfully, but then continued before Dad could promise. "I swear I am not crazy, but I am pretty darn sure I saw…a person…leap across the road. Above my car. *Way* above."

Oh jeez. That swerving white car. I had forgotten all about it.

Dad laughed—a very forced laugh. He's a horrible actor. When I was nine I saw him in a Community Theater play about a smart butler, and even then I could tell. "Gosh, Rev," he was saying, "good thing I know you don't drink or I'd have to tell you to lay off the sauce." See what I mean? I had to come to his rescue.

"Oh, hey, Reverend Paula. Over on the big hill? Yeah, I saw something there too…last week! I swear it looked like a…a monkey or something. You know what I think it was?" *Yeah, what, Smart Magic Girl? Go ahead, throw her off your trail.*

Dad and the reverend waited.

"I think it might have been a condor! Aren't they, like, releasing them into the wild and stuff? They're really big…" I trailed off. *Wow. So that's what you come up with? What Nate said when he almost Saw you in the orchard last year? Brilliant.*

Reverend Paula considered. "Well, I don't know. Aren't they desert birds? I never heard of any condors in the Santa Inez Islands. It certainly was big, though. And it had—"

"Joss could be right," Dad said firmly, nodding way too much. "Or more likely a heron. Don't you think? I mean…how would a person get way up in the air like that?" He laughed again, heartily.

"It *was* way up," the Rev said. With her eyes narrowed, she looked like a sharp old hen. "Higher than a person could get. Was yours that way too, Jocelyn?"

I nodded. "Yup. That's how come I figured it was, you know, a bird. And then I told my science teacher about it, and he was going to look it up, but he forgot." Wow, was lying to a minister worse than regular lying? What if it wasn't *your* minister?

"Well, you are undoubtedly right," sighed Reverend Paula, "and I am undoubtedly hungry, which is why I stopped by to pick up a can of tomatoes for my soup. Really, though, I just had to tell someone who would listen. Mr. Howe at the gas station just laughed at me."

"Oh, so you told Mr. Howe, huh?" Dad smiled, but he shot a sideways glare at me. "Anybody else on the island think you're crazy now?"

"No, just you and your lovely daughter. It's nice to see you, Jocelyn. Say hello to Savannah for me, will you? Tell her we miss her. The church seems to be running out of young people these days…"

Their talk dribbled into Boring Mode as Dad helped her ring up her soup ingredients and I made my escape. I needed to think about cocoa and nothing else.

Didn't help much. By the time Lorraine called me to set the table, the cold was still lingering in my hands and feet, I hadn't done any homework, and Dad had had a whole thirty minutes to work up his next lecture.

Wasn't my fault about the homework. I needed to kind of hover over my cocoa to get warm, and of course I didn't want to spill it on my social studies book. So I went back to Harry Potter Six, the part where Harry and Ginny finally get together. I love that part. Book Seven was due out in July, so I knew I'd get it as a late birthday present. Ever since Book Four, Savannah and I used to take turns reading chapters out loud to each other. *Yeah, that little tradition may be about to die off.* Ginny was giving Harry a "blazing look." I was trying that out on my own face when Lorraine called me.

"Way, way, WAY too close." Dad's lecture started before he had even pushed through the curtain, and it kept going as he held out his bowl to Lorraine for lentil soup. "Broad daylight, across the road, as though we'd never even talked about exactly that scenario. If *she* Saw you, who else did, huh? And she told Mr. Howe! Now what's *he* going to think? And who else will she tell?"

"She believed you about the heron thing." I had planned just to sit there and let Dad wash his temper out on me, but suddenly I didn't feel like it. "Why would she tell anybody else? She just said she didn't want people to think she's crazy."

"She's a *minister*, Jocelyn. What if she decides to make her little sighting the subject of next week's sermon? Believing the unbelievable? What if she decides she saw an angel, fer-crying-out-loud?"

I would have said that was stupid, but Number One, Louis's Mom's old boyfriend had once said exactly that after he Saw me, and Number Two, backtalking Dad didn't seem like a good idea right now.

"Wait a minute," Lorraine interrupted slowly, which sounds impossible, but that's what she does. "Are you talking about Reverend Paula? *She* saw you flying?"

"Yes, didn't you hear her back there?" Dad jerked his chin toward the curtain. "I'm surprised the whole town didn't hear her. We're just lucky no one else was in the store when she came in and announced that my daughter had flown right over her car."

Wow. Totally unfair and ridiculous. "She did NOT say it was me! And I wasn't 'right over' her, she said WAY ABOVE."

"Reverend Paula." Lorraine stared hard into her soup, which seemed to remind her that Dad and I hadn't eaten a bite yet. "Hey, don't let the cornbread get cold." She nudged it toward

Dad, which stopped him from launching Lecture 2.0. *Hey, thanks, Lorraine.* But then she kept going. "Reverend Paula was there when Beth got herself trapped, you know. So that makes twice that she's seen a Flyer, even if she didn't know what she was seeing. And if she told Mr. Howe, that's almost twice for him too."

Thanks, Lorraine.

"Which is exactly my point!" Dad didn't even wait to swallow his cornbread, so, yeah, *see-food. Gross.* "Every time you or your mother breaks the Rule, the one single Rule that you both agreed to, someone else gets in on the little secret. How many sightings will it take till some of these people realize they're not crazy after all? How long till one of them notifies the media? They'll get hold of that old video of your mom, analyze it…you watch!"

"I've only been Seen once," I muttered, and even if this was not true, well, Dad didn't know about the others so it wasn't fair of him to assume. But I was spared his next attack by my brother, of all people.

"Kneel before me," Michael declared as the back door banged open. He was waving a small, official-looking paper. "I have passed."

It's only your permit, dork, I wanted to say, *you still can't drive without an adult.* But I was grateful for the interruption.

"Oh, well done," Lorraine smiled, so maybe she was glad too. Dad had to do that face-rearranging thing grownups hate to do when they have a good Parenting Moment going.

"Proud of you, son," he managed, bobbing his head. Guess he hasn't had too many chances to praise Michael over the last year, so he's a little out of practice. "Come on and have some dinner."

So we actually got to talk about other stuff for a good ten minutes or so, like the gruesome crash stories Michael's driving instructor shared with the class. Michael seemed to have forgotten he was pissed at me for flying without him. The lentil soup chased out the last bits of cold from my stomach, and Lorraine's cornbread was amazing. But then Michael had to go and say this word...

"...grounded. By his grandma! Grounded for three months."

Dad turned to me, his eyebrows going up. "Ah, yes. This brings me back to the evening's paramount subject." Damn, I hate when he starts talking that way. "Jocelyn, the point I was working toward when we were so—" he nodded at Michael—"pleasantly interrupted, is this: you're grounded. Not in the traditional sense," he added quickly as we gaped at him, but I knew exactly what he meant. "I laid down the Rule. You broke it, what? The very next day? Therefore: grounded. No more...flying. For a month."

"Whoa," Michael breathed. Seeing me get in trouble for a change must've been like dessert to him. Me—so many emotions struggled to get out of my mouth, I was suddenly breathless.

Dad hesitated a moment, not quite able to believe he had won so easily, then gave a satisfied nod and helped himself to more cornbread.

"Ron," Lorraine said, "if I may...I don't think it's quite as simple as that."

"Of course not!" I burst out, ready to flood the table with all the reasons Dad was being ridiculous. Mrs. Mac taught me how to Craft an Argument, okay, and I'm really good at it, but sometimes you just have to rush on in there like a firefighter. *No flying? For a* month? "You never said that's what would happen, you just said there was a rule, so that's not fair. And I only got Seen once! Mom's roof thing doesn't count for me! And Reverend Paula didn't even know it was me! And—"

"That's not what I meant," Lorraine put in, giving me an odd little smile. She turned to Dad, who stopped chewing. "Flyers have to fly, Ron. You can't keep their power from them. We've seen what happens when that occurs, and it's extremely...unhealthy."

Dad looked stony. "That was different. I never kept Bethany from flying. That was her choice. Don't put that on me."

Suddenly this was not just my argument. Michael and I looked at each other. His eyes were wide.

"No, no, of course not," Lorraine said gently, but I could hear steel underneath the tissue paper of her voice. "Beth made her situation worse by inflicting the punishment on herself, being her own jailer, so to speak. In some ways I think she's still at risk of that, even though she's acting so free now." Michael's eyes narrowed; he usually defends Mom, I guess because she's the only one who screws up more than him. "But Beth isn't the only example. I've been doing more research on the topic of harnessing powers, controlling them. I've been reading some books...I wish you and Joss would take a look at them. They're ancient, they're hard to read, but I think they would help you understand..."

"I don't care about other examples! Jocelyn's a child. And I'm her parent. So how could 'harnessing' her be wrong? Kids need harnessing! It's called discipline." Dad's face was getting pinker. *Uh-oh. Here's the part where he mentions that these are his children, thank you very much, and what does she know about parenting?* Suddenly I wasn't sure whose side I was on.

"Yes, honey. But not just any child. This power in her is real, she can't control it—"

Excuse me, Ms. Know-it-all? I anchored myself all day!

"—and if we force her to try, we may inflict real damage." Lorraine the Librarian was smart, using "we" to sound less accusing.

"What are you talking about?" Dad snorted. "'Damage?' Lorraine, look at the damage she may have already done to herself, and to us fer-crying-out-loud, by being Seen! What harm can possibly come from telling her to keep her little butt firmly on the ground for a few weeks to avoid becoming a freak?"

All the soup-warmth was sucked out of me. I stared at Dad. *Is that what you think I am?*

"Oh, maybe we should finish this conversation later," Lorraine said, sounding distressed. I could feel her glancing between me and Dad. "I'm sorry, Ron, I should have…but when you said… oh, it's just so complicated." *Ya think*?

"Right." Dad tightened his lips. "Sure. Later." He pushed away from the table. "I'll be in the living room watching basketball if anyone needs me, *later*." Wow, hadn't ever heard him use that tone with Lorraine. He stalked out.

I could feel Lorraine looking at me, but I kept my eyes firmly on my empty bowl. The squeak-and-roar of a basketball game came on in the living room.

"Is there any dessert?" Michael finally said.

"Yes," sighed Lorraine, and left us.

Wow. Their first fight, and I caused it. I had absolutely NO idea how I felt about that.

Michael found the tin of Valentine's cookies and plopped it by my elbow. "Have a good flight?" he said nastily. So he hadn't forgotten. Now even my dessert stomach clenched up.

What a perfect Valentine's Day. I went into my room, ignored my homework and read Harry Potter until I got sleepy. But as soon as I turned out my light and closed my eyes, I saw Savannah jumping up, Nate moving in closer…I turned my light on and read some more.

Before I became a Flyer, reading Harry helped me have flying dreams. They were awesome—though not as awesome as real flying, of course. But now that I can do the real thing, those dreams don't come anymore.

I lay awake for a long time, missing them.

CHAPTER FOUR

WIND ONE, JOSS ZERO

"C'mon, Joss, you're wasting perfectly decent weather!" Michael started in next morning, low-voiced so Dad wouldn't hear through the store curtain. Lorraine was already at work; Saturday's busy at the library. "Don't give me any more of that 'I'm too tired' crap. You weren't too tired to go and fly in front of half the island last night, right? Yeah, okay, it was just one person," he added quickly. But then he tried guilt. "How would you feel if you couldn't do this amazing thing and you just had to sit around and watch someone else do it all the time?"

Yup, that stung. "You don't just sit around. I've taken you up tons of times."

"Not for two whole weeks! The last time we went flying was February First. I remember 'cause I…I'm writing a song about it." Michael looked like he hadn't meant to let that slip out, but he couldn't have picked a better argument if he'd tried. Wow, my brother writing a song about flying with me?

But I knew I shouldn't take the bait. Michael lives for trouble; there's no way I could follow Rule Number One with him on my back. "It's been raining, so that's not my fault. And yesterday I just had to be alone, okay? And it's hard to fly with you, Michael, you're heavy, you make my knees hurt! Plus it's totally windy today." Spraying arguments out of a firehose might have worked with Dad. But Michael? Hah. His flight-desire just burned hotter. We were working ourselves toward the yelling-in-whispers stage when Louis walked in through the curtain the way he always does, grinning his squinched-up grin, and distracted us with his gimongous stash of on-sale Valentine's candy.

"This is just from the grocery store, Joss, we should go to Howe's and see what they have fifty percent off!" Louis urged as we wildly unwrapped half a bag of Reese's cups in red and pink foil. Chocolate may not taste any better when it's all dressed up, but it does when it's on sale! Even Michael joined our feeding frenzy, and I let him 'cause it got him off the topic of flying. For a while, anyhow.

"Oh yeah," Louis said, stuffing three Reese's in his mouth, "thish your valentine, Josh. Fergot-ta-tell-you."

"And thish ijj yerjj," I imitated, mashing another one into his disgustingly sticky mouth. But I really hadn't got him anything. And I hadn't even apologized for being a jerk yesterday.

"Oh, gross, I'm outta here," Michael said. But he stopped at the door. "So Joss, how 'bout later? I mean, if you keep pigging out like this you can't be too worried about getting off the ground, right?"

I was not going there, not with Louis looking at us. "Later, sure, whatever," I said, and Michael nodded and left. What else could I say? But my chocolate-happiness started to drain away.

"So you and Michael are gonna—"

"Maybe," I frowned. Great, now Louis was going to start bugging me. But he just nodded and unwrapped another Reese's. That boy can eat.

"I got a couple nice ones," he said a moment later. "Valentines. We had a party in Mrs. Mac's, and she had everybody write something about—"

"Mrs. Mac let you have a party? She never let us!"

"—three other people, kind of like Secret Santa, and then she checked 'em to make sure they were Appropriate. And mine were cool. Elana, Becky, and Erin. Erin said she liked my smile." He showed the smile that Erin liked, all chocolate-smeared. Then he asked, "So'd you get any nice ones?"

"Hah. Right." *Wow, Louis, thanks so much for sharing your happy day and opening up mine.*

"Why, what happened? Was Savannah being a, you know?" I get that Louis doesn't like Savannah because she's snotty to him, but it was none of his business what she said, or what Nate did, or what they might have done together.

"Savannah's fine," I said forcefully. "We had a party too, in Ms. Vaughn's. I'm just pissed because..." *Nope, did not want to go there.* "...because Mrs. Mac never let us have one, and she let you guys. That's just wrong."

"Well, she probably thought Tyler and Nate wouldn't be Appropriate." *And she'd sure be right about that,* I thought, but I really, really wanted out of this topic.

"C'mon," I said, pushing away from the table. "Howe's is open. Let's go get some more chocolate."

The wind blew away some of my grouch on the way over. *Poor ol' Dad,* I thought—this was one of those mornings when he would be pining for his old fishing days, before the bank took his boat away: full of fresh life, the world getting aired out. But then I forgot all about Dad. It was impossible not to feel cheery with the sun glaring off the harbor and people carrying blooming things out of the garden store.

Mom was behind the Howe's counter, looking reasonably fresh for the Not-A-Morning-Person she always describes herself as. She greeted us with a casual wave. Even though I was still a teensy bit mad at her for the getting-trapped-on-the-roof thing, (after refusing to fly with me! Okay, more than a teensy bit) I felt a little rush of pride at seeing her by the register, all normal like any other working mom.

Whoa. The hottie I'd seen there last time was in the candy aisle, repricing and moving all the red and pink stuff to make way for the next color wave: pastels for Easter. He stood up when we entered his territory, and I thought, *Wow, tall,* and then, closer up, *WOW.* I know this sounds cheesy, but he looked like a magazine cover, all blond and, you know, manly. Never saw anyone like that on Dalby—or anywhere else, for that matter.

"See, told you, Joss—fifty percent!" Louis crowed. He can be such a little kid sometimes. Imagine getting that excited over candy. I suddenly felt embarrassed by our mission.

"These ones are seventy-five, or they will be as soon as I tag 'em," the hot guy said, indicating those nasty little hearts with words on them—honestly, who eats those?

"No, those are nasty, we just want chocolate," Louis said without looking up. I wanted to kick him.

"Thanks, though," I said. *Oh, wow, we must look like total pigs.* "We're getting these to share with our class," I mentioned. I could feel Louis turn to stare at me, but so what? We might do just that.

"Oh, yeah?" Hot Guy kneeled down again and started slapping on stickers with a little plastic gun. His hair was cut short in back and I could see where his shoulder muscles sort of flowed under his collar. "My cousin in your class?"

"C'mon, Joss, I got all mine," Louis said, and I swear he sounded whiny. But this whole chocolate thing was his idea, and then I heard Mom call, "Hey, you two, save some for the rest of the island!" and even though I knew she was kidding, I felt even more embarrassed. So I just said, "Um, yeah," even though I had no idea if that was true.

Suddenly Hot Guy sat back on his heels and looked at me. "Hey, you're Beth's daughter, right?" I never saw golden eyes before! Seriously. "She's a crazy lady," he said, like it was a huge compliment. "So did you learn at a young age never to talk to her before she's had her morning coffee?"

"Oh, she…we don't live together," I babbled. "She, like, lives in my Dad's wife's old house…I mean his new wife. She just moved back here…my mom, I mean."

But Hottie just kept those eyes on me and nodded, so I added, "See ya," and headed for the cash register like a dork.

"Woo-hoo. Can I come to your party?" Mom sang out as she rang up Louis, then me.

"Shhh," I hissed, slapping down my allowance money. "It's not like these are all for us."

"Yuh-huh," Louis started, but Mom was now looking at me with that mischievous grin that Michael gets from her. *Uh-oh.*

She said, "Ahhh, I see. Met the boss's nephew, have we?"

"Shhhh!" Hottie was only about thirty feet away. The store's not that big. I was ready to join Louis and head on out of there before she said something really loud, when her words sunk in. "Mr. Howe's nephew? So that guy is Tyler's…"

"Cousin, yup," Mom nodded. She was enjoying herself. Louis looked revolted. "Just moved here from Seattle. Very industrious kid. Shall I introduce you?"

"No!" Jeez, he was probably hearing every word. "We don't care, okay? We just wanted the stuff on sale. C'mon, Louis," I added as though he was the one holding me up.

"Don't forget your change, ma'am," Mom called playfully, and I snarked back, "I'm not old enough to be a ma'am, unlike some people."

I apologized later, okay? But she should have been more sensitive.

"Let's go to your house, I don't want to deal with Michael."

"'Kay," said Louis, and he was probably thinking, Great, more candy for us. All I could think was, *That guy? Cousins with Tyler the Gangsta-Wannabe Jerk? But he seemed so nice.* "Can't believe that guy is cousins with Tyler, he seemed pretty nice," Louis added, making me feel guilty about him as well as Mom.

Louis isn't really such a baby, I reminded myself. *He's a lot smarter than he looks. And by the way, he happens to be pretty much your only friend right now, so you might as well start being nicer to him.* "I know, right?" I started on my new resolution as we walked through the village to where Louis and his mom, Shasta , live with their goats, and Shasta's latest boyfriend. "Well, maybe he gets it from his uncle. Mr. Howe's cool."

"Really?" Louis sounded exactly like this word from our last vocab. list in Language Arts: skeptical.

"Yeah, really. I even, like, invited him for Career Day. He's going to be my speaker."

Louis stopped in the middle of the street. This is not a problem in Dalby Village in February, even on a Saturday. There's no Farmers Market, no tourists. "You *what*? Seriously? Why?"

"Why not?" I shrugged, still walking, but then: *Nicer to Louis, remember?* "He's not at all like Tyler," I explained. "He's polite, and, uh, interesting, and, duh, he's a good businessman, right? Oh, and he has a great vocabulary." *And he's probably going to be totally boring, but too late now—he's invited.*

Louis followed me across the street, shaking his head.

"Why do you even care? You're not in my class."

"Yuh-huh, they're doing it different this year, 'member? Middle and upper school together. We get to sign up to go hear different speakers and stuff."

Oh yeah, I had forgotten. "Well, just don't sign up for Mr. Howe then."

Louis glanced at me. "Yeah."

"What?"

"Well. I thought we were gonna get to go to the same speakers that day. You know. Since you're not in any of my classes any more."

Wow. I really am a bad friend. Here Louis had probably been looking forward to spending a whole school day with me like in the old days, and I'd invited the one person guaranteed to make the day of Louis's worst enemy—if someone who calls you "Fag" all the time is an enemy. More like a nightmare. Usually Louis manages to stay away from Tyler, but if Mr. Howe was guest-speaking, Tyler would be there all right, puffing himself up worse than ever.

"Oh," was all I could think of to say. Outside Louis's house, some crocuses were blooming on the damp little lawn, looking ridiculously tender and hopeful on this wintry day. A guy in a denim jacket stopped to admire them. "Sorry. I don't think…"

Whoa. That's Hot Guy. What's he doing out here? On a break from Howe's? A bright flash of a face—hair and eyes and shining teeth—then he hitched his jacket collar higher and strode off toward the bike shop next to Louis's.

"What?"

"Sorry," I repeated, coming back to Louis. "Umm…I don't think Mr. Howe'll be very interesting, anyway."

"That's okay," Louis said, his response to everything. Suddenly it wasn't okay with me. I couldn't un-invite Mr. Howe, but there was something I could do to make it up to my friend.

"Hey. Know what? Let's go flying."

"What, now?" His little face blazed—so that's what it looks like!

"Yes, now. Let's dump this stuff and go. You done with your chores?" Louis milks their two goats and cleans the pen behind their house.

"Yeah! Lemme just tell Mom we're going, like, out." If Louis told Shasta he was going "out" at three in the morning, she'd be fine with it, but he still likes to tell. It's kind of cute.

The wind grabbed the back door and slammed it against the side of their house as we entered—it's really more of a shack, built onto the side of the Food Co-op, but it's cozy—and I briefly wondered if flying in this weather was the best idea. But there was Shasta in jeans and a UW sweatshirt, and she was giving me a hug like she always does, and introducing me to someone, "Janice, my new roommate." Huh, so maybe she was done with live-in boyfriends for a while. Janice looked like she might be part Japanese or something, with short, chopped-off hair, sharp cheekbones and sparkly brown eyes, and she shook my hand in a firm, grown-up way. Louis was so excited about flying that I got the giggles watching him tell his mother we were going for a walk, and watching Janice wonder what's wrong with this kid who gets so hyped up about walking. So I pretty much forgot about the wind and just felt happy.

"Oh, you guys," Shasta said when she saw our loot. She doesn't "do" candy, which is why Louis is so crazy about it, but I knew she wasn't mean enough to toss it out while we were gone. Louis's house smells like candles and oatmeal and peppermint—good, old-fashioned smells—and the giggles warmed me up. The Flying Burgowski was going to fly with her friend. All would be well.

I know, I know. Rule Number One. Lorraine had kept Dad from grounding me, but if I was going to fly in broad daylight, the least I could do was hide a little.

So we went to the Toad. Our old rock is about as secluded as Dalby gets, and even though I'd made the mistake once of showing it to Savannah, who'd shared it with Guess Who, I hadn't seen them out there since way last fall. Too far to walk when all you want to do is get high or do whatever Tyler and Savannah do on their "dates." Yuck. It's not real close to the village, but I didn't feel like going back for my bike. Plus, the walk felt good after all that chocolate. *Maybe it'll give me more energy in the air.* As we pushed through the prickly scrub of the shortcut, the wind tried to blow us back to the village and I thought, *I'm gonna need it.*

And I did. Three fast takeoff steps off the spongy lichen, and the next thing I knew the air was being sucked out of my lungs and the wind was trying to flip me. Us. *Whoa, whoa, whoa.* Louis gave a little scream, not a whoop but real fear as the sky opened above us and I flailed like crazy. The aerodynamics of doubles is completely different.

"Help me flail!" I shouted at Louis, or tried to, but he was choking me. Even if he heard, he'd have no idea what I meant. When had I bothered to give him flight lessons? Lesson Number One was going to be Choking the Flyer Doesn't Help Her Fly.

Fir branches whacked my legs and I kicked up, getting some height, which is better than crashing, but up here was the wind's home territory. No nice "*Whssshhh*" this flight; it roared and ripped, clawing its way up my pant legs. It spun us like Tion with her catnip ball. Probably it took only a few seconds, but it felt like forever as I used all my chocolate-fuel to pull Louis's arms off my neck with one hand, while still flapping the other and kicking my legs like a drowning person. Must have looked ridiculous, but it worked. I got us leveled out at last, and did a couple of slow circles above the Toad, finding the right height for avoiding the worst punches of the wind and still staying safely out of the trees.

Louis had stopped screaming after that one little burst, but he was still panting in my ear.

"You okay?" It's hard to see a person who's piggyback, especially when you need to keep your eyes out for waving treetops.

"Yeah," he puffed. "Did you...did you do that on purpose?"

Man, you gotta love Louis. Here I'm trying not to let us crash and he thinks I'm just showing off my flying skills. I wanted to hug him for having such confidence in me, but I just patted his leg—then quickly got my arm back out, airplane-style. I needed every bit of balance I could find. "Ah, not exactly," I told him. "And if you could, like, twine your arms under mine and hold them out, that would...Yeah. Much better. Thanks." Louis is a quick learner.

"Pretty windy, huh?" he said, which made me giggle, which made him laugh, because it's really hard not to when your stomach is pressed against someone who's laughing, right? So we flew some more circles, laughing like idiots.

"You better not get snot in my hair," I said, feeling my own nose dripping like a faucet.

"Yeah, you're snotty enough already!" Louis shrieked, so proud of himself for the joke I started cracking up all over again and almost let the wind get back under me. In case you're wondering about a guy mashed onto a girl like that...let's just say it's not a problem with Louis, okay? His body doesn't, you know, seem to care.

"Erin said she's gonna ask Janice to be her Career Day speaker," he said a few minutes later. I was back in control, but having trouble keeping the sun from blinding me every time we circled toward it. "She's a marine biologist."

"No way! Didn't know we had any of those on Dalby."

"She moved here after Christmas, from Thatcher Island. She met my mom at a Save the Orcas meeting, and they got to be, like, friends."

"That's cool. Marine biology is awesome, I'll come to her talk." *Nice to see Shasta with a friend for a change instead of one more man who ditches her.* But Louis didn't need me to say that.

"Yeah." *Brrrrffffrrr,* said the wind. We flew a while. I was starting to get a teensy bit bored with these low, careful circles, and wondering where else we could go that would be safe on a Saturday, when Louis said, "Hey. Can I tell you something?"

Usually when someone has to ask that instead of just coming out and *telling* whatever, it's what Mr. Evans calls a Watershed Moment: one minute everything's flowing one way, the next, the world has changed. You see it all the time in movies. Sometimes at night, when I think about...a guy...he says that to me, and that breathless feeling it gives is almost better than what he actually says. But this was Louis, and even though he was talking into my ear, it wasn't giving me that feeling. "Yeah?"

"I think Janice is...I think Janice might be girlfriends with my mom."

"Yeah, so? She could use a girlfriend."

"No, I mean…" I swear I could feel his face get warm, right over my neck. "*Girl*friend. Like boyfriends and girlfriends."

"Oh!" I was surprised, but not shocked. I mean, Shasta sure likes men, but she hadn't had much luck with them. And there are plenty of gay people on Dalby, it's a pretty free place, so why not? Maybe she just felt like branching out. A tree branch hit my hand as I thought that, and even though it hurt, it made me giggle.

"What?" said Louis. Now he was frowning, I could feel it. "You think it's funny?"

"No, no—I was just…thinking of something dumb. But Louis. Are you sure? She said 'roommate,' right? Maybe that's all it is." *I mean, Shasta really does like men.*

"Nooo," he sighed. "Janice doesn't have her own room, she shares with Mom. And there's only one bed in there. And they really seem to like each other."

"Oh. Well, okay. I mean, that's cool, isn't it? If your mom's happy? And Janice seems like a cool person."

"Yeah." He sighed again, and suddenly I saw the problem. One more strike against him at school. *"Louis has two mommies!"* I could hear it now, and it wouldn't just be Tyler. Dalby might be free, but there are still plenty of mean people here.

"Does Erin, like, know? That your mom and Janice are a thing?"

"No. But she's gonna figure it out. Mom and Janice are starting to hold hands sometimes. Pretty soon they'll go to the store like that, and then everyone will know."

I thought hard. This was like the opposite of my mom. A picture of her at Howe's flared up, wearing that little blue apron with a name tag, working so hard to be normal. She'd practically killed her wild self to be that kind of mom. Now here was Shasta, trying to get out of her own box, and Louis wanted her to stay there. He was too nice to say so, especially after hearing my enthusiasm, but Louis really didn't want his mother to change.

Well, I wanted mine to. She was the Flying Burgowski Mother and she belonged in the sky, with me. And we hadn't been flying together in, what? A month! She must feel shy with me, maybe afraid of the powers she might have lost in fourteen years of not-flying. She looked like a perfectly good Flyer to me, even once tried to teach me her swimming-in-the-air style, but now…she resisted. But she couldn't resist herself. So she flew solo and crazy. No wonder she ended up on Howe's roof.

The weight of Louis and his problems on my back disappeared as the excitement of my idea surged through me. *Mom needs to fly with me. She just doesn't know it. She can let off steam, but I'll keep her safe. Rule Number One can push us back together. I can talk her into it. We'll go tonight—*

Louis screamed for real this time, as a wild burst of wind caught me in mid-thought and rolled us sideways. One of his arms un-twined from mine and I felt him slide off me, felt nothing but cold air on my back as I scrabbled desperately to grab his other hand, the one that just a second ago had been splayed below mine, helping me bank the turns. In the movies someone always grabs the guy's hand as he goes over the cliff and pulls him back up in agonizing grunts. This happened way too fast. One second here, the next—tumbling. *Mom, help!* I thought wildly, as Louis slipped from my grasp and crashed into the top of a tree.

I didn't even think. I dived after him.

A tornado of crack-crack-crash! Grabbing needle-tufts—no way to stop. Snap-snap-stab, all the way down. One branch clonked me under the chin and I felt the jaw-slam in my feet. Blood in my mouth. Eyes shut tight. *Louis—where? Below? Did he—*

I hit the ground on my back with a thud that took away all the air and light in the world.

CHAPTER FIVE

MY MOM'S VALENTINE

*D*ad is going to kill me. That was my first thought. Then came *I'm alive, I think.* Then: *Omigod, Louis.*

But when I opened my eyes, Louis was hovering over my face. His own was bright with scratches and streaked with tears. "I thought you were dead!" he wailed, and threw himself onto me.

Oh, *ow.* The breath that must have come back while I was blacked out went squooshing right out of me again. "Uhhhh…"

"Oh, sorry, sorry!" Louis scrambled off me, wiping his eyes and getting a big smear of blood on his hand. "Joss, are you okay? We fell into a tree!"

Oh, Louis. Laughing, it turns out, hurt even worse than not breathing. I spit out some of the blood that had scared Louis so badly and concentrated on not barfing chocolate all over him. When I finally felt like sitting up, we took turns examining each other to calculate the damage. Amazingly, no broken arms or legs, but my ribs felt like that time I got too close to the back of Heather Angstrom's donkey. *Oh, wow.* And my tongue wouldn't stop bleeding.

Louis's face looked like he'd been experimenting with the different sides of a cheese grater. But nothing had seriously clonked him; he'd even managed to land on a bush, which kept him from going all rag-doll like I had.

"What're we gonna do?" Louis said when he finally got tired of "I can't believe we just fell into a tree!" That didn't make me laugh any more. My ribs hurt horribly, and what if I needed stitches in my tongue? What was I going to tell Dad?

"'FAh cud juth mek de bleeding thtop," I said thickly, wiping my mouth again on the sleeve of my windbreaker. Lucky it was red.

"Yeah, we need a rag or something we can throw away. We can't walk back in the house looking like this." *Like wiping those scrapes of yours is gonna help.* Too hard to talk, but Louis was right, I did need some kind of rag for my tongue. Slowly I started removing my windbreaker to get at the sweatshirt beneath. *Oh jeez*, that hurt. I blinked hard, trying not to cry, when something bright green caught my eye. Unnaturally green.

"'Uith. Get 'at fo' me." Carefully, I pointed to the green thing. There were two, actually, and I knew exactly what they were. Tampons, thank you very much. Individually Wrapped for My Convenience. It was that time of the month, and hey, a girl's got to be prepared, right? I had stuffed them in my jeans pocket that morning. They must have fallen out as I crashed through the tree.

"Oh, GROSS!" was Louis's reaction when he realized what he was handing me. And what I was planning to do with them.

Hey, it worked, okay? I stuck 'em both in there above my tongue, closed my mouth hard and lay back, looking up at the tree and feeling my ribs throb. Of course every time Louis looked over at the two strings hanging out of my mouth like long, floppy fangs he'd say something like, "Uhh, I'm gonna hurl!" I closed my eyes to shut him out. And to keep the tears down.

I wasn't crying from pain. It was more…well, the tampons. Louis was such a good guy; he would never hurt my feelings on purpose. But the tampon thing made him want to vomit, and I suddenly knew that Savannah would have loved it. Would have named me "Sanitary Mouth" or "Tampon Tongue." And we would have laughed about this moment for, like, ever. That pain of yesterday came whooshing back through me, and our disappearing friendship hurt worse than my ribs. Louis's mom was not the only one who could use a girlfriend.

That was it. I opened my eyes and sat up suddenly, then squeezed them shut against the immediate stabs. *Idiot.* But what had I been thinking about when I crashed? Sisterhood, right? Savannah hurt too much—it was Mom I needed to be with. Even if she wouldn't fly with me, she could tell me what to do about…stuff. Even if she wouldn't fly, that didn't mean she wouldn't talk.

And maybe she would fly.

"Leth go 'oo my mom'th," I said, testing my tongue after taking those useful little Feminine Products out of my mouth. The bleeding had stopped, my ribs weren't broken. Probably.

"Isn't she at work?"

"Yeah. Tho we c'n get c'eaned up whi' shee'th gone." *And take the time to invent a good story for Dad. Hoo, boy.*

Mom lives on the far side of the village, in Lorraine's old house—I know, pretty weird—so we trudged the long way around, me breathing carefully around my ribs. I buried my tampon-fangs under a blackberry bush, and Louis used his sleeve to clean the worst of his scratches. None of the cars that passed us screeched to a halt, so I guess we looked okay.

Tion met us at the door and couldn't understand why I wouldn't bend down to pick her up. She did figure eights around my ankles, meowing for an explanation.

"Here, girl, I'll take you," Louis said, picking Tion up. She got all rigid in his arms, which is not like her.

"Maybe sheeth juth mad a' me," I suggested. Talking didn't hurt too much if I lisped like a four year-old. Then I realized. "No, I know! You thmell funny! You're all cover' in tree thap! Be' she doethn' like tha'."

"So are you," Louis retorted, setting Tion down on the back of the couch before she added to his scratches. "You have a big gob of it in your hair."

"Oh, maaaan…" I tried to reach back to feel it, but my ribs stopped me.

"Hey," a muffled voice said. We jumped. The crumpled old quilt on the couch was talking to us. "Either shut that door or bring some more wood in. I'm not heating the whole damn village."

"Mom!" I don't know which shocked me more, the fact that she wasn't at work, or the fact that she was lying on her couch in the middle of the day, completely covered up. Or her voice. Last time I heard that wavery sound, she was in a hospital room in McClenton. It was a bad time.

"Wha' are you doing here?" I asked stupidly. *Duh, lying in the dark.* But we had just seen her, looking all chirpy at work! Only a couple of hours ago, right? *Oh jeez, I was so rude to her when we left, what if—*"Mom, I'm thorry I wath thnotty to you a' Howe'th, okay? Are you… upthet with me?"

She pulled the quilt off her head as we came around the couch. Her eyes looked too big for her face. I hated seeing that pale mousiness again.

"No, no." Slight head shake. Her pupils were gigantic. "You're fine, babe. Just got sick, that's all. Came home early." I could tell she was making an effort. I knelt down by the couch and sort of hugged the top of her, ignoring my ribs.

"Ugh. What do you have—that *is* tree sap, isn't it?" Now she sounded a little more like herself. "How in the world did you get that in your hair?" Then she must have looked up at Louis. "And Jesus, what happened to your face?"

"We…" Louis started. We hadn't had the chance to come up with our story yet.

"Don't tell me," Mom said, pushing me off her so she could sit up and look at me, and through my shock I remembered, *We don't need a story for her.*

"We crashed," I said at the exact same time Mom said, "You crashed, right?" Oh, it was a relief to see her smile. She must not have taken too many of whatever pills she took.

"Yeah!" Louis jumped in excitedly. Apparently he had also just remembered Mom was one of us. "We fell into a tree! We were flying doubles and it was really windy and Joss was doing great and all of a sudden we went sideways and I rolled off, and…we fell into a tree."

"You fell too?" Mom focused her gaze on me with an effort. "You mean you lost your power all of a sudden?"

Had I? With the terror of being inside that crazy tornado of branches, and the varieties of pain that followed my big thud, I could barely remember what led up to it. Louis had rolled—no, we had rolled, then he slid, then his hand disappeared, and then…

"No!" I said, triumphant with the recovered memory. "I di' i' on purpothe."

"You did? You, like, tried to save me?" Louis sounded impressed. I've only ever saved one person while flying, and that was Mom, back in McClenton. And that memory comes with too many other yucky things attached.

"Well, that's something anyway," Mom said, but she was back in that weak voice. I got up from the floor and made room for myself on the couch by her feet. If she noticed me wincing, she didn't say anything. Louis perched on the edge of the rocking chair.

"Tho, like…" I searched for the right way to ask what happened, to lead into my plan. She needed to fly with me—flying *was* her medication! But right now Mom wasn't looking much like a Flyer.

"Did you throw up?" Louis asked. I whirled to glare at him. *Oww*, my ribs said. "At work? I hate when that happens. I did that once in second grade. First day of school," he added sadly.

So that's why they called him Barf Boy for so long. But what kind of idiot asks a grown-up that? Now Mom would really be pissed off.

But all she said was, "No." We waited. "I just felt crappy, okay?" she added. "I'll be fine, just need to lie down for a bit. Zach's got everything under control, he said he'd cover for me."

Zach? Oh. Hot Guy had a name. It fit him. *But so what? Mom's in trouble again*. I had to do something to get that weakness out of her face, her voice.

"Mom, when you feel be"er, will you pleathe pleathe PLEATHE go flying with me?" So much for careful arguments. "I really wan' you to."

I don't think there is any worse expression to see on your mother's face than sad. Give me furious any day. "Babe, I'm sorry. I think that's gonna be a No. I think I'm about done."

I felt cold in my stomach. "Wha' you mean, done?" She frowned, and I made a huge effort to speak correctly. "You're gonna take some time off? 'Cause of what Dad said? Don't worry, Mom, he can't make us stop flying. I mean I crashed, but I had to save Louis, and it's not like we got Seen!" *Enough*, said my tongue. Mom looked at me steadily. "You can't be *done* done. You're a Flyer."

"Yeah, well." She closed her eyes. "Being a Flyer is all about controlling the power, isn't it. And right now I'm exercising my control by taking a break. Which is something you look like you two could use," opening her eyes again to look right into me like she was x-raying my ribs.

This was not where this conversation was supposed to go. "Whaddya mean, taking a break? You took a break for, like, fourteen years!" *And it almost killed you*, I did not say. "What just *happened*, Mom?" *Omigod—did my crash somehow do this to her? Maybe we were magically connected, like Harry and Voldemort...*

"Valentine's Day," she said. Nope, did not expect that. "You know, I just got to thinking about...love, I guess. Selling those ridiculous cards all week. Made me think about how I ...feel about you guys." Now she was looking at the quilt under her chin. "If I want to be a better mom, I'm not gonna get there by zipping around in the air, almost blowing the whole thing for all of us."

"That's what I mean! You shouldn't fly alone, you'll just get into trouble—" her eyes flashed at me but I kept going, "but if you fly with me, we'll be twithe—*twice* as careful."

"You'll have each other's backs," Louis put in helpfully. Mom's mouth twitched for a second, like she was about to burst out "Gotcha! Had you going for a minute there, didn't I!"

But she didn't.

"Joss, I just really need to take a rest now. I feel like crap." Her eyes closed again. "And you two look like crap. Go find something in my bathroom to patch yourselves up. Try some makeup on those scratches, Louis." Tion climbed back onto Mom's shoulders, where she likes to be when people are sad.

We were being dismissed. My stomach hurt worse than my ribs. We did what she told us. Louis put some concealer on top of the antiseptic and it looked okay, like a weird tan. I found some aspirin and swallowed two. But I had to use scissors to cut the sap out of my hair. And yeah, I was ready to droop on home, if Louis hadn't made me stay.

"You should make her some cocoa or something," he whispered to me in Mom's bathroom. "That's what I do when my mom gets bummed."

"No way, she'll be totally pithed if I don' leave! Di'n' you hear her?" I lisped back.

Louis shrugged. "She'll probably be more pissed if you do. I don't think moms ever really *want* you to leave."

Did he have to sound so superior? "Wha' you even know about my mom?" I whispered nastily.

Louis just shrugged, "Whatever, Joss. Thanks for flying. See ya."

"That makeup lookth ridiculouth," I snarked as he tiptoed out. I heard the front door open and close. Oh, man, I'd lived with Pissed-off Mom for four months, back in her little McClenton apartment. Sure didn't miss her. *Damn, I hate when Louis is right!*

So…make her laugh, maybe? I called from the bathroom, "Hey Mom, how come boyth are thuch athholeth?"

I heard a snort from under her quilt, so maybe it worked. "I'm gonna make cocoa," I announced quickly, heading into the kitchen. "Oh, I don't mean Louis, he doesn't count." I forced my tongue to speak correctly. "I mean regular boys. Like yesterday? Valentine's Day? You wouldn't believe what…this one guy did."

"Who?" *Hah, got her attention!* Her voice was still quilt-muffled, though. I found a canister of instant cocoa…with about a half-spoonful left. Shoot, I was going to have to make the kind with milk and sugar. Did she even have any? Not that I could find. Looked like Mom had become a little better about groceries since McClenton, but that wasn't saying much. I tried her tiny pantry.

And that's where I found it, stuck behind a can of soup.

A valentine. Folded red construction paper—what else could it be? But who puts valentines in their pantry? And who wouldn't look at one if they found it there?

On the outside it said: *To the Flyer.* So I had to open it, right?

But inside was no valentine. It was great big computer-printed words, each line cut and pasted separately like a ransom note in a movie. It said this:

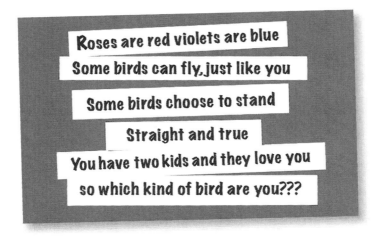

Roses are red violets are blue

Some birds can fly, just like you

Some birds choose to stand

Straight and true

You have two kids and they love you

so which kind of bird are you???

My brain got numb.

Beneath the poem, a plain rectangle of computer paper was glued on. Plain font. It said:

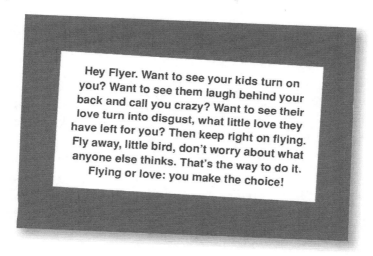

Hey Flyer. Want to see your kids turn on you? Want to see them laugh behind your back and call you crazy? Want to see their love turn into disgust, what little love they have left for you? Then keep right on flying. Fly away, little bird, don't worry about what anyone else thinks. That's the way to do it. Flying or love: you make the choice!

I dropped the horrible thing like it was poison. Which I guess it was.

Who gave this to her? Who would care if she flew or not? Who had Seen her? Why did they call her a Flyer? Why had she kept the thing? Why hadn't she told me?

And what was I going to say to her now?

Mom made that part easy. "Hey," she called from the couch. "You still here or what?" I stood paralyzed—*put it back and pretend nothing happened? Confront her and watch her fall apart even more?*—until she padded into the kitchen and that was that.

"Oh," she said.

I wanted so much to wrap my arms around her skinny little self, but the way she stood there, stiff as a doll… "Mom. Why?" That's all I could manage.

"Ron was right, huh." She gazed out the window, squinting at the brightness. "You get Seen, bad stuff happens. Not quite what he predicted, but," she laughed roughly, "just as effective, turns out. Makes you think."

"Think abou' wha'?" I lost control of my poor tongue. "Mom, thith ith horrible! Thomeone knowth abou' you, and they've gone all nathty! Why they wan' you to thtop flying?" *And why didn't you* tell *me?*

"Y'know, I have no idea," Mom said, so casually it made me shiver. "Anyone could've Seen me, pretty much. I was up on Howe's roof for a long time, lots of folks around. And that's hardly the only time I've been Seen. There's that video, remember? Maybe someone figured out it was me. Plus there was that time I kind of forgot that school was letting out…wrong place, wrong time, you know? You would've Seen me yourself if you'd looked up. And over the harbor a few weeks ago…"

"You flew over the harbor?" I've done it myself, no right to sound so shocked, but the reality was sinking in: Mom was just as reckless as Dad had said, and way worse than I had imagined. I spoke slowly. "Mom. Thith…this stuff is whack!" I poked at the letter, not wanting to touch it again. "Why didn't you just burn it up?"

"Yeah, not much good in that, is there. Since my secret admirer kind of has a point."

I stared at her. She stared out the window.

Finally I said, "Mom. It's crap. Can't you see that? Why are you letting one crappy person tell you not to fly?"

"Because the truth doesn't always come wrapped in pretty packages, babe. If I've learned one thing from therapy, it's that." I really wish she hadn't said that. But I had to try again.

"Mom, this…*thing* isn't the truth. If it means anything," I said louder, as she started shaking her head, "it means we Flyers have an enemy, right? Someone has a problem with *us both*."

"Oh, so you got a letter too?" Mom demanded. I dropped my eyes. "Right. So *I'm* getting threatened, babe. Me. Not you."

Her cheeks had those red spots, but at least she was calling me "babe" again. "So it's my problem. And my solution. And I happen to think whoever wrote this..." the cheek-spots faded, "is right. So."

"So? We need to figure out who this weirdo is..."

"You do whatever you want. I'm going back to bed." She sounded exhausted again. "Make yourself some cocoa, I don't want any." There went the quilt: off the counter and back over her head. And there went my mom, back to the couch.

I wanted to cry with frustration. "I don't want cocoa either! I'm gonna find out, Mom! I'm gonna...do research." I heard a snort from the living room. "I am! Lorraine has these old books about witches and what happens when they get Seen—I'm gonna look in there! Bet I can figure out what to do when someone threatens one of us! When Lorraine sees that valentine, she'll..."

"No," Mom said distinctly. I followed her into the living room. "You burn that thing if you want. But I'm not bringing Lorraine in on this, or anyone else."

"Mom, wh—?"

Quilt off, cheek-spots bright as paint. "I'm sick of everybody hovering over me, okay?" she hissed. "Just let me figure out one damn thing on my own, will you? If I'm controlling my powers, then I'm controlling my powers."

"But the person who wrote that thing—"

"—will probably write me another, and if he does, I'll burn it up, happy? But leave Lorraine out of it." She sat up straight, eyes all laser-y. "Promise me, Jocelyn."

I promised. Didn't even think to cross my fingers. Didn't even make her promise me anything back, like flying with me again, just to show Valentine Sicko that she wasn't scared of him.

I burned the letter in the woodstove, but I still felt gross, as if it had breathed some horrible germs into me. Like it had with Mom.

CHAPTER SIX

GOOGLING THE ENEMY

The snappy, sunny day seemed like a joke after all that drama. My ribs and tongue *killed*. Too much talking. All I wanted was to go back to my room and let Harry Potter take me away. Not think about that horrible thing in Mom's pantry. Or how Mom had made me promise not to tell.

I love Harry. He carried me off for a good hour—till Michael got home.

"Doofus Louis practically crashed into me coming out of the Co-op," my darling brother said, barging in without knocking, which is a huge no-no when I do it to him. But he cut me off before I could protest. I was deep in the chapter where Dumbledore takes Harry to the cave, and it took me a second to notice that my brother's face was flushed like he'd been running. Michael never runs. "He looks like crap. Told me you guys fell out of a tree."

"What were you doing in the Co-op?" I said stupidly. My tongue felt way better after an hour of not talking.

"Guitar strings, dumbass. They order stuff like that for musicians," like of course who could forget. "Anyway. Fell out of a tree, he said." *Oh, Louis, did you really just spit the whole thing out to Michael?* "Like you guys have been climbing trees together every weekend for the last hundred years." I hate when Michael uses...oh, what's that word—hyperbole! It's immature arguing,

Mrs. Mac used to say, and then she'd add, "I've told you a million times!" to make us laugh. But I was proud of Louis for coming up with a cover story, since we hadn't agreed on one.

"You really think I'm that stupid?" Suddenly Michael was all up in my face. I dropped my feet off the bed and onto the floor. He looked like he might punch me.

"What're you talking about?" I grabbed my ribs automatically before the ache hit.

"You. Flew." Michael breathed through his nose, about two inches from mine. "With Louis. Not with me. You went flying doubles with him after you promised Me. That We. Would. Go."

"Yes, I did!" I yelled right in his face. He backed off a step. Who did he think he was, barging in here? "Louis is my friend, and he asked nicely, and I can fly with him if I want to!"

"And I'm your brother," Michael snarled. "And I asked nicely too. But I guess that counts for s--- around here. I'm done with this s---. I'm done with you."

"Good! I'm done with you too!"

"Yeah," Michael sneered, turning at my doorway. "But you're not done with Dad. Not after he finds out what happened."

"Finds out *what* happened?" came Dad's voice, sounding dangerous. Michael and I scooted into the hallway. There was Dad's head sticking through the curtain. "This better be good, and it better be quick. Do you two realize I can hear you all the way into the store?"

"Jocelyn says she and Louis were climbing a tree and fell out of it," said Mr. Virtuous.

"Sounds pretty idiotic, but nothing to yell about," Dad said. "You okay, Joss? Good." He glanced behind him. Saturday's pretty busy in the store, even off-season. "So if you two don't mind…"

"But it's b.s., Dad!" Michael had the sense not to cuss now. "They were flying and they crashed! Flying doubles, in the middle of the day! After what you said and everything."

Dad peered at me. "Yeah, you're banged up all right." He frowned. "Is this true?"

Whoa. I was not ready. Technically, we hadn't been Seen, but treetop crashes seemed like they might fit into the same category in Dad's mind. Couldn't take that chance. "Of course not. It's too windy to fly today." Well, that part was sure true. "I told Louis about this thing we read in Language Arts about a guy who climbed a tree in a storm, and he wanted to try it."

Mixing a little truth into a lie makes it stronger. I have no idea why I know this.

"She's lying to you, Dad." Michael shook his head, like the whole thing was Such A Shame. "I *know* they were flying."

"And how do you know this?" Dad turned on Michael.

"Because—jeez, Dad, look at her! Of course she's gonna fly if it's windy, she's just like Mom…"

"I don't have time for this. Michael, leave your sister alone, go play your guitar." Back to work went Dad.

"So you're just gonna take her word for it?" Michael yelled after him.

No answer. Michael slammed into his room, but I knew I had to get out of the house before he worked himself up to come back at me. Great, so who to hang out with? Louis, whom I'd have to apologize to again, or Savannah, who needed to apologize to me but wouldn't? I tried Molly. "She's over at Savannah's," her mom said. Of course.

So I spent the afternoon with Harry Potter, outside. I wrapped my quilt around me like Mom—*argh, Mom!*—and plonked myself down against the sunniest side of our house, out of the stupid wind. But this time, Harry couldn't seem to work his magic on me. *Why didn't I tell Dad? Even if I didn't mention my crash, shouldn't he know about Mom's poison valentine? I know, I promised, but…*By the time the sun got too low to warm me, I felt as bummed as Harry.

"Hey, Jossa-lame, come set the table," I heard Michael call from the back door. Then, in a completely different voice, "What the..?"

I heaved myself up and came around the house to see my brother picking something up from the back steps. "Is that a doll?"

Michael held the thing up. It was a doll, sort of. A soft, shiny one, dressed in a little red toga. With wings made of silvery fabric. "Oh, it's a Cupid! For Valentine's Day."

"Duh," said my brother. "But what's it doing on our doorstep? And—oh, man. Look at that. That's just not right."

It wasn't. Cupid has arrows, right? To shoot love through your heart? And this cute little Cupid doll had arrows too, a tiny plastic one set in his plastic bow, and two more in a quiver on his back... plus a fourth one, stuck right through the glossy fabric of his wings.

The chill of the air swooped into my stomach. I couldn't stop staring at the fake-feather end of that little arrow, its point buried in the silvery wing-sprouts.

"Wow, Joss, one of your boyfriends sure has a jacked-up sense of humor," Michael muttered, tossing the doll to me.

I threw up my hands, letting the freaky thing drop to my feet. "That's not mine! Don't give it to me!"

"What, you think it's for me? Valentine's was yesterday, dumbass," Michael snorted, like that was the point.

"Prob'ly," I ventured. *Oh jeez—was this like my version of Mom's poison letter? But I couldn't tell Michael about that, I promised Mom...* "Bet it's from Moira. Bet she was too scared to give it to you at school yesterday." This was stupid; even gothy Moira Elwes wouldn't be that lame, though she did have a crush on Michael. But everyone likes a secret admirer, even one with infected piercings.

"Huh," he said, picking the Cupid up again. "Maybe. Whatever." He stuffed it into his sweatshirt pocket, then glared at me. "So you just keep your mouth shut about this."

"Whatever," I snipped back. *OK...so I don't have to explain this* to Dad. But... Mom's the one who needed to know. Because that was no valentine, to Michael or anyone. That doll was shot through the wings, not the heart.

Lorraine was taking a quiche out of the oven. I hate quiche. What a horrible thing to do to pie crust, fill it up with gloppy eggs. And now I had to pretend to like it so's not to hurt the Stepmother's feelings.

"Sweetie, I need you to do me a favor," Dad said to Lorraine as she cut slices and let the glop loose. It smelled disgusting. Michael slouched in, his sweatshirt pocket empty, so he must have stashed the Cupid in his room.

"Settle something for us, would you?" Dad continued. "You can smell when a Flyer's been flying, right? On their skin?"

Lorraine looked at him in surprise. "Yes..."

"So, what about this little Flyer? Give her a sniff and tell me what you smell, okay?"

Oh, wow—did not see that coming. Dad was smiling like this whole thing was just a harmless joke, but I knew better. He has plenty of time on his hands in that store, and he'd obviously spent it figuring out how to catch his flying daughter in a lie.

"Why?" Lorraine asked, like she couldn't guess, but Dad shrugged and said, "Humor me."

I sat there as she let go of the stinky quiche and moved behind me. What was I going to do, slap her away? I wanted to. Across the table Michael was grinning at me.

Lorraine bent, then straightened—who sniffs that quietly? Then she pulled her own chair out and sat down beside me.

"Well?" asked Dad. Now he didn't sound so casual. *Oh jeez. Here's where he remembers he started to ground me yesterday. Maybe if I told him about the Cupid? No, that would only make it worse.*

"All I smell is tree sap," Lorraine said. "Have you been climbing trees, Jocelyn? What a lovely idea. Oh, Michael, would you grab the salad dressing?"

I guess it tells you what a little Flying Burgowski Family we'd become. Dad and Michael automatically believed Lorraine's nose, like of course you can smell supernatural powers, who doesn't know that?

Dad nodded. "Okay, little jet, you're off the hook this time."

Michael got all quiet and didn't try to argue. The grown-ups spent dinnertime talking about someone's car getting smooshed by a falling tree. That really was some strong wind I'd crashed in.

"Great quiche," I said finally. I had managed to eat most of it; it felt nice and soft on my sore tongue. Lorraine smiled.

See, I believed her nose too. And I knew perfectly well it had smelled the truth. So if she was willing to lie to her very own husband, for me…I could lie for her, too.

"By the way," Dad added, "Lorraine and I had a good, long talk last night and she convinced me that people like you can get pretty messed up if they can't fly when they need to."

Thought Number One: *Duh, tell me about it—can you imagine keeping yourself from going to the bathroom for a month?* Thought Number Two: *"Messed up?" You mean depressed? Or addicted to pills like Mom was? Is that where Lorraine thinks I'm headed?*

"Uh-huh," I said.

"She showed me this passage in one of those old books of hers which talked about… what can happen to Flyers who stop flying. Explains a lot about…you know." He meant Mom. "So I promised her I would not use grounding as a punishment if you can't handle our flying rule." He was clearly getting more comfortable with the Burgowskis' own personal f-word. "However. I am taking the threat of discovery as seriously as ever, and I need to know that you are too. So…if I catch you taking any more risky flights, like yesterday…you do Michael's chores for a month."

"Two months," Michael suggested.

"Okay," I said immediately. *Chores? Hah. Deal!* "Sorry about yesterday," I added. But it was Lorraine I really owed.

Apparently she thought so too. I was washing dishes, so as soon as Dad settled himself in front of the TV, she cornered me easily. "How'd you crash?" she demanded, low-voice.

"The wind! It was really strong, right? It just flipped us!"

"Us? Did you have Louis? Did anyone See you?" I started to feel annoyed. I mean, yeah, she'd covered for me, but did that gave her the right to get all FBI on me?

"No, it's fine! I'm fine!" She arched her eyebrows at me, which irritated me even more. "Hey, don't worry, I'm not gonna go all Mom-like, just 'cause of one little crash."

"What do you mean, 'all Mom-like'? What's wrong with Beth?"

Oops. "Nothing. I just meant…"

I'm a wimp, okay? All she had to do was look at me. *Being bitchy to Louis, flying along all happy while my mom was crashing, keeping my mouth shut about the poison letter, then the Cupid doll…* My guilt-load hit its limit, and I unloaded. Told Lorraine everything: the poison valentine, Mom's reaction, the Cupid. *Oh, Mom's gonna kill me.* But I told.

Lorraine was as horrified as I'd been, but didn't waste time asking why I hadn't shared sooner. "You can't make Beth fly again," she said, zeroing in on my main worry. "At least not right now, Joss. But if we help her understand that Flyers—other Flyers, like her *daughter*—have an antagonist, maybe that'll bring the fight out in her."

Antagonist. Every teacher since third grade had taught us that word: the one who causes problems, gets in the way of the hero. The enemy.

"I already told her that, even before I got the doll! And she didn't care."

Lorraine shook her head. "It feels personal to her right now, and Beth's used to everyone coming down on her personally. Remember that video? Her own personal stalker, all those years ago? So she needs to know that letter could be part of some-thing…larger. Kind of a… campaign."

"No way." I felt creeped out all over again. "You think, like… someone really has a problem with Flyers in general? But who would know? And who in the world would be against flying?"

"I don't know," Lorraine said grimly, but she had that teacher-glint in her eye. "So why don't we take a look at the history?"

So, that thing I said to Mom about research? I was just shoot-ing my mouth off. But Lorraine? *Holy shih tzu.* Here she came, staggering under the largest book I've ever seen in real life. It looked like one of those giant old leather ones that Gandalf the Grey does his research in, even worse than the one she gave me last fall, *A History of Witches.* I couldn't make out the title.

"You gonna tell Dad?" I mumbled as she laid the monster book on the kitchen table.

"Shouldn't I?"

We looked at each other. Then we both looked at the book. No way could Dad handle this stuff—he can barely say "fly"!

I shook my head. *She'll tell him anyway. She's his* wife.

Lorraine stared at the book for a long moment, as though it was whispering a secret message. Then she nodded. "Well, you may be right about that. Let's get to work."

So we did.

Lorraine gave me a pen and a pad of yellow sticky-notes. She slogged through a couple of pages, reading some parts aloud, and if they sounded useful, I wrote them down with the page num-ber. Then we switched: I read, she took notes.

You'd think a book that size would have big writing, but this stuff practically needed a magnifying glass, plus it was that ridicu-lous script where the *s*'s look like *f*'s. It was all about witches— what the rest of the world tends to call us Flyers.

Oh, WOW, it was boring. Took us a whole hour to get to, "Ye witchef ðo flye by ðay anð night," which, duh, I already knew, and the slightly more interesting fact that "Thoſe who do ſtande beneath ye witch and praye aſ ſhe do flye" might be able to "caſt ye witch down." But nobody had "cast" me down yesterday— I'd been saving Louis! And there was nothing in there about witches being "cast down" mentally by threats. We did find a part which mentioned "ye ſcent of flowreſ be on her ſkin" after a witch flies, which made me feel kind of proud, like: Yup, that's me they're talking about! But mostly it was endless warnings about the signs of Satan. Stupid and useless. My head ached like my ribs.

But after maybe the twenty-eighth sticky-note, I noticed something.

"Hey, that's like the tenth time I've written the word 'stand.'" The note in my hand said, "Stande alwayſ for righteouſneſſ leſt ye ſuffer ye powerſ of ye dark to flye." I sorted through the other notes: "And ye ſhall Stande and do the Lord'ſ work." I stuck that one next to, "He who do Stande ſhall never fall into ye pit," and "Without thoſe who do Stande, ye witcheſ ſhall flye until ye ſun be blotted from ye ſkye."

Lorraine nodded, nose still in the giant book. "There's more." She started reading this whole nasty story about a mother and daughter in France, 1621, and I quit taking notes and listened.

"Ye watchmen did Stande" as the girl and the woman flew over the village gate "by midnight," and after this had happened a bunch, they told the magistrate, who got all the villagers to "Stande and praye" in the middle of the night in a kind of trick to "caſte ye witches down." The poor things crash-landed "on ye greene" and got arrested. The magistrate talked a whole lot about "Standing for ye goode" at their trial (which happened the very next day) and told the "wymen" that "Satan and hiſ impſ do flye, but they who love the Lord do Stande for Him alwayſ."

And then they burned them at the stake.

I knew that already, all right? People throughout world history have tried to destroy witches. But I'd never thought about who those people were, or why they cared so much.

Or when my brain had started filling in the word "Flyer" for the word "witch."

There was a picture, an old engraving. The girl's mom was small, like mine—they were about the same height, tied back to back. They weren't screaming. Yet.

"It's always capitalized," Lorraine murmured. "The word 'stand,' like it's some kind of secret invocation…"

"Yeah." I looked at my stepmom's wrinkled forehead, thinking of the brain cells marching around underneath like little robots. *It should be Mom sitting there all comfy in her bathrobe, solving this mystery with me.* She'd feel the same stab of horror, seeing that poor girl and her mom straining against the ropes, so terrified: that's *us*. And Mom wouldn't use words like "invocation." She'd say something smart like…

"I know!" I said, "let's Google 'Stande.'" The look Lorraine gave me felt satisfying. *That's right, Ms. Boring Books, it takes a crazy Flyer mind to come up with something so simple and obvious.* Dad had lumbered off to bed, so the living room was all ours. We lugged the giant book to the coffee table and fired up the computer.

But the internet didn't help. I Googled "stand" with and without capitals and the "e." Zero matches.

I tried Yahoo and all the other search engines we could think of.

"This makes absolutely no sense," Lorraine said. "It's just a word. Try 'stop.'"

I did. Thirty-four million, eight hundred thousand matches.

"Try 'cast down witches.'"

Seven million, nine hundred and ten thousand. The first ten were about Sabrina the Teen-aged Witch.

"Now try 'stand' again."

Zippo.

We stared at each other. I have no idea how the internet works—who does?—but I'm pretty sure it's not supposed to just skip a word, especially one as ordinary as "stand."

I tried a few other random ones—"fly," twelve and a half million; "pray," over five million—while Lorraine wrinkled her forehead and stared at nothing.

Then she said, "Try 'Flyer.'"

"With caps?"

"Both ways." And guess what: no hits for either one.

Lorraine saw me rubbing my shoulders and laughed softly. "You got goose bumps too, huh?"

I nodded. I'd been magic for eight months, so you'd think a little cyber-weirdness wouldn't be so hard to handle, right? But this was such creepy, normal-seeming magic! An unsearchable word? One that stood like a rock in a stream and made the whole internet go flowing past? And not a magic-sounding word like "Alakazzam," but…"Stand"? "Flyer"?

"I told you this was something larger," said Lorraine, but her voice was grave, not nyah-nyah.

"But what does it mean? Why's it even matter if we can't search…"

I expected Lorraine to keep staring and sigh, "I don't know," but she looked at me, hard and serious. "It means your magic is bigger and older than cyberspace. Magic doesn't have to bend to the rules of technology."

"Like vampires and mirrors! That is so cool! But," a thought hit me, "what about that video of Mom? Somebody uploaded that, only last summer. So the internet does work for some magic."

"That's true…But that was just an image, right? The person— or people—who filmed it and uploaded it never added any theories about what it meant, did they?"

"Let's watch it again," I said. So we did. There she was: a pale, fuzzy image, above the level of the muttering cameraman. The sudden leap into the air…*ah, the feeling of that final bound!*…and the cameraman's voice, now clear: "There she goes! Did you see that? Did you see that?"

We watched it twice.

"Well, you got me," Lorraine said. "Obviously the internet can *show* the magic. It somehow can't *explain* it. But apparently, Flyers aren't the only ones entwined with this magic. It involves your antagonists too."

"Ye people who do Stande?"

"Let's call them Standers, shall we? That seems to be their identity."

I Googled "Standers," just to check. Sure enough: nothing. "So whoever sent me that doll and sent Mom that letter is, like, a modern-day witch-hunter? A Stander, not some random kook? Is it the same guy who filmed Mom? Or uploaded her?"

"I doubt it," Lorraine sighed. "This video was taken in 1992, before you were born. The letter and the Cupid sound more… targeted. Someone's trying to stop the Flyers *right now*. As they've always done. "

"So maybe the poison-letter person found that old video and uploaded it! To try to stop her, only it didn't work, so they wrote the letter. No, wait—when that video went out, Mom wasn't flying. And neither was I. So, why…?"

"They might not be connected, Joss. Say the video was uploaded as a joke. Then some modern Stander saw it, and recognized your mom. They felt that ancient call to 'cast ye witch down.' Only these days they can't exactly burn her at the stake."

I shivered. "They don't need to. They've already stopped her."

Lorraine nodded. "Looks like they're trying to stop you too, with that doll, but you're a little tougher than Beth."

I felt a weird mix of pride and irritation. *Whaddya mean, Mom's plenty tough.* Then Lorraine's words sunk in. "Trying to stop *me*…"

"Well, sure. They delivered the doll to you, not Beth, right?" Suddenly her face got harsh. "Joss, you haven't had any other… interference with your magic, have you? What about your crash?"

I blushed. *Forgot she figured that one out, didn't you?* "No, no. That was just the wind. I'm sure of it. But I did think…my crash might be connected to Mom's, you know, mental one."

"You are connected," Lorraine said firmly. "I'm not sure how, exactly. But see how much we've learned just tonight? We know you two have an enemy, part of something big and ancient. Standers. We know how Standers defeat Flyers: stand beneath them, praying as they fly overhead."

"Stand and pray? Sounds like a preacher," I said.

"Hmm, yes," Lorraine nodded. "Makes you feel bad for real Christians, doesn't it, seeing their faith twisted like that? But let's not jump to conclusions. What we need to look for now is the counterattack. What can Flyers do to defeat Standers?"

I thought of my mom's pale face beneath a hood of blanket. And that horrible illustration of the French girl and her mom, flames rising beneath them. It made me shiver again. "What if we can't?"

"Oh, we're not there yet," Lorraine said, smiling grimly. "More research is all we need. I'm going down to Seattle later this week to pick up a special book from the university, a restricted one. I have great faith in books, in case you haven't noticed."

"You sound like Hermione," I couldn't help saying. A huge yawn erupted out of me and I realized I was exhausted. What a day.

Lorraine's smile softened. "But I have even more faith in you and Beth. You can't keep a good woman down."

But she didn't look at me, and we both knew what she said wasn't true. Keeping good women down seemed pretty easy.

CHAPTER SEVEN

NICE AND NORMAL

*T*here be ye witch!"
"*Stand fast! Cast her down!*"

Mumbling. A bunch of those tall, Pilgrim-y hats, seen from above, but pointed forward like the people wearing 'em had bowed their heads. More mumbling.

Would you call that a nightmare? It wasn't exactly scary, but I woke up late Sunday feeling hollow inside. Yesterday came rushing back: my crash, Mom's nasty valentine, that mutilated doll. Nope, none of that was a dream.

"Ready to fight the Standers today?" Lorraine asked, as soon as Dad left the kitchen.

Oh jeez, that crusty old book. I did NOT want to spend my day giving myself another nightmare. I rubbed my eyes. "Umm… sure. Maybe later? I have some homework," I added vaguely.

I just wanted to have a normal day, okay? Lorraine wouldn't understand. So when Louis stopped by, all friendly like I'd never hurt his feelings, we made brownies and hung out. And when Lorraine came through the kitchen and looked at me meaningfully, I ignored her.

And no, I didn't tell Louis about the Cupid doll, or what Lorraine and I had discovered about the Standers. I'd have to explain about Mom's poison letter, and I wasn't going to break my promise twice. Once felt bad enough. The day went by, nice and normal, except for my sore ribs.

But at dinnertime Mom didn't show up like she always does on Sundays. And when I called, she said she "might be coming down with something, babe—better keep to myself tonight."

"Coming down" sounded like "cast down," what the book said about stopping witches. And "cast down" sounded like "depressed." Which is how Mom sounded, blurry and muffled. The conversation lasted about fifty seconds and cast me down too.

After dinner Lorraine looked at me hard, but right then Dad called from the living room, "Hey, here's that National Geographic thing about volcanoes."

"Oh, my science teacher said we should see that!" I plopped myself next to him on the couch. I could feel Lorraine's disapproval trailing after me, but... *you know what? I'm the Flyer, not you, and if I want to take a night off from research, that's up to me, right? I don't need another nightmare on a school night. And I really ought to spend some time with Dad, seeing as how we're not even telling him any of this.*

The volcano thing was cool. My ribs felt better after my quiet day, and my tongue was almost back to normal.

Right before bed, though, that big leather book finally got to me. *Fine, I'll just take a quick peek at this Flyer-Stander stuff.* I grabbed a couple of sticky-notes and a pen and hunched over the teensy print. Of course it made me sleepy in about two seconds. I forced my eyes along, and all of a sudden, there was Lorraine at my shoulder.

"Oh, good," she began.

"I got this," I said, and watched her face battle between approval and disappointment. Couldn't tell which won, but Lorraine said, "Okay, honey, take it away," and disappeared back into her and Dad's room. *Deal with it.* I'm *the Flyer, and we're the ones being threatened.* It should've been Mom there helping me take notes, but if she wouldn't—I could handle it myself.

So now I really did have to keep going. I slogged along grumpily, until I found something that made me forget all about my stepmother.

"But beware ye power of ye witch to defeat ye Goode. For if she do knowingly drinke from ye cuppe wherein ye inner power of Goodness drippeth, then ye Goode do drinke again thereof, so be all his power forsaken, and none shall further Stande."

I shook my head hard. It was past my bedtime now…but that part definitely said something about "ye power of ye witch," right? "Ohh-kay," I said aloud. So I read the passage again, and the page leading up to it. Oh, wow, that tiny print hurts your eyes. But nothing. The next page? It blabbed on about the *"End of Dayes"* when the witches take over and mate with imps. Gross, but no help. So I read that stupid passage again. Out loud. Three times.

The first sentence sounded just like what we were looking for: witch power. *That's Mom and me.* So "ye Goode" in this case is the nasty person who wants us not to fly. *Okay so far.* But… "'Ye cuppe wherein ye inner power of Goodness drippeth?'" *Sounds like some kind of ceremonial, Harry-Potter goblet, all ancient and crusty.*

"Where are we supposed to get something like that?" I muttered. "This book is, like, five hundred years old."

"Four hundred and eighty," said Lorraine from the doorway. How long had she been standing there? *What, Librarian Lady, couldn't trust me with the research after all?* "And I need to return it to the university soon—my librarian friend will get in trouble if it's discovered missing. So did you find something useful?"

"Umm, maybe." Dammit, my headache was back. I shouldn't have let myself get pulled back into this. *How's all this stupid "ye olde" stuff supposed to help me get Mom back in the air?* "You can look if you want. I gotta go to bed." *And don't look at me like that; it's not my fault you stole a giant book!*

I don't know what Lorraine would have answered, because the

telephone rang then. Yeah, ten-thirty on a school night. Who else but Savannah?

"I need to talk to you," she announced. Apparently she'd forgotten all about how bitchy she thought I was.

"'Bout what? Savannah, I have a headache."

"Oh, I can't tell you over the phone, Joss," sighed Miss Phoneaholic. "But I have a doctor's appointment tomorrow morning, so no carpool, 'kay? Tell your dad. I'll see you in second period, 'kay?" And she hung up.

So now my head had two aches: what the heck was "ye cuppe wherein ye inner power of Goodness drippeth?" And what did my not-so-forever-BF have to say that was so frickin' important? No nightmares that night—but not much sleep either.

I didn't realize how tense I felt about seeing Nate next morning until he was absent from math. My whole groggy body relaxed, and I learned enough to be able to help Molly for once. But of course Savannah wasn't there either, so by Language Arts I was stuck back in my rut of *Maybe she's gonna apologize/Maybe she's breaking up with Ty and switching to Nate/Maybe both???* until Mr. Evans, of all people, came to my rescue.

Hard to ignore a teacher who, instead of "Good Morning" says, "Hey, what's a tree hugger?"

"Hippies." "My mom." "Someone who hugs trees." "Molly's mom."

Me and Louis this weekend, I thought, *trying to break our fall.* I touched my sore ribs gingerly.

"Okay. And thinking back to when we read about the Witch Trials in Salem, Massachusetts…where did the Puritans think the Devil resided?"

"In the woods!" "In the *trees.*" "Anywhere outside of the village." "Out in nature."

"Ah," said Mr. Evans. "So. Three hundred years ago nature was the Devil's lair, yet today we love it, or at least we *say* we love it, even if we don't do the best job of showing that. Doesn't any-body wonder when and how this monumental switch in mindset took place?"

Suddenly we all wondered. Turns out it started with the TRANSCENDENTALISTS. Okay, he got me: this was inter-esting. We started taking turns reading a thing about nature by Ralph Waldo Emerson, and I forgot all about Savannah.

We all got to choose our favorite quote and write about it. I liked, *"In the woods we return to reason and faith,"* but I really meant *above* the woods—zooming above the trees, and I couldn't write that. So I picked *"In good health, the air is a cordial of incredible virtue,"* once I found out "cordial" means, like, medicine. The air sure makes *me* feel better! I wrote that, then figured Mr. Evans would think it was dumb, so I erased it and wrote some b.s. about getting outdoors to improve your blood circulation.

Halfway through class, Savannah breezed in.

"Doctor's appointment," she said, plopping herself next to me. Then she leaned in and whispered, "Talk during break, right?"

"Not if you don't tell me what about." I didn't want to start another fight, but honestly...

"For reals, girl, don't you know?" Her face danced with ex-citement.

"Just tell me!" I hissed. Too loudly—got Mr. Evans's attention.

"Miss Enderle, thank you so much for joining us, and have you found a quote to share with the class?" *Jeez, she just got here,* I opened my mouth to say, but Savannah was ready for him.

"'I am not solitary whilst I read and write, though nobody is with me,'" she read promptly. "And I like it 'cause it's true. When-ever I'm reading or writing, it's like I'm having a conversation through the paper."

Mr. Evans looked impressed, and I wanted to laugh out loud. *Oh, she's good, Savannah!* That quote just happened to be the second sentence in the reading. All she'd done was glance down, read it, and fake the rest—just what I would have done! She caught me grinning and grinned back with her little head-toss, and suddenly my beef with her seemed ridiculous. I missed my bestie too much to let a stupid boy mess us up.

"So here's the thing," Savannah said during break. It felt good to be sharing snacks again. "You know Nate likes me, right?"

Ouch. "Duh. He made me give you a choc—a valentine, re-member?" She didn't need to know about that heart; it wasn't like I'd eaten it, right?

"But what I'm *saying* is…" Savannah paused dramatically, "he likes you too. He told me! So I said—"

"Cut it out," I interrupted. "He does not, Savannah. You told me that last year too. He likes *you*, and I'm fine with it, okay? So you can quit trying to make me feel better."

I even believed myself. Till Savannah tossed her head and showed me what Nate had made me give her.

"TOP SECRET," said the folded front of the construction paper Nate had stuffed down my back last Friday. *Wow—very second grade.* Inside: a drawing of a big, grassy field, and what looked like…lions??? perched on a rock in the middle. At the bottom it said, "WHEN YOU GET TY-ERD, SEE WHO ELSE IS LION AROUND. J/K." He'd used Flair pens.

"Yeah, Savannah, this is definitely all about me," I said, giving her a disgusted look. "'Ty-erd?' Seriously? He's saying it right here, he wants you to ditch Tyler and be with him!"

"Oh, I know that," said Savannah all casual, like, *whatever, I've got the two hottest guys in ninth grade lining up for me.* "Even though it says 'J/K,' he has to say he's kidding just to protect himself, right? Boys hate being vulnerable. But that's not—"

"And what's up with the stupid African scene? He's a lion, he's gonna, what, pounce on your heart? That is so lame!"

"It's the savannah, the grassland they have there," Savannah smiled, but gently—no smirking. "It's supposed to be me, right?

Yeah, I told him how lame it was. But Joss. Guess what Nate said about you, when we talked."

Oh yeah. The two of them sitting thigh to thigh outside the marina, Savannah jumping up, Nate moving in... "You talked about me? Right."

"I'm telling you! I said he was sweet, but my heart belongs to Ty, so he should like another girl." Savannah made it sound like those romantic vampire books. "And he said, 'But I don't like any of 'em,' and I said, 'What about Joss?' and he said, 'Yeah, I like her.'" She waited, like she was expecting thundering cheers.

"Savannah," I began. Where to start? *Nate doesn't mean that kind of like. Nate would say anything if it made you happy. Nate is... not in my league.* But Savannah was gazing at me with such honest joy that I didn't have the heart for another argument. She really did mean well. "You're a crazy bee-yotch," I mumbled.

She gave a little shriek and hugged me. "I know, right? Told you! So go for it, Joss! Let him know how you feel, 'kay?" Holding onto my shoulders, she added: "We could double date!!!!" and that thought brought on another hug.

Oh, wow, was I more relieved than ever Nate was gone that day. How could I even have a conversation with him now, knowing Savannah was cheering us on from the sidelines? But through the rest of that finally-pretty-normal day, I felt a weird lightness inside. Not the flying kind, more like...

...happiness. *Whoa.* It came to me in art, when I was painting my coil pot in purples and greens. Savannah can be a drama queen, but she's super smart. *What if she's right about Nate? What if he does like me and just hasn't figured it out yet? And...what if he does figure it out?* By the time the bell rang, I felt just like my coil pot: bright and ready for firing.

And I wanted to fly like crazy.

On the carpool home, the day matched my mood, with huge, puffy clouds and sun warm enough to draw that sweet, grass-shoot smell out of the cold ground. Savannah's mom suggested ice cream in the village—well, I couldn't turn that down, though Michael did, slouching home in his usual sulk. By the time we'd finished our sundaes, the anticipation was fizzing through my limbs like happy electricity, and I practically scurried home. *No need to sneak, Michael's quit bugging me about flying since that last fit of his, just let me dump the backpack and—*

And there was Mom, sitting in our kitchen with Michael like it was the most natural thing in the world. "Hey, turbo," she said.

Michael got up fast. "So, yeah," he said to Mom, and his voice sounded almost as scratchy as hers. Had he been crying? I stared, but he turned his back.

"Hey," I told Mom brightly, dropping a kiss on her head, but she spoke to Michael.

"Just to finish our conversation, babe: I think you're on your own with this thing. I'm sorry, okay? But we can talk more."

"Yeah, it's all good," my brother muttered, and disappeared into his room.

I was smart enough not to ask what they'd been talking about, but my mood couldn't be contained. "Guess what I'm about to do?"

"Ahh…get your mom a snack, maybe? Your brother has a lot to learn in the hospitality department." Man, sometimes I can really see why Mom and Dad got together: same sarcastic sense of humor.

"Sure. Want some popcorn?" I could have kicked myself; popcorn takes too long, and I needed to GO. But too late, Mom was nodding. *Okay, make the microwave kind.* I tossed it in, pressed some buttons, and gave her my best smile. "It's a beautiful day, Mom. You don't think you might wanna…?"

Her look cut me off. "Just the popcorn, thank you."

That should have stopped me. But my blood was practically singing with energy, every muscle pushing upward, and here I was with the one person who could understand. "Wow, I'm about to float right off the floor!" I blurted. "Mom, don't you remember how that feels? Really, I think I could hover right here—want me to try?" My heart pounded at the idea, and I grabbed the side of the table, ready to keep myself from launching straight into the ceiling.

Her face twisted, but I didn't care—it *should* hurt not to fly! We are Flyers. "No, you'll kill yourself," Mom managed, half-smiling. "And yes. Of course I remember. We've been through this, Jocelyn. And I don't want…"

I'm not sure why she broke off, because I had my eyes closed, feeling the warm buzzing under my skin. I'd never realized how pleasant that feeling is, if you force yourself to ignore the urgency. It's like all your cells are working to the max, all at once.

"Of course I remember," she repeated quietly. "It's only the best feeling in the world."

My eyes flew open. "So who wants to stop you, Mom? We have to figure that out, at least. Then if you fly or not, it's…it's up to you. But you can't just let somebody else stop you." And now, drumroll, it was time for the Flying Burgowski Mother to bite my head off, or go back to her couch. One or the other.

"I told you before," Mom said. "Could've been anybody."

OMG, we were going to have an actual conversation about this. *How to turn this moment into research? What would Ms. Boring Librarian do?*

"I know! Let's make a list, right now. Of who's Seen us." I grabbed the notepad and pencil by the telephone. *Quick, before she changes her mind.* "I'll start: Reverend Paula. Now you go."

For once Mom's feelings were dancing all over her face, a perfect picture of that Inner Conflict Mrs. Mac used to talk about. "Me too," she finally said. She ignored the popcorn.

"Oh right, Reverend Paula counts twice," I said, and made two tally marks by her name. "So who else? Oh, duh—the Mystery Video Person, whoever that was." I wrote down "MVP."

Mom got up. "I need a beer," she said, opening the fridge. She must have felt my glare behind her, because she added, "Mr. Howe, probably." She cracked the can and sat down with it, looking at me challengingly. "Your turn."

Flying could wait; my blood continued to churn. She was drinking, but talking: that was good, right? "Umm…Nate, I guess." *Oh, Nate. Will I ever get to talk about this with you?*

"Oh yeah, the condor thing last summer. All right. I know I got Seen over your school that time, so name some people who are always there to pick up their kids, okay?"

I took a deep breath, wondering how I was going to manage such an amazing memory feat, when Lorraine breezed into the kitchen.

"Beth!" No way could Lorraine fake a smile like that; she was really pleased to see Mom there. And Mom real-smiled back. I let them chat for a moment, thinking, *Huh. Sometimes I forget how lucky I am.*

That thought must have blocked out my real brain, because the next thing I said was, "Hey, did I tell you about this weird thing I found in your book?"

Lorraine shot me a frown. Mom asked, "What book?"

"Oh, this big, super ancient one," I told her, still not getting it. "We were researching in it to find out who wants to stop the Flyers, right? And guess what we found, I was going to tell you—"

Mom interrupted me, her voice down below zero. "And how did 'we' know that someone wants to stop the Flyers? Did 'we' happen to forget a certain promise 'we' made not to share certain private information?"

My cells didn't exactly stop buzzing; they sort of curdled. I felt limp. Mom was glaring at me fiercely. Lorraine looked at the floor.

"I kind of forgot," I whispered. Not true; I'd told Lorraine about the poison letter on purpose, out of fear for my mother. But telling this to Mom right now didn't seem like the best idea.

"Well," she said. "I guess I kind of forgot I can't trust you after all. And I kind of forgot you live with someone who can't keep her nose out of other people's business." She stood up, quivering. "And since I'm the subject of your little research project, I think I'll kind of forget to mention all the other people who've seen me fly on this piece-of-crap island, so your little list is worth s---." She turned on Lorraine, who looked pale but lifted her eyes. "You. Stay out of this. This is between me and…me. Nobody else. I don't care what you find in any f------ book. You have NO IDEA what this feels like."

She slammed out, taking the beer.

Michael appeared in his doorway. "Dude. What the hell did you say to her?"

I couldn't move. Lorraine said, "Oh dear."

"Wonderful, this magic," my brother snarled, and slammed himself out too.

Yeah. A nice, normal day.

CHAPTER EIGHT

A LITTLE GIT-TAR ACTION

My brain felt like a hopeless tangle of Christmas lights with no plug to light the way out of the mess.

Lorraine tried to cheer me up, but I kept my head in my hands. *You and your know-it-all book—now Mom's further away than ever.* Finally she left me alone.

Then something weird happened: my flying urge unsnarled me. Don't know how long I sat there, but after a while I started noticing more than the sticky spot on the linoleum by my foot. I felt the energy-hum—in my butt, of all places, and then it swarmed up my body and plugged in my poor brain.

"Oh," I said out loud. *I still gotta fly.* And I jetted out of there before someone could tangle me up again.

No way was I going to let myself be Seen now, so I ran for my old launching-rock in the woods, The Toad. My ribs stabbed, but the flight-pull was stronger than the pain, my legs on fire with it…

Never made it to The Toad. Halfway down the path I let go and hurled myself into the narrow avenue of sky.

Yessss.

Tunnel-flying, I call it, and it doesn't work with doubles. Even flying solo I get whacked and scratched, zooming through the space below the fir branches and above the brush. Think *Return of the Jedi* where they're riding those speeders through that giant forest, ducking and weaving, only the forest isn't giant, it's right up against you. And you *are* the speeder. When I busted out into the open above that old rock-hump, my heart just about busted too. The joy of it. No one could take this away. "Oh wow," I said to the air.

I zoomed across the woods to somebody's sheep farm, then a quick road check—no Reverend Paulas, all clear!—and over to the next woods, following their rise to the center of the island. My heart soared with me, and my ribs quit throbbing. *Hey, just like Ralph Waldo Emerson said!* The air really was "a cordial of incredible virtue." And, thinking of those quotes, above the woods I "returned to reason and faith."

Reason: *Okay, so no more "research"—I could have told you breaking your promise to Mom would piss her off like that, and now she'll never fly with you! If she ever flies at all.*

And Faith: *But! I have to help her more than ever, if she wants me to or not. How could I let some crazy Stander take away her power?*

Reason: *Don't tell me you believe that mess about "ye cuppe wherein ye inner power of Goodness drippeth?!"*

Faith: *Why not? That book is OLD. Lorraine is SMART. You got anything else to go on?*

"Ark," said something behind me, and I squawked back, swerving hard. *Whoa—!* Two ravens zipped past, one on each side of me like I was the slow car on the freeway. Then one of them rose and, I swear, did a barrel roll before dropping down to chase his buddy across the island. Okay, *that* is confidence.

"I can totally do that," I said, and—*whew!* Dizzy city! I did two more before I realized I was freezing again.

Duh, said Reason, *still February, and where's your jacket?* The air's "cordial" was wearing off; I could feel my ribs again. I dropped down, below the wind, and banked for home.

But don't you see? Faith persisted. *You didn't think you could even move after Mom screamed at you, and now look—barrel rolls! You didn't think Nate could ever like you, and—*

Really? You want to go there? Reason snorted. *Nate likes you… why? 'Cause Savannah says so, and he wasn't at school to say "Nuh-uh"?*

I could feel myself slowing down, and gave a little Mom-style flutter-kick to counteract the draggy thoughts.

He could like me. Savannah's too dramatic for him. He just doesn't know it yet.

Nate Cowper, with those eyelashes and that sarcastic mouth.

Reason got brutal. *Get real. She's gorgeous. You're…not. You can fly—isn't that enough?*

Fine, then. The Toad came in sight, my arms sagged, but Faith wasn't giving up. *I'll just focus on defeating the nasty Stander and saving Mom, and I won't even think about Nate.*

Then why are you? Reason wondered, reasonably, as I landed.

But after dinner, Lorraine had to go and mess me up.

"I found the weirdest passage in our book, hon," she confided as I cleared the dishes.

Wait—our book? Are we really back to being a cozy little research team? After what that did to Mom?

I cut her off. "Thought you had to return it to the university."

"My friend gave me one more day," she breathed, and pulled a sticky-note out of her pocket. I saw the word "cuppe."

"Yeah, I already read that part. The 'cuppe' thing, right? I had an idea about that. Just need to, you know, think about it a little."

"Really? Tell me about it!" She read from the sticky-note: "'*For if she do knowingly drinke from ye cuppe wherein ye inner power of Goodness drippeth, then ye Goode do drinke again thereof, so be all his power forsaken, and none shall further Stande.*' Inner power of goodness *drips*? Do you think they mean some kind of magic potion? Or the sacred wine of communion?" Lorraine gazed at me, all hopeful and encouraging, and suddenly I couldn't stand to be in the same room with her.

"I said I need to think about it, okay? I have to do my home-work. And jeez, it's not like the stuff in that book is real, anyway!"

Luckily I was done clearing so I could huff away into my room. But it's hard to focus on Transcendentalism when your stomach is full of guilt-rocks. So I reread Harry Potter Six's horrible ending.

The rain came back on Tuesday, but Nate didn't. I started passing notes with Savannah like the good ol' days. But she kept writing stuff like, "Nate: boxers or briefs????" So by Language Arts I was ready to listen to Mr. Evans.

It was more about nature today. We read something by another Transcendentalist, Henry David Thoreau, who lived out in the woods by himself for two years and said things like, *"Time is but the stream I go a-fishing in."* That made me think of Mom, flying without her watch. Maybe she'd say, "Time is but the sky I go a-flying in." I should tell her that. Tonight. I'd go over after dinner. *But what if she's back under the quilt? Help Lorraine catch the Standers—that's what I need to be doing.* And then Mr. Evans assigned us a prewrite for the humongous essay he was scheming about.

At lunchtime Tyler Howe circulated a new nickname for Louis—I won't repeat it here. But when I complained to Savannah she tossed her hair and said, "Oh, tell Louis to get over it." Then she ignored me for the rest of the day.

By last period, I decided those Transcendentalists had it right. A cabin out in the woods by myself sounded pretty good.

That afternoon I was settling into the kitchen with some Thoreau quotes and a bowl of goldfish crackers when I heard someone through the store-curtain ask, "Is Michael around?"

Normally I tune out the store—if I didn't, I'd go nuts with boredom listening to Dad chat with customers. But that voice made me stop chewing. I'd heard it a week ago, saying something about candy on sale.

Apparently Michael heard it too, because he appeared at his doorway even before Dad called him. Like he'd been wait-

ing for whoever it was. I decided right now that I needed...
something...from the store. Following my brother through the
curtain, I found him saying "Hey, bro," and fist-bumping Zach
Howe like they had just scored a goal together. When did they
get to know each other? And how come I didn't know about
it? Now Michael was introducing Dad, and they were shaking
hands. I drifted toward the snack aisle.

"And have you met the other one? This is Jocelyn," Dad said,
waving toward me. I took that as a signal to come over.

"We've met," Zach said, but he shook my hand too, all formal.
His hand was warmer than mine. "So, what're you up to, bro?"

Damn, Michael just glowed. I had no idea when or where
they'd met, but being called "bro" by this older, magazine-y guy
was making Michael's day. Come to think of it, I had no idea
how old Zach was. Maybe twenty? Those golden-brown eyes
didn't look anything like Tyler's.

"Y'know, just chillin'," Michael mumbled. "You scouted a
good spot for a jumps course yet? Out where you were headed
on Saturday?"

"Jumps course?" Dad asked.

"Yeah, Zach's got a killer bike, he's checking out this place in
the woods to build some, y'know, dirt humps. Hey man, I'll give
you a hand when you're ready to dig."

Wow, my lazy brother offering to give a hand.

"No doubt," Zach said. "That's how you can pay for your
sessions." Wow, when he smiled, his whole face sort of threw
light on whoever he was looking at. Michael bathed in it. "Little
git-tar action going on," Zach explained to Dad.

"Oh, you guys starting a band or something?" Dad's pretty
clueless when it comes to Michael's music.

"No, dude," Michael frowned, but Zach just smiled wider.

"Maybe some day, Mr. Burgowski. I told Michael I'd give him
some tips. Then maybe we can jam together when he's had a
little more practice."

If anyone else had suggested that Michael wasn't already a stud guitar player, he would've bitten their head off. But here he was, nodding like a little kid.

"Well, great. That's nice of you." Did I mention my dad loves to chat? If he worked in a real grocery store, his checkout line would always be the longest. "So you're new here. Where'd you come from?"

I pretended to study my cracker options. This was riveting.

"Seattle," Zach said. "Finished up school a semester early, but I wasn't ready to dive into college yet. So I'm taking some time, putting some cash away, and my uncle offers me this job."

Huh. So he's younger than he looks…eighteen? That's not that old!

"Wow, all the way to Dalby for a job? I'm impressed. Or is the economy that bad in Seattle?" I'm serious, Dad could do this all day.

For the first time Zach's face clouded over a little. "Oh, there's jobs," he said. "I just…needed a little space from the family, if you know what I mean."

"Gotcha." Dad nodded. "So, you have sisters or brothers back in—hey, Joss. You looking for something?"

Shoot. I wanted to hear about Zach's sisters or brothers. And his parents. And what his room looked like. And when his birthday is. "No, I…we don't have any," I fumbled, and turned back to the curtain. "See ya."

What an idiot. But I'm pretty sure Zach said "See ya" back.

I had a hard time focusing on Thoreau, as Zach and Michael made plans for guitar lessons later in the afternoon. *Here? What time?* Couldn't hear. When Michael came back through the kitchen, I asked him casually, "So, lessons, huh?" hoping he'd brag the rest of the information, but he only said, "Yup," all smug, and disappeared into his room.

So back to homework, till Lorraine hurried in. Awkward; I hadn't apologized at breakfast for blowing her off the night before. "What're you doing home from work?" I blurted, adding to Jocelyn's Pile of Rudeness.

"Needed to get my bread started for dinner, so I just zipped over for a moment," Lorraine said, assembling ingredients and pans with lightning speed. *Great—homemade bread. Is she* trying *to make me feel guilty?*

So I dived in. "Sorry for being rude. I don't really have an idea about that 'cuppe' thing either. I just don't want Mom to..." Dammit, my throat was closing up. I've only ever cried in front of Lorraine once, last fall when she caught me trying to sneak off the island to save my mom. I lost it like a baby and she held me like...a mom. Yeah, it brought us closer. But no, I do not like thinking about it.

Lorraine dumped a large mess of flour into a bowl but didn't say anything.

After a few moments I was ready to look up again. "I think I understand," she said then, breathier than ever as she stirred furiously. "You promised Beth. But Jocelyn, this thing is real. These people exist. They're not going away because you don't want to hurt your mom. She's going to be hurt a whole lot worse if we don't help her."

This time that "we" didn't bug me. I gave a huge sniff. "Okay," I said. I closed my notebook and went back to Ye Olde Research.

But, *man.* Do they have to make the print so tiny?

I woke up to find myself alone, my cheek stuck to a sticky-note that said, "*Stande and pray and ye shall never...*" I think the word was "*doubt.*" Oh jeez, what if Zach had come in while I was snoozing away like an idiot? Rubbing my eyes, I squinted again at the horrible print. *Maybe Zach will talk to me some more when he comes for Michael's lesson!* No, dummy, Michael won't share him. *Maybe if I'm researching while they play...*This was hopeless.

I remember in fifth grade reading *The Phantom Tollbooth*, where "killing time" is seen as a horrible crime, but that's exactly what I did. Ditched the giant book. Put away some clean clothes, stuffed some dirty ones under my bed. Rearranged the shells and rocks and feathers on my dresser. Put my series books—Harry, Narnia, *The Chronicles of Prydain*—back in order. Finally I got so tired of myself I plopped down on my bed and went back to my stupid Transcendentalist homework.

I was finishing the last Quote Reflection when someone knocked. "Jocelyn?" Lorraine's whispery voice. *She's back from work already?* I looked at my watch: four forty-five. Wow, I'd killed time all right. "You have a visitor."

"Be right there," I called. *Great. Zach could be coming over any minute, and now's when Louis shows up to ruin the moment...*if there was going to be a moment.

"Hey." Nate Cowper was standing in my kitchen.

WAY too many reasons why I couldn't get a word out.

"Guess I could've just used this door, huh," he said, like that was the important thing. "I just came in through the store and your mom...I mean your stepmom..."

"You know Lorraine," I said accusingly. It's true, but it was hardly the point.

"Yeah. Sorry." I'd never seen Nate look awkward before. "Um...Savannah said you might wanna hang out."

Oh jeez. What else did Savannah say? I sat down at the table, feeling my face getting warm. "How come you haven't been in school?"

"Sick." I didn't invite him, but he pulled a chair out cautiously and sat across the table from me. "I'm fine now. My mom just didn't want me infecting people."

"Oh, but it's okay to infect me?" My heart was hammering so hard, the chest-revving was bound to start.

Nate laughed. "Yeah, Burger, that's why I'm here—to take you down." He fiddled with the salt shaker.

Why are *you here?* I did not ask, not sure I wanted to know. But I had no idea what to say. The only real one-on-one conversation we'd ever had was last summer, and that turned into lame jokes about tide pool critters. I was ready for something a little deeper. But what came out was, "Want some popcorn?"

We were still talking in embarrassed circles as the popcorn popped, when Nate said, "Hey, put some paprika in."

"Seriously? That red stuff?"

"Yeah, and garlic salt. My mom does that."

So I did. "Hey, what about Parmesan?" Then we needed to put in more butter to make it all stick. Pretty soon the popcorn looked like a science experiment, and we were grinning at each other. We carried it into my room and he plopped down on the floor where Savannah always sits, like, *of course I'm here, so what?* I lounged on the bed. And…we talked.

About Mr. Evans: "Dude, he made me rewrite my project intro, like, three times. And then he only gave me a B. My mom was mad, 'cause she wrote most of it."

Wow, can't believe Nate Cowper is sitting here in my room.

About clothes: "How come you wear those sneakers all the time? Aren't girls supposed to be, like, into shoes?"

He notices my feet? "I like my sneakers!"

"They're cool. Did Savannah draw that horse on 'em?"

"Yeah." But I didn't want to talk about Savannah right now. "Hey, no offense, I know Tyler's, like, your best bud, but really? He makes the nastiest jokes."

"I know, right? Tyler's a moron. But he's got my back."

Jeez, it's like we're having a real conversation.

Then here came Savannah again. "I don't know what you guys talk about. But Tyler…" he paused. "Tyler talks about it all the time."

"It?"

"Her, I mean. Savannah. And stuff they do. Together." Was he blushing?

"Is he saying they're, like, having…?" Hey, *you* try saying the word "sex" in your own bedroom, in front of the boy you've liked for three years!

"Dude, forget it," Nate said quickly. "It's none of my business what she…"

His voice trailed off. Half of me felt hurt by his tone: *He's still crushing on her, isn't he?* But the other half was going, *Sex? No way! Savannah would have told me!*

But all her talk about maturity…maybe she is telling me. And Nate's here to check my reaction, because he…

I glanced down to see Nate looking up at me. His eyelashes are so long, they cast little shadows on his face. My mouth felt totally dry all of a sudden. All that salty popcorn.

"It's pretty cool just talking," he said.

I guess I am an idiot. All those stupid fantasies—flying doubles, swooping through the dark, his hands on my shoulders, his breath in my ear, moon peeking through the clouds—I hadn't thought about being *friends* with a boy. Well, not this boy.

"Yeah," I smiled. Then someone knocked on the door.

Not my door. The outside door to our kitchen. The door people use when they're coming over like they said they would.

"I'll get it!" Michael yelled, banging out of his room. *Oh, yeah.* Zach Howe and his *git*-tar.

"I should prob'ly go," Nate said.

Whatever "moment" we were having ended, but for some reason I didn't mind too much. "Okay." We went into the kitchen, where Michael was handing Zach a dish towel for his dripping hair.

"Totally guessed wrong on the rain." *Whoa, when had it started raining?* Zach rubbed his hair, leaving it tousle-y. "Really slow day at the store, so I actually got some practice in, working on a little run I'll show ya. Thanks, man." He tossed the towel back to Michael.

"Hey, Zach, wassup?" Nate got the fist-bump treatment.

"Not much, bro," said Zach. *Hah,* I thought to my brother, *you're not so special.* "Well…" he patted his guitar case, "where you want to go to work, boss?"

"My room," Michael said quickly. *Well, of course, what had I expected? A little concert in the living room?* "C'mon," he added, like the rest of us might not let Zach go. I could understand, actually. Zach made you want to be where he is. Magnetic, that's the word.

"So, um," said Nate behind me.

"Yeah," I said. "Guitar lessons, that's pretty cool."

"Yeah," said Nate. "I might take guitar."

"Cool."

It was hopeless. The awkwardness was back, and I wasn't up for another round of popcorn. We blabbed a little longer, not looking at each other, and then Nate remembered he had homework.

After he left, I sat back on my bed and looked at the spot where he'd been sitting. It had been a good visit. More than good—*amazing*. But as I listened to the sounds coming through the wall, I wasn't really thinking about suddenly being friends with Nate. Or how much he still liked Savannah. Or whether Savannah had lost her virginity. Or how hard it was going to be to solve that stupid Stander riddle. I wasn't really thinking about anything. I was too busy losing myself in the slick bursts of Zach's guitar.

CHAPTER NINE

STEP FORWARD, STEP BACKWARD

Too bad I didn't get to dream about hot guitar players. Instead, those nightmare people in the Pilgrim-y hats were back, shouting at me. Or at Mom. Is that why she'd grounded herself, to make the poison-letter nightmares stop?

"Okay, okay, I'll go back to Lorraine's book after school," I grumbled to myself, splashing water on my face. *Unless she's returned it to the library…in which case I'm off the hook.*

On the way to school Michael sat in front, since it was his turn to Not Speak With Joss. Savannah dived right in: "Wonder if Nate's gonna ask you to go with him?" I kept my mouth shut about his visit—no way was I giving her that to chew on.

So of course Nate said exactly nothing to me all day.

"Told you he likes you," Savannah whispered as we slid into our seats for Language Arts. Mr. Evans was writing another great big word on the board.

"Right, 'cause he just can't keep himself away from me."

My bestie gave me a pitying smile. "Seriously, Joss. The more he likes you, the less he'll talk to you! He's a *guy*."

I rolled my eyes at Miss Relationship Advice. *This is why I don't tell you stuff.*

"Double-dating would be so fun…" Savannah continued, but Mr. Evans came to my rescue.

"Good morning, my fellow Transcendentalists," he said. I kept my eyes on our teacher like a good little student, though at the edge of my vision I could see Savannah shaking her head with exasperation. "Last couple of weeks we've delved into the fascination with nature that made our boys Emerson and Thoreau so unique to their time. Today we're going to examine the concept of uniqueness itself. Hence, this word." He pointed to the whiteboard. "Repeat after me: 'NONCONFORMITY.'"

We did. Savannah kept glaring at me.

"Now write it down. This is Point Number Two of Transcendentalism; you may go back and label Love of Nature as Point Number One if you like." We all obeyed. A minute later, when Mr. Evans explained that "conformity" meant doing what everyone else did, and "nonconformity" meant being different, I thought it was pretty funny that we all just followed along like that.

We spent the period going back through Thoreau and Emerson, finding quotes that illustrated nonconformity. This was my favorite: *"If a man do not keep pace with his companions, perhaps it is because he hears a different drummer. Let him step to the music which he hears."* In other words, if you don't fit in, don't sweat it. This reminded me of McClenton High School last fall. Boy, did I "not keep pace" with those kids! They never even believed me that Dalby Island was in the United States.

"Joss, it's no fun having a boyfriend when you don't." Now that we were working in pairs, Savannah was back at it—who knew you could whine in a whisper?

"Really, no fun? I'll be sure to tell Tyler that," I grinned.

"You know what I mean! Why do you always have to be such a goober?"

"Me? I'm just stepping to the music which I hear," I told her innocently, but an image from one of my early flying dreams popped into my brain: me and Harry Potter, flying side by side like superheroes. Only these days Harry was Nate.

Flyers are nonconformists, I realized—duh, right? We have to be. But it's pretty lonely up there when the only other Flyer I know in the world won't fly with me. What would that be like, to be a regular girl with a boyfriend! To be like Savannah, sharing boy-talk. Clogging up the school hallways with PDA. *Could Nate keep my flying secret? Oh, if he cared enough about me...* Even Savannah and Tyler wouldn't share that kind of closeness.

Mr. Evans hovered, so we had to shut up, but toward the end of the period, the class discussed how Thoreau moved out of his lonely cabin when he noticed that he'd worn a path by walking the same way every day. "See how hard nonconformity is? It's human nature to fall into patterns, to follow," said Mr. Evans. And I thought, *Yeah. 'Cause it's a lot less lonely.*

"You could go talk to *him*, you know," Savannah said around her burrito at lunch.

"Savannah, shut UP about him."

"About who?" Louis joined us as he's been doing lately, since Savannah's started being nicer to him.

"Mr. Evans," I lied. Savannah looked hard at me. I looked at my burrito. Wasn't trying to be snotty—I just didn't feel like Louis needed to know about Nate.

As soon as we got home, Michael disappeared into his room. But no guitar this time—he started banging around. Last thing I needed was to get him in my face again, so I couldn't ask what the hell he was doing. No way could I do my Transcendentalist pre-write with that racket, so I decided to go to the library. *Maybe Lorraine won't see me, 'cause the last thing I need is for her to start asking me about that wacko "cuppe"...* which was the whole reason I couldn't talk to Mom, even though I really really REALLY needed her advice about boys... *Aaarghhh,* people*!*

Then I saw something white sticking out behind the flag on our mailbox.

My first thought was, *Why not put it* in *the mailbox?* Then I saw the block letters on the envelope: **FLYER**.

I hugged myself automatically as the temperature seemed to drop. "Oh, not again," I said aloud.

It wasn't here fifteen minutes ago, I walked right by! Glancing wildly down the street, I saw only a gray-haired lady getting into her car. I circled the mailbox like it was a bomb I had to defuse.

Don't open it. Don't give them the satisfaction. The Pilgrim dream-people flashed through my brain. "Dammit!" I said. "Leave us alone!"

Of course I opened it. Whoever left it there knew I would.

It was a sweet little greeting card, or it used to be, before someone tore apart the hand-holding cartoon boy and girl, right where their hands met. Above them, thought-bubbles connected them to a cartoon light bulb, which was left un-ripped.

I opened it. Inside it used to say, **You Light Up My Life**. But someone had written a big "F" in front of the word "light," then slashed the whole word through with a red marker.

No Flight.

"Uhhh," I said, and dropped it. Then stood there like a paralyzed idiot.

Tell Lorraine. The Standers are real. "Hah, Lorraine already knows that," I muttered, poking at the card with my sneaker. "She'll just say I told you so." *Well, who else—?*

I needed my mom.

As soon as I knocked, I knew this was a lousy idea. If Mom wasn't at work, then she wouldn't be in any kind of shape to talk. But too late. Tion was meowing at me from the other side of the door and I heard Mom say, "Come in." So I did, carrying my evil little card by one corner.

Let's hear it for talking-gerbil ads on TV: Mom was laughing. Before she could reharden her face, I held up the card. "Mom, I got one too."

She got right up off the couch. "Oh, babe," she said. I stared hard at her old rug, holding the tears down. Mom's never been real touchy-feely, so I wasn't expecting a hug, but... *Hey, she got up, didn't she? That's a step forward.*

She turned off the TV.

"Hmm. That's a Step Backward," Mom said.

"What?" I faltered, wondering if she'd read my mind.

"Something my therapist says. She keeps this little chart for me, you know, Steps Forward and Steps Backward. Gives me a better way to deal with bad days. Which it looks like you are having."

Oh wow. Mom's seeing her therapist instead of using substances again. And she's talking to me. HUGE Step Forward. A little sob of relief bubbled out of me.

"Cocoa, right?" Mom said, and disappeared into the kitchen.

So we talked.

I showed her the card. I told her about the Cupid. I apologized for telling Lorraine about the poison letter.

She stayed silent, so I took a deep breath and continued. "But they're real, Mom. Those old anti-Flyer people in the book. Standers. They stand against magical powers. They're our enemy. And one of 'em lives on Dalby."

At that point Mom, who had been nodding at her mug, turned her sharp, dark eyes on me. "You show Lorraine this?" She jerked her head at the latest Stander gift.

"Not yet."

She took a short, hard breath through her nose. "Well, do. Bring her in. Lorraine's a smart cookie. Looks like we're gonna need some of that."

GINORMOUS Step Forward. So I told her what we'd read so far, and about the weird riddle that was stumping both of us.

"'Ye inner power of goodness *drippeth*?' Sounds like tears to me," Mom muttered. "Maybe if you drip some tears on the Stander's writing?"

But by this time I didn't need to cry anymore. I told her about the Transcendentalist stuff we'd been reading and how it reminded me of flying, and of her. She got a little quiet then, like, *Uh-oh, I know what's coming and the answer is No,* but I was smart enough not to go there, and she lightened up again. She even teased me about inviting her boss, Mr. Howe, to be my guest speaker next day. "Crushing on the big guy, huh? He is quite the hunk."

Well, I said I wanted to talk to Mom about boys, right? Like a dork, I blushed—and got my wish.

"Aha…" she said. "Who is it? Zach Howe, am I right?"

"Mommm! Come on." I felt myself blush harder. "He's way too old for me."

"Yes, he is," she said firmly, sounding more like a mom than I had heard her in weeks. Step Forward.

"But there is this guy at school…"

"Louis? Babe, he's a sweetie. Love that kid. And they say redheads are supposed to be trouble."

"No! Louis is my friend, okay? I'm talking about Nate." *There—said it. I'm having a Guy Talk with my mom!*

"Aha," Mom said again. "Bottom line. You like this Nate guy?"

"I don't know."

"Is that, 'I don't know if I want to tell you,' or 'I don't know how I feel?'"

Wow, when did she start taking Mom lessons? "Ummm…the second one."

She nodded.

"Yeah, I like him. A lot. But he likes Savannah. But she says he likes me. But I can't tell."

Mom shook her head hard. "Oof. Such intrigue. But even if Savannah's right, babe… aren't you wondering about…boys and flying?"

"What do you mean?"

"Well, that card you got, right? And my letter? The Flying

Burgowski Mom giving up flying in order to be a good wife and mother? You're worried that you're going to have to choose between your flying and your relationships."

Holy shih tzu. She was way ahead of me. Well, duh, she'd lived it already. And she was right. I was worried.

But. "I don't even have a relationship."

"Oh, you will, it's only a matter of time. And the big question is, then what? You've already handled your power way better than I did at your age. I mean, you've shared your secret with your buddy and your brother—two boys! I'd always thought that would kill the magic, but you went ahead and you're fine. So maybe it wouldn't be any different with a boyfriend. When you have one," she stopped my interruption.

Whoa. A tide of warmth pushed through me. If I could tell Nate…if I could *show* him, then…it would our special secret. Not like *Harry Potter*, where everyone's magic. More like those vampire books Savannah reads. *Bound together with a magical bond…*

"On the other hand," Mom added.

"What other hand?" The warm tide ebbed away.

"Well, your Cupid doll," she murmured. "Love. Shot-up wings. Pretty accurate symbol for us."

"But you just said I could share my secret with boys!"

"It's the love part, that's what's different." She sounded like she was talking to herself. "When you love someone, you give part of yourself to them. Less power for you."

"Nuh-uh!" I burst out. "You're talking about *you*, not me! You said it yourself—*you* gave up flying when you met Dad 'cause you thought you had to. You even let the Poison-letter guy make you stop flying 'cause he said it interfered with your love for me and Mich—"

I stopped. *Oh great, she's gonna go back under the quilt now.*

Her voice got scratchy, but all she said was, "Well, maybe I was wrong. Maybe I could've told your Dad. Maybe I could've kept flying. But I didn't want to take that chance. Flying's a magic power, and love's a magic power. Kinda makes sense that they mess each other up."

"But—but—you flew with me! And you love me! And you let Dad see you fly"—it's true, last fall, and that one time was all Dad could handle—"and he still...he still cares about you! So they can't be messing each other up!" *Because if they did, that would* suck.

"Yeah," my mom said thinly, "But maybe I wasn't wrong. Flying with you guys was wonderful. Honestly, it...it brought me back, you know? But now it feels more like...something I want to give in to."

"So give in to it!"

She gave me a hard look. "I don't have a real good track record when it comes to giving in to stuff, do I."

"But flying's different, Mom! It's—flying is healthy!" "*The air is a cordial...*" "We're Flyers!"

She shook her head. The wide-open, vulnerable Mom of the past few amazing minutes was closing up like a window shade. "I had my time, Joss. If I'd given up flying right when I met Ron, I think I would've had a fine life. It was trying to keep flying that messed me up, not quitting."

I looked at her in shock. "So you're telling me if I start going out with...a boy...I have to give up flying or I'm gonna be as messed up as you?"

It was a horrible thing to say to anybody, let alone your mother. But she didn't snap at me. I wish she had. Instead she said, "I'm not telling you anything about you, babe. I'm just talking about me."

"But I *want* you to tell me about me." Tion crossed into my lap from Mom's, like she could hear how pathetic I sounded even if Mom didn't. That freed up Mom to pull the quilt off the couch and wrap it back around herself.

STEP FORWARD, STEP BACKWARD

"Sorry, babe. You're on your own with this. The more I think about it, the less I have to say." She closed her eyes, and—bam—we were right back to last weekend, like this whole cocoa-happy evening hadn't happened.

The only thing worse than trying not to cry is knowing that you can go right ahead, but it won't help. Thinking of how Mom might react, or not react, made me want to cry even more. So I got up fast, dumping Tion.

"Thanks, Mom," I told her from the doorway. *Thanks for all the great advice.* No, I did not go and hug her. "I'll see ya, 'kay?"

Her "'Bye, babe," came out quilt-muffled as I left.

Big, huge, ginormous Step Backward. I walked home with all my muscles clenched. When my door was closed I let everything come loose.

Mom won't help me. Mom wishes she'd never met Dad and had us. Or she wishes she'd given up flying sooner than she did. Because Mom thinks Flyers have to give up flying if they fall in love.

I stopped crying just in time for Lorraine's tap at my door: "Set the table, hon?"

Wonderful. I splashed off my face as best I could in the bathroom, but of course Lorraine gave me the Concerned Parent look as soon as she saw me.

"What is it, Joss? Something you can tell me?"

I shook my head and kept my eyes down as I dug out the silverware. If she'd only asked that first question, yeah, I might have told her. Even Mom said it was time to bring Lorraine in on this! But that second question, dripping with concern—all that did was piss me off. Dinner was leftover meatloaf and silence.

Later, lying in bed after giving up on my essay prewrite, a thought hit me like a cartoon punch: first I'm upset about having to sacrifice a boyfriend when I don't even have one. Then I'm upset about not having a loving mom, and I get one. The wrong one.

That Stander card should've said, "Joke's On You, Flyer."

CHAPTER TEN

WHY THEY CALL IT DRAMA

Thursday was a horrible sit-com: *Right, He Definitely Likes Me.*

(Scene: Dalby Island School, soccer field, PE class, two days after Nate's visit to Joss)

NATE: "Burger! Behind you!"

JOSS: >*grunt*< *(Turns and crashes into Greta, who takes the ball away and scores.)*

NATE: "Nice one, Burger."

JOSS: "Shut up."

(Scene: Dalby Island School, lunch room, later that day)

SAVANNAH: "Hey, look who's here."

NATE: "What's up?"

JOSS: "Unemployment. The sky." *(Savannah kicks her.)* "Ow."

NATE: "Wow, you're funny. Hey. Who's your guest speaker for Career Day?"

JOSS: "Tyler's dad. Who's yours?"

NATE: "I couldn't get one."

JOSS: "Oh."

NATE: "I know, right? See ya." *(Wanders away.)*

SAVANNAH: *(Kicks Joss again.)* "See??"

JOSS: "You are so incredibly idiotic…"

Pathetic, right? I wouldn't watch that show.

By the time Career Day came along on Friday, I was a mess. Why had I thought the owner of a drugstore would be a good speaker? Mr. Howe was going to be *lame*. Michael still wasn't speaking to me, so Dad kept asking careful little questions while I did the dishes, like, "Joss, is there anything you need to tell me about what's going on with you and your brother?" I didn't growl at him like Michael would've, but I used "I'm fine," and guess what, it works great for getting people off your back. No wonder Mom does it.

And Nate kept on not talking to me. When he did, it wasn't quite what I expected.

Louis's big worry on Career Day was Janice, who was now pretty officially his mom's girlfriend. Even I could tell by the way they looked at each other when they came into our store. So I signed up for her presentation, to be there for my buddy. Plus Marine Biology sounds ridiculously cool.

Everyone else thought so too, so there was a limit on how many people could get in. Savannah didn't make it, but she seemed happy that I did. "Nate," she pointed to his name on the list. "Sit next to him, 'kay?"

But Tyler made the list too, and he beat me to it. So what: Janice's presentation was in Mrs. Mac's room, and it felt good to be back in a room with a teacher who thinks I'm smart. She gave me a hug when I walked in. Her hair's mostly grown back since her chemo, and yeah, it's grayer, but it still looks great.

Louis had to introduce Janice, and I thought he might pass out. There were maybe twenty-five people in the room—for Louis, a huge crowd. He turned totally white and got stuck on the word "oceanography," and I heard Tyler laugh, but then Janice sailed in and shook Louis's hand and thanked him, and he sat down, shaking.

Janice was awesome. She started with a story of herself at our age, how her aunt took her whale-watching and a whale looked her right in the eye and that did it—she knew what she wanted to do with her life. She had a Powerpoint of her work with the orcas who live right here in the Santa Inez Islands, and she could name each whale just by looking at the shape and pattern of its big fin. She showed us a chart of their family structure and talked about how many females each dominant male usually mates with. Then she asked if there were any questions.

Tyler raised his hand and it kind of went downhill from there.

He was giggling even before he spoke. "Yeah, so what do the other males do? Do they, like, mate with each other?"

The room shifted uncomfortably. Mrs. Mac used The Look on Tyler, but he's pretty much immune.

Janice explained pleasantly that the less dominant males often were not able to pass on their genetic material, and that this actually helped the overall strength of the group, or pod. Tyler raised his hand again.

"What about the dominant females? Do they get to ignore the males if they want to and, like, just do it with each other?"

This happened all at once: Janice's bright face froze and turned red. Louis put his head in his hands. Mrs. Mac said, "Mr. Howe, step into the hall with me." And Nate said, "Dude. Don't be a douche."

With Mrs. Mac outside, it took a couple minutes for the room to settle down. I wanted to jump up there and yell at everyone to shut up and let Janice talk, but I didn't want to embarrass Louis any worse. Luckily Janice is really cool. She put a hand on Louis's shoulder and murmured, "Well, you did try to warn me, didn't you?" Then she cleared her throat and asked, "Does anyone have any questions worth answering?"

People did, so the presentation limped back to life, and so did Louis. When Mrs. Mac led Tyler back in, Nate moved his chair to turn his back. At the end, as Mrs. Mac was making Tyler apologize to Janice for being inappropriate, Nate suddenly crouched down by me.

"He's a total douchebag, okay? Tell Louis 'sorry.'"

I think it was the nicest thing he'd ever said to me. But he took off before I could answer.

Mr. Howe's presentation was next, in Mr. Evans's room. Not very many people had signed up to hear him, big surprise. Louis had, but he didn't come and I didn't blame him. Not with Douchebag Tyler standing at the door high-fiving people, shouting, "Welcome to the Money Show!" Mr. Howe was too busy clipping on his name tag and looking at his notes to say anything to his son, I guess. But after Tyler's third yell, Nate went up and kicked him behind the knee. Tyler sat down suddenly, Nate smiled at me, I smiled back, and suddenly we were friends. Just like that. This time he sat next to me.

I don't have any problems speaking in front of people, so I introduced Mr. Howe very professionally, if I do say so myself. All our Transcendentalist quote-posters were up on the wall, so I picked up on mine and said, "Here's someone who definitely hears a different drummer, because he started a store on Dalby that isn't like any of the others."

The first thing Mr. Howe said was, "It's so interesting that Miss Burgowski chose that quote to start us off with. I was looking at some of these posters earlier, and you know, that's exactly what I want to talk about today." Then he started his Powerpoint with two pictures: a Coke and a Pepsi.

"I did the graphics for him," Tyler whispered loudly.

"Choices," said Mr. Howe. "We're faced with them every day. Coke vs. Pepsi. Chevy vs. Ford." He showed that picture, which started a brief, hissed argument among some of the boys in the room: "Gotta be Ford." "Ford sucks."

But Mr. Howe cut through them. "Not all of our choices are so trivial, though. Sometimes the choices we make about spending our money say a lot about the kind of people we are. For example, my store." A picture of Howe's Drugs. "We sell things like jewelry." A picture of the earrings rack. "Or, you could buy this." A picture of handmade leather-and-bead earrings set against a tie-dyed cloth.

"Hey, my mom makes those!" Molly squealed.

"We also sell pottery…" He showed some factory-made mugs with "Dalby Island" in curly script over a leaping orca. "Or, you could buy this." Brown-and-green pottery on a table at the holiday fair. I didn't recognize it; too many potters on Dalby. "My point is, you need to have choices. Just because we live on an island, that's no reason to pretend we don't need the real world. And that's why I opened my shop…to give people choices. So, are there any questions about running a small business?"

Just what I was afraid of—LAMER than lame. Nate and I looked at each other and shrugged. Then Mr. Evans raised his hand. I thought he was going to do that teacher thing where they ask something they already know just to start a discussion. But he was frowning. "So, are you saying, then, that cheap, mass-produced items are preferable to locally made?"

"Not at all, sir, but I'm glad you asked," Mr. Howe said heartily. He looked like Mr. Evans's opposite: suit and tie instead of work shirt and jeans; smooth, dark hair instead of bushy gray; tall and bulky instead of short and round. "Please note that I am not, repeat *not*, preaching one particular lifestyle. I am merely offering, through my store, a way to partake of the regular life of mainland America. A place for those Dalbians for whom the freedom of the island has proven to be, shall we say, a false freedom. A freedom to go their own way, like Mr. Thoreau says—" he waved at the posters, "which can lead people to feel that society's rules no longer apply to them."

I was totally lost, and judging by the fidgeting in the room, so was everyone else. *Oh, jeez, I should've invited Dad after all!* He might have embarrassed me a little, but at least he wouldn't use words like "advocating" and put the room to sleep.

But Mr. Evans wasn't done. "Could you give us an example of this 'false freedom' you're describing?" His tone was polite as ever, but his eyes were narrowed. I sat up; Nate did the same.

"Absolutely. When I wanted to add the deck onto my store, I went to get a building permit, and you know what the inspector told me? I was his first customer in five months. Now, do you folks really think five whole months went by on Dalby without anybody building anything?" He smiled indulgently at us. "Of course not; only nobody here bothers with things like building permits. They just go their own way." Mr. Evans opened his mouth, but Mr. Howe carried on happily. "Another example? My own firstborn." It took us a second, but then everyone stared at Tyler, who grinned and waved. "He's fifteen. Last week, when we were discussing his academic future, I told him he could start taking Drivers' Ed this summer, and you know what he told me? Quote, nobody bothers with that stuff here, Dad, they just let their kids start driving. Unquote." He looked around the room, still smiling. "Well? Was he right? Search your souls—you know the answer perfectly well."

I thought of Michael. Yeah, Dad hadn't let him drive before he got his permit, but he was pretty much the strictest dad we knew.

"So island life breeds lawlessness, is that the point you're making?" This time Mr. Evans didn't bother to raise his hand.

Mr. Howe tilted his head politely. "Nonconformity was celebrated by Mr. Thoreau and, I can tell, by this classroom." Again he gestured at the posters. "But let us not forget that Mr. Thoreau went to jail for refusing to pay his taxes. And as a small business owner, I know that paying my taxes is part of the deal; if I decide to be different and not pay, if everyone decides that, well, then, society falls apart, doesn't it? No nice roads to drive on, or schools to go to, right? So," he added as Mr. Evans seemed to be trying to interrupt, "my point is this: there is such a thing as too much freedom. Dalby Island has about as much freedom as a society can handle, maybe a little more. And my store, I'm proud to say, offers a way for people to spend their money to support the society of the entire United States, not just local...individuals."

"I thought you guys just sold aspirin and stuff," Molly piped up. She wasn't trying to be funny—Molly never is—but everyone laughed, even Mr. Evans, and the tennis-game tension between him and Mr. Howe faded away as people started asking stuff like, "How do you know how much to charge?" and "What do you do with the stuff that doesn't ever sell?"

Thank goodness, my speaker's presentation didn't totally suck. I shook Mr. Howe's hand politely at the end and thanked him for coming.

"So him and Evans, what was that about?" Nate was holding the door for me like the most natural thing in the world.

"I have no idea," I said. I really didn't. And I was too happy to care.

We had one more set of speakers—I didn't get into the Veterinarian one and had to sit through some architect who nearly put me to sleep—and then lunch. Nate sat with me, and I saw Tyler hesitate with his tray, but then Savannah came up and steered him over. They sat at the end of our table, but still—Louis took one look and went to sit in his old spot by himself. I felt kind of bad about that.

School got out an hour early so we could start the goat pen work party, and all the speakers, after eating lunch with the teachers, were invited to join. Mr. Howe came over to me as lunch ended and gave his "regrets," because he had to get back to his store. "Otherwise your mom won't get to eat *her* lunch," he added, with that same formal smile. It gave me a little jolt, and I realized I had completely forgotten he was Mom's boss. I muttered, "Okay, thanks," and he left, probably shaking his head over the rudeness of kids these days. But then he has Tyler to live with, so maybe he didn't notice.

Tyler's rude, but he's not dumb, and he spent most of the goat pen time working his way back toward Nate so he could start speaking to him again. From what I've noticed, when boys get mad at each other, they never need to Talk About It, they just wait a while and then move on like nothing happened. Or they punch each other. Sounds okay to me; I'd take a punch over Drama any day. But Nate wasn't being a typical boy for once. As we took turns digging postholes with the architect-mom, Nate even explained to Savannah why he wasn't speaking to her BF. I had to fill in the details, quietly, because Architect Lady didn't need to hear.

"Huh," said Savannah. "So Nate, are you mad at Ty for embarrassing Louis, or for being homophobic about his mom, or what?"

She's amazing, Savannah. I had been wondering the same thing, but my brain hadn't boiled it down like that. I mean—embarrassing Louis had never been a problem for Nate, or for anybody. And I'd never noticed him leaping to defend gay people before.

"I guess both," Nate said, shrugging. He had taken his jacket off, wearing only a white T-shirt in the clammy air, and I noticed his arm muscles bunch up like little potatoes as he grabbed the posthole digger. Then I noticed Savannah beaming at me, and it hit me: *Oh. Nate's not embarrassed because of Louis or Janice or Shasta, but because of me.*

Oh, wow, I dug some great postholes. All manual labor should be done by people who feel liked.

Pretty soon our digging squad met up with Janice's, which included Louis and Molly and Heather. They were all laughing about something, and I felt happy for Louis, but then he saw us and his face just fell. Seriously, I finally understood that expression:

one minute, eyebrows, smile, chin, everything's pointed up—the next, down they go. But then something weird happened.

Out of nowhere, Tyler loomed up behind Louis. Louis flinched, but Tyler leaned down and muttered something, and then walked away to the far corner of the new pen, where they were already working on the roof. Louis cast us a helpless look, but he followed Tyler. Savannah opened her mouth, then closed it again.

Janice said quietly, "Last hole? Who wants the honor?" Nate dug the hole, but it was a crappy one because he, like the rest of us, was trying to see what Tyler was doing to Louis. *He wouldn't dare hit him in front of all these grown-ups, right?*

Right. "Apologized," Louis said to Janice when he returned a few minutes later. His face was red as his hair, but he was smiling, and she gave him a hug. I wanted to too, till I realized Louis still hadn't looked at me.

Savannah busted in. "For reals? He said he was sorry for being a jerk? Did his dad make him?"

"Um, no," Louis said, still looking at Janice. "He just said his questions didn't come out the way he meant them to, and he wanted me to know he thought you were, like, cool."

"Well, it's a start." Janice smiled, reaching to take the digger back from Nate, who was nodding at Louis in this really adorable way. *Whoa, Nate and Louis friends? Wouldn't that be something?* "Here, let me just trim up that hole a bit..."

"Told you Ty can be sweet when he wants to," Savannah said to all of us. "Joss, I'm serious, we should do something together after school—watch a movie or something."

"Uh-huh," I said automatically, and dang—there went Louis's face again. Janice put a hand on his shoulder as she had back in Mrs. Mac's room, and steered him away, saying "Okay, my group, let's go brag on our progress to the Person in Charge." Molly and Heather both threw me "you-go-girl!" smiles as they trailed after. Architect-Lady took our digger and followed.

Nate frowned after them. "You know Tyler's just trying to get in good with us, right? He still hates gays. And he doesn't give a crap about Louis's feelings."

"Neither do you," Savannah retorted. "I heard you make that joke last week in math, about the bartender who—"

"I know," Nate said hurriedly. Oh, man, is he cute when he's embarrassed! "But I feel bad now. I was just going along, you know? It's what you do, you go along with people."

"*Whoso would be a man, must be a nonconformist,*" I quoted. Nate stared at me. He has Mr. Evans for Sixth Period, and that was the Emerson quote he'd chosen for his poster, a tiny stick figure facing off against a crowd of stick figures. But hey—Nate's no artist, right? Remember that valentine?

Savannah laughed. "Oh, she nailed you, Cowper. I'm just saying, that's all Ty does, right? He just goes along, like you do. And when he goes too far, he fixes it. Like today: problem solved. That's pretty mature, if you ask me."

Nate was blushing big time. "Yeah, mature," he muttered. "Hey, my dad's here. See ya." And he took off.

If I'd bet a million dollars on what Savannah said next, I'd be rich. "Told you he likes you!"

"You told me boys *don't* talk to you when they like you," I reminded her. But it still felt good to hear.

"Oh, you're past that stage now," she smiled, perching her butt on the hood of someone's car next to the furthest posthole.

I joined her. "You're full of it. But…he did come over and hang out the other day."

"No WAY! Why didn't you TELL me?"

Should've bet on that too. So of course she had to mine me for all the details. Hearing myself, I started wondering if she was right. *Wow. Nate Cowper?*

Then Savannah lost me. "So, girlfriend. Nate's pretty hot, but he doesn't, you know, know stuff like Ty does. Should I tell Ty to give him some tips?"

I looked at her. *Is she saying what I think she's saying?*

"Sex, you idiot," she said boldly. "He's a *guy*, Joss. I keep telling you. When he asks you out, that's the first thing he's gonna be thinking about."

So that was why Nate blushed when he said, "Mature"—the same way he'd looked in my room, saying, "stuff they do... together."

"Just 'cause Tyler does..." *But what do I know about guys?* "And, yeah, Savannah, you better watch it, 'cause I heard Tyler's been bragging about...stuff with you."

"Sex, Joss—you can say the word," Savannah snapped. "And so what? People can say whatever they want—I don't care."

She sounded like my mom, and I felt a flicker of admiration. "What if your parents hear? Won't they, like, freak out if they know their daughter's having...sex?"

"They're not gonna find out. We're, like, careful."

I'm such an idiot. I thought Tyler was only bragging.

"Well, don't look at me like that. You seriously didn't know?"

I shook my head. Savannah put her hand on my leg and smiled at me like her mom does. "Joss, I'm sorry. I would've told you, but I thought you knew. Or I thought you wouldn't want to know. Whatever." *Ouch.* "Anyway, it's really not that big a deal. Not like the books make it sound." *Really?* I found that vaguely disappointing. "And he's so sweet about it, Joss." Her face melted into this kind of joy; for a moment my best friend looked like a woman in one of those old oil paintings. Her voice dropped into a whisper. "He says he loves me. When we're...together." Then it raised back up in triumph: "And that's the Tyler Howe nobody knows but me."

"Phooo..." Too many things to say. *Savannah was right: I am totally immature. My best friend lost her virginity and thinks I can't handle it. But!!* I'm a Flying Burgowski. We have power. We have a secret enemy. And it's not like I'm totally out of it: I fantasize about Nate all the time. *Yeah, right: about flying with him. Wow.*

Savannah gabbed away, kind of impatient since she'd figured out how far behind I was, and how disappointed. Told you she was smart.

"…so if you don't want to hear about it, Joss, fine—then don't bring it up, okay? And," looking suddenly fierce, "don't you dare tell my mom."

"I would never do that," I said, shocked that she thought I might. But Mr. Howe's last comment stuck in my mind: *There's such a thing as too much freedom.*

"Yeah, okay," Savannah relented. Then that laugh of hers, like a jingle for an ad. "Bet you really want to double-date with us now, right? Seriously, Ty could teach…"

"Don't be disgusting!"

She actually hugged me then, which felt like a kind of apology. The lady whose car we were sitting on was approaching with a frown, and Savannah slid off.

"Really, I hope you do get with Nate, okay? But don't worry about me and Ty. We know what we're doing." I slid off too and smiled politely at the annoyed woman. "Oh yeah," Savannah added as her mom's car pulled up, "if it doesn't work out with Nate, I can always get Ty to introduce you to his cousin, right? Have you *seen* that guy?"

CHAPTER ELEVEN

THE IMPORTANCE OF DROOL

Think I'll quit writing for a while. Things are going great, but I don't have time to write now that Nate and I are hanging out more. Plus the pregnant goats showed up at school last week—Pansy and Dora—so we have to observe and take notes on them in Science, on top of our textbook work. And Ms. Schneider seems to think we were all born with algebra-brains like hers. And when Mr. Evans piles that Transcendentalism essay on, it'll probably kill me.

At least Lorraine's cooled it on the Stander Research: she hasn't found one thing more on defeating them in that whole Gandalf-y book! She says her UW librarian friend has another moldy old book for her, but she doesn't have time to drive down and get it. But Mom and I haven't had any more threats, so it's all good.

Man, I did not mean to be gone for two whole weeks! Feels like my life's a treadmill that someone keeps speeding up. Get this: Savannah and I finally double-dated. It's not like there's a movie theater on Dalby, but we all sat in Nate's family room and watched *Shrek II* on their HDTV, popcorn and everything, and Tyler acted like a human being for once. Nate didn't put his arm around me, but when Savannah and Tyler started kissing, he did smile and roll his eyes. And we've started doing homework on the phone sometimes. Haven't hung out with Louis at ALL, but we still high-five in the hallway. So it's all good.

Hey, it's a week later, thought I'd check in. Mom said she'd join us for Sunday dinner again! She seemed pretty cheery.

Oh, and Lorraine brought that other ancient book back from Seattle yesterday. It's a lot smaller and dark green, but even more crumbly than the giant one. Can't believe they let it leave the library. Lorraine dived right into it and found another part talking about "ye inner goodness." She thinks it means blood. Blood dripping into a "cuppe"? Sounds crazy satanic!

I told her I'd check it out when I can, but…really? Number One, I have WAY too much homework, and so does Nate, and I have to call him. And Number Two, if Mom's given up flying for good, why bother figuring out how to defeat the Standers? Those weird threats last month were probably some kind of Valentine's prank. I didn't say that to Lorraine, though. I'll probably end up helping her research when she starts bugging me to. But for now it's all good, right?

When I wrote that thing about the treadmill, I just meant lots of stuff was happening. But after a month, my metaphor felt real. I was getting nowhere. My "relationship" with Nate was stuck pretty much where it had started on Career Day. We ate lunch together, passed some notes, saw some movies, but always with Savannah and Tyler acting like a married couple with us as kids. Oh, and we talked on the phone, but always about homework. Wow. And Lorraine kept dropping hints about researching, but New Cheerful Mom made me think, *No, thanks.* Every part of my life felt stuck in a rut—even the weather, with endless rainy reruns. And my essay was stuck worst of all.

I don't know which is worse, not knowing what to say, or not knowing how to say it, and this Transcendentalism thing was taking turns: one totally b.s. paragraph followed by a brilliant thought hopelessly tangled up in words like "furthermore." My favorite Thoreau quote said, "*Simplify, simplify*," but I was going in the opposite direction. Rough drafts were due next day.

So I went flying.

Instead of taking off at the edge of the woods, I walked my soggy-brained self to the Toad. I needed a boost, so maybe my faithful ol' rocky launchpad would help. It had finally quit raining, and the sun felt afternoon-y, though it was past five. *Oh, yeah*—March 21, the official first day of spring. On Dalby you don't wake up one day and go, "Hey, it's Spring!" Someone's crocuses start blooming, then a few trees, white and pink, and pretty soon you see daffodils and wonder how long they've been there. *Nice.* As I pushed my way through the brambles of the shortcut, a bald eagle soared right over my head. They make it look so easy.

Somebody had left an empty garbage bag at the base of the Toad, which bugged me, but I decided to get it on the way home, and up I climbed. Turns out I was right about my old friend. With each step up his craggy gray back I felt more alive, and by the time I was on top, I was striding over the squooshy lichen and moss with takeoff steps. One, two, three, *push*—*ah, how ya like me now, Mr. Eagle?* I did my own soar in a tight circle, not too high—people would be out on this nice sunny day. Ever since those stupid Valentine's threats, I've been more cautious—about being Seen, I mean. Not about flying: barrel roll! *Oh yes,* that felt good. I tried two, nearly caused another tree-crash, laughed out loud and tried again. And that's when I heard the sound.

A low whimper, on the other side of the Toad. Some animal? I flew over to look.

Crumpled in the brambles, some bright blue plastic, like a tarp. Only this tarp had been stretched and attached to a kind of wooden frame. Pale, thin, splintered boards stared up at me like ribs. And sticking out from underneath this mess of plastic and wood was a purple-sleeved arm.

"Michael!" I dropped straight out of the sky and was yanking away the plastic thing before my feet had even touched the ground. There he was, on his back, his other arm covering his face. "Are you okay? What happened?"

"Uuhhh," he said. His nose was bleeding, but it tends to do that pretty easily ever since he got punched out last fall when we were rescuing Mom. I couldn't tell if anything was broken. It's hard to check somebody out in a bramble bush.

"Can you move? Move your arms and legs," I ordered, and he did. "Good," I said, feeling more in charge. "Come on, let's get you out of there."

Both of us thrashed around for a moment, which led to more scratches, but reassured me he probably didn't have any broken bones. When we got out of the bush, I dragged the tarp-thing off to the side. *Jeez*. All that banging in his room last month. The garbage bag. *A home-made hang-glider? Are you insane?* I turned to say this, but Michael had rolled over and lay there on the damp grass.

"You look like s---," I said instead, hoping my cussing would make him laugh. He mumbled something into the grass. "What?"

"Never mind," Michael said distinctly, and sat up. "Doesn't matter." He didn't look too bad except for the blood, which he started wiping away with his sleeve.

"What happened?" I asked again, but he didn't need to answer. I knew perfectly well what he had tried to do, and why. And for the first time ever, my heart ached for my brother.

Everybody wants to fly. No one believes they can. But to have that power so close to you—your sister, your mom—and have it pass you by…yeah, I think I'd try wearing plastic wings and jumping off a giant rock too.

"It's okay," I told him. I may even have patted him on the shoulder. "It's gonna be fine."

"Easy for you to say," Michael retorted, but he didn't sound mad. More like exhausted. I realized we were having our first real conversation since he'd screamed at me a month ago. "You didn't have to jump-start yours."

I probably looked pretty stupid while I figured out what he meant. "Ohhh. You're trying to...you think the magic's in you, you just have to kind of drag it out into the daylight?"

"Gotta be. It just doesn't make sense for it to skip me like that. I'm the oldest."

So that was his logic. I guess it made sense, if you really wanted it to. If you hadn't been studying ancient books which made it crystal clear that a) the magic did whatever it wanted to, and b) if you weren't female, your chances of flying were pretty close to zero. Lorraine and I had found only two stories about flying men in all of our research, and one of them was thirteen. And no—I'm not describing what they did to him. I opened my mouth to tell my brother he was wasting his time. Then I thought: *So what?* Dreaming and scheming to make yourself fly sounded better than shutting down like Mom had.

Something else clicked. "Is that what you and Mom were talking about, that time in the kitchen?"

"Maybe. Yeah."

"Well, what did she say?" I had only heard the tail end of it; had Mom encouraged Michael to try this?

"She said go for it. On the first day of spring. So I did. Hah." Michael wiped his bloody sleeve on the grass. "Maybe I shoulda waited till Summer Solstice. Isn't that when it worked for you? Doesn't the power get stronger then?"

"Well..." First of all, I was pretty sure that Mom hadn't actually *said* "go for it," that's just what Michael heard. Which meant that he was going to hear whatever he wanted to hear from me.

"Kinda. But, hey. Maybe you should talk to Mom some more. Get her to show you how to take off and stuff." *So why don't you offer to teach your brother, Brilliant Girl?* But I was counting on Michael's pride; no way would he ask for my help now that I'd seen him like this. And meanwhile, maybe he could do what I hadn't: get Mom excited about flying again. That *was* brilliant.

"She really didn't want to talk about it," Michael said gloomily.

"Oh." So much for that idea. We sat there for a minute. I could feel the damp seeping into my jeans.

When it reached my underwear, I stood up. Maybe it took breaking the hold of the wet, depressing earth, but I felt suddenly light and special, like a princess. *I can fly! I have a gift, and no one can take it away.* "If you want," I told Michael, "I could fly you home. We can come back for the thing later." Flying doubles into the village on a lovely spring day was an idiotic idea, but I felt royally privileged. Happy to share my gift.

But my brother shook his head and heaved himself to his feet. "F--- that," he said. "I'm done." He started lumbering through the shortcut. The princess stayed put, turning back into normal old me.

As he reached the trees, Michael turned. "Hey," he called. "You better keep this to yourself."

I almost wished he'd said it nastily, so we could've had a good ol' argument and gone back to the time when Michael wrote songs about flying with me. But it's hard to get mad at someone who sounds like he's already lost whatever argument you might have. So I called back, "I know," and waited another minute, pushing my fingers into moss clumps, before following him home. Thinking about how distant I had become from Mom and Michael, since she wouldn't and he couldn't fly. Wondering: *Is my gift naturally selfish? Or is it me?*

Walking home, wet and scratched, I understood for the first time why someone might want to put flying away for a while.

No wonder the Transcendentalists were giving me trouble. You try being a Nonconformist, flying free and pure like an eagle, and next thing you know, someone's netting you in guilt and pulling you down.

Fine, I'll call Nate. He never makes me feel guilty. I could read him my essay over the phone, like I do with math. One of these days he'll be the one calling.

"Hey, Burg," someone called as I hurried across the grass. Nate was standing in my driveway.

Whoa. It's like I magicked him here! "Hey. What's up? C'mon in. Want to make popcorn?" I couldn't remember the last time we'd been alone.

"Nah, 's okay, I just wanted to talk," Nate said, like, *doesn't everyone lean on mailboxes for that?* Our box's flag was sticking up, right where that horrible Stander card... *Wow, almost forgot about that.*

"Yeah?" I gave him my best smile. The sun was spreading dark gold over the village, lighting up the tops of the fir trees. Actually, this was more romantic than my kitchen.

"Yeah," Nate said. He shifted his feet like people do when they have to give a report. *Oh wow, he's nervous. That is so cute.* "You like me, right?" He looked up, without really looking at me.

"Duh," I said, still smiling. But my heart sped up. "Why? Don't I act like it?" *He wants to kiss me, but he's scared. Oh, Savannah, was your boyfriend ever this sweet?*

"Shyeah. But I have to ask you something, Joss."

Wow—even all this past month, he'd never called me by my name before. His mouth looked adorable, forming the word. I leaned my elbow on the mailbox. Our faces were very close. *It's really happening.* "Yeah?" *Oh, if he kisses me I'll tell him my secret. I'll take him to the air, hands on my shoulders... I'll show Mom those letters were wrong about flying and love.*

"'Member that thing I gave you to give Savannah, back, like, a month ago?"

I giggled. "That lion valentine? Yeah, that was cute all right. But Savannah said she just wanted to be friends, and you were cool with it, so it's okay." *I'm not upset about that anymore. I trust you now.*

"Yeah," Nate said. "Thing is…" *He feels bad about it. He wishes he'd never admitted that crush—he's so over her.*

"It's okay," I repeated. "I know how you feel."

"Really?" Nate looked right into my eyes, and his were wide with relief. "So, you think Savannah would ever go with me?"

I don't really feel like describing the rest. Guess Nate wasn't cool with being Savannah's friend after all. Guess he hoped hanging out with me all month would get him closer to Savannah. Guess it wasn't working out so well. So he turned to his ol' buddy Joss for advice.

That's what I was to Nate: his version of Louis.

I set the table without being asked and mumbled my way through dinner. And afterward I sat down on my bed with the crumbly green book and our pile of sticky-notes. Not because I was supercharged with guilt about taking my flying gift for granted when Michael craved it so bad. And not because I really believed I'd find anything to stop the Standers. I just needed something to get my mind off Nate's expression when he'd thought I knew how he felt about my best friend.

It worked pretty well. After half an hour reading that ancient print, my brain went numb.

Scanning the pages with my mouth open, I drooled a little gob right onto the page. *Oh, shoot*—I dabbed it with my T-shirt, careful not to tear the browned paper…and read the passage again: "Guard ye every drop that falleth from ye lipf of ye Goode, for if ye witch do drinke knowingly thereof, fo fhall fhe vanquifh all power to recover her from Satan."

And once more, as the words sunk in.

And then I solved the riddle of the "cuppe."

"Spit!" I yelled.

"Ex*cuse* me?" Dad had heard me all the way from the living room.

"Nothing, sorry. Where's Lorraine?" I called.

She opened my door immediately, as though she'd been waiting for an invitation. "What is it, honey?"

I kept my voice low. "'Ye cuppe wherein ye inner power of Goodness drippeth':—it's *spit.*"

"Spit?"

"You know—saliva. What drips into a cup? Your spit. It comes from inside you, right? And if you're one of the Good People, your spit would represent your inner power of goodness."

Lorraine looked at me with her mouth so open I thought she might drool too. "Ohhh…" she said at last. "So all Flyers have to do is…spit on a Stander?"

"Nope," I said, feeling myself come back to life, "Easier than that." I read it out loud: "'*Guard ye every drop that falleth from ye lips of ye Goode, for if ye witch do drinke knowingly thereof, so shall she vanquish all power to recover her from Satan.*' They say it's the devil who makes us fly, right? So to keep ourselves from being 'rescued' from our satanic flying power—Flyers just have to drink out of a Stander's cup!"

The look she gave me lit up the room. "Jocelyn. That is brilliant."

"I know." My heart still hurt, but this moment felt like comfort.

Lorraine flipped through the stack of sticky-notes. "Then I suppose they have to drink out of it again right away, like it says: '*then ye Good do drinke again thereof.*' So you're mingling your power with theirs, I suppose. Yes! '*…so be all his power forsaken, and none shall further Stande.*' Your spit cancels out theirs."

"Yeah, I guess." I looked at the passage again. Hard to believe something so major and magical could be so simple and obvious. Really hard, in fact. *And I'm kind of done with believing in stuff.*

"So…what? I'm supposed to go around town drinking out of everybody's cups?"

Lorraine shook her head. "*Knowingly* drinke," she reminded me.

"Meaning…"

"Meaning you need to *know* you're drinking out of a Stander's cup when you do it. You can't just guess."

"Great," I muttered.

"Well, we don't have too many candidates, do we? It must be one of the people who've Seen you and Beth—probably the same person who uploaded that video of her." Lorraine sounded cheerful, and irritating.

"If you even take this stuff seriously." Sharing spit? I know it was my discovery, but—*really?* I was already feeling silly for my earlier excitement.

"Oh, I think we need to," Lorraine breathed. "Let me read some more…you've done wonderful work, honey," she added, maybe picking up on my expression. "Don't worry, we're on the right track now. We'll get Beth back in the air."

Oh yeah—Mom. I rubbed my eyes. So I'd solved the riddle— yay. Where did that leave me? A useless plan to defeat an unknown enemy. A boyfriend who'd turned out to be imaginary. And a horrible, horrible essay still waiting in my room.

CHAPTER TWELVE

SIMPLIFY, SIMPLIFY

Mr. Evans called me purple again.

My essay, I mean. The one I spent gazillion hours revising. The one I was looking forward to getting back—the *only* thing worth looking forward to in two awful weeks of sharing a classroom with Nate and Savannah. Mr. Evans gave it a big fat B-.

"Too many clichés, Jocelyn," he said. "Your idea is wonderful, but you have to tone it way down. Like Thoreau says, 'Simplify, simplify.' You want to sound like yourself, right? Not like those cards Mr. Howe sells."

Ouch.

I *hate* crying in front of people who don't know how to handle it. Mrs. Mac would have put her arm around me and said sarcastic things to make me smile, but Mr. Evans just fussed around the room looking for Kleenex, then handed me a paper towel and stood there making us both feel more awkward. Luckily it was his planning period. When I could talk again, I asked him what I was supposed to do now.

"Remember what I told you about your potential? I want you to rewrite this." He nodded at my stinky essay. "But this time, don't reach. Don't preach. Just *tell* it, sister, as though we were talking."

Yeah, right, like I'm ever going to talk to you about writing again. But all I said was, "Can you write me a note? I'm gonna be late for class."

*Re*write that essay? I may not write anything, ever again—period.

Two birthdays finally started me journaling again, in the middle of May. It's hard to stay bummed after that much cake. First came Michael's: seventeen, and gonzo about practicing for his license after waiting so long. Too bad for him no one needed to drive for groceries. But Dad's present fixed Michael's mood better than anything: weekly guitar lessons with Zach. At our house! Didn't hurt my mood either.

Unfortunately, the next lesson conflicted with Louis's birthday "party," a.k.a. me and Erin. *Hippo Birdie, Louis. Hope you have as much fun being fourteen as I have. Hah.* At least this year someone else came. But no one could give Louis a better gift: I was going to take him flying as soon as Erin left. Probably would've done it anyway—I kind of owed him. First I'd practically ignored him for a month to hang out with Nate—*yeah, that worked out well.* Then I'd ignored everybody for another two weeks, until they left me alone. Only Louis didn't.

Erin gave Louis this card game called "Set," and the three of us were playing and eating the cupcakes Janice had made—yup, real cupcakes, with frosting and everything. Not like those whole-grain ones Shasta makes. Janice has been a good influence on Shasta.

"Louis, you are *so* lucky," Erin sighed, after Janice brought us a bottle of sparkling cider. "Your moms are *so* cool. They just get you. Last year my parents asked me if I wanted treat bags at my party, like I was eight or something."

Louis opened his mouth and closed it again, then looked at me. I shrugged and smiled. So what if Erin didn't know that Janice had only lived here since January? She was right; Janice was a better parent than any of Shasta's boyfriends. And if Erin was cool with it...

"Yeah," I said encouragingly, "your moms rock, Louis."

"Thanks!" Louis's voice kind of squealed and he blushed, but then Erin and I busted out laughing and he joined in. Hey, even Nate's voice used to do that sometimes. Plus, Louis can't help it if he hasn't, you know, totally Matured yet. "We were all three going into the grocery store yesterday, and Tyler was coming out, and guess what: he held the door for us."

I was surprised Louis hadn't told me at school. Tyler the Hater being polite to gay people—that was big news. *Wow, we really have gotten out of touch.* I turned another card over without looking at it.

"Ooh, *Set!*" screamed Erin, scooping up three cards. She was totally winning, but I didn't care. It was the prettiest day of the year, and my buddy and I were going to fly.

Cutting across our lawn, we saw Michael and Zach sitting on the picnic table with guitars. "A bass run's your best friend," Zach was saying, and demonstrated with a series of low notes that slid perfectly into the melody. Then he looked up. "Hey, kid."

I stopped and Louis bumped into me. "Hey."

"Hey," Louis said in my ear. "We're still going up, right?"

"Right." *Get a grip, it's his birthday.* "See ya," I added as we turned for the woods. Michael ignored me, but Zach nodded, in time to the music.

"BEST....PRESENT...EVER," Louis whooped as we took off—but he managed to whoop in a whisper. Louis knows what's important—*not like some guys.* He eagled his arms like I'd taught him, and I settled myself in for the nice, long flight he'd earned.

"I have tons to tell you," I started, as we circled over the Toad. I felt as bright and glowing as the day. "Want to go to the Bluff?"

Louis whooped again, so we banked left and headed for the south end of the island.

On the flight down I filled him in on stuff I should have told him weeks ago: Mom's poison letter, and how it had depressed her that day we crashed. My horrible Cupid, and the "No Flight" card at my mailbox.

Louis was horrified. I could feel the stiffness of his muscles on my back. "You mean you guys actually have an *enemy*?" he marveled. "Someone *hates* you?"

"Yeah, I guess. Kinda Voldemort-y, huh?"

"*Hates* you," Louis repeated.

We were flying along the cliff edge, checking to make sure the beach was empty, by the time I got to the part about discovering Standers in my research with Lorraine. Whittier's Bluff is our special place. Tourists don't come there, and I braced myself for Louis's whoops to start again, but he stayed quiet. *Okay, let's get this party started.* Without warning, I dived, brushing the stiff leaves of a madrona tree on the cliff-top before plummeting toward the giant rocks by the beach. Plummeting—I love that word, and I love the feeling, and so does Louis, but still, no whoops. He gasped, and gripped my shoulders. But when I pulled up, practically skimming the rocks, and rose high, high, nearly straight up into the sun, and Louis continued to do nothing more than breathe in my ear, I began to feel annoyed. A kingfisher chattered at us and I went "Chattadaddadaddadda!" right back just to make Louis laugh. He didn't.

"What?" I demanded.

"So the Standers," Louis said slowly, like he was thinking out loud. "They're real? Lorraine says so?"

"Yeah, well, you know Lorraine," I said, circling the crest of the bluff. "If it's in a big fat book, it's gotta be real."

"And Standers are magic too? You can't Google them?"

"Yeah—that part's true. I'll show you later."

"And they can defeat you? I mean, just take away your power? Without burning you at the stake?"

"Well, that's what the books say. Standers try to say a prayer as a Flyer flies over them. Sounds pretty hard, though. Guess that's why they just burned 'em without waiting for proof, back in the day."

"Or they could just scare 'em down," Louis mumbled. I could barely hear him. "That's obviously not too hard."

I banked into a tighter circle. From this height the ocean looked like a piece of blue satin. "Oh, you mean Mom? I know, that's messed up. But she's been fine lately. She'll fly again when she gets good and ready. And the whole Stander thing...? Modern-day witch-hunters—really? Come on, Louis, they'd have their own TV show if they were real. Those 'threats' were just somebody's stupid joke."

"WHAT? You must be high." Louis hardly ever says things like that. "Anonymous letters? A stabbed doll? What kind of joke is that?"

"Duh. Tyler Howe would think it was hilarious."

"Huh." That got him thinking. "Tyler's not that smart..."

True, even his best friend says he's a moron. Nope—don't want to go there. I sent us plummeting again. Still no whoops.

"But he is smart enough to get close to you," Louis added, catching his breath as we rose again. "Through other people."

Ouch. "Seriously—Tyler Howe's a Stander? Why hasn't he sent me any more threats, then?"

"Maybe he knows you don't scare like your mom. Maybe he *wants* you to fly now, so he can, you know. Pray you down."

A cold blob formed in my stomach as I began a new circle. "But..."

"So all he'd have to do," Louis continued, "would be to, like, learn your movements. So he could predict where and when you'd fly, and hide out there. And you'd have no way to stop him stopping you."

"Yuh-huh!" What an idiot, I hadn't told Louis this part yet. "There's, like, a counter-attack—if you believe this stuff. Lorraine and I figured it out. You have to drink out of the Stander's cup, then they have to drink again, so, like, your spit mingles with theirs…" I snorted.

"And you haven't done this because…?" Louis said, not in my ear, but to the sky in general.

"It's ridiculous, okay? It says you have to KNOW they're a Stander before you use their cup, or you give yourself away. How're we supposed to prove…" I could feel Louis shaking his head. *Dude, this isn't even your problem!* "And we don't really need it now anyway! I mean, Mom's okay with not flying. And I'm being careful, right? So. Yeah."

"Yeah, 'cause you have x-ray vision to see through all those trees where Tyler could be praying right now. Or anybody."

Wow. Fourteen year-old Louis is sarcastic. I stopped in midair, but hovering doubles is really tiring.

"Let's go home," Louis said. He sounded disgusted.

The wind picked up as we flew back over the fields and woods, slowing me down just when I most wanted this flight to be over. I concentrated on my breathing as we approached the school.

"Wait," Louis ordered. "Soccer practice just let out. Hover by that tree or something till we make sure no one's coming."

Somebody was. A blue pickup crawled away beneath us as we hid behind cedar branches.

"See?" said Louis. "What if they'd looked up? What if they were the Stander?"

"That's Mr. Evans!"

"So what?"

"What's your point?" snapped Stupid Jocelyn.

So Louis told me. "You don't even care. You have all this power, and somebody wants to take it away, and you're not even trying to stop them. You're not even *trying*, Joss."

I didn't want his birthday to end totally snarky, so I kept my mouth shut as we landed and climbed back down the Toad. Or maybe I agreed with him. *Selfish, selfish.* That's what Thoreau would have written about me, not "Simplify, simplify." I wasn't even trying.

"Thanks for my present," Louis said at the edge of our lawn, friendly again. "Wanna come over and finish the cupcakes?"

"No, I gotta go set the table," I muttered. It was true. But it was also true that someone seemed to be under our picnic table. He seemed to be Zach.

"Okay." Louis gave me a hard look. "But that guy's Tyler's cousin. So…"

"…so I won't ask him if he can steal his cousin's cup for me," I interrupted. "I'm not an idiot, okay? Sorry. Happy Birthday. I mean it."

"I know," Louis sighed, walking away.

Zach was crawling out from under our table. "Hey, kid." He held up a small metal object. "Dropped my capo down there. Didn't notice till I got home."

"Can I see?" *Need to clear my head about this Stander thing.* But I'd never talked with Zach alone.

"Well, sure," Zach said. "Without the guitar, though, I can't show you how it works. It's just a clamp." He clenched and un-clenched the thing, smiling at me.

"You could show me on Michael's," I said. *You ditched Louis on his birthday for this? Wow.* But Zach was nodding.

"I'll just get Michael to let me…" I began before realizing: no truck. No Michael! He and Dad were probably off unloading the recycling. Even better.

Zach followed me into the house. "So you're interested in gui-tar too?"

"Yeah." It wasn't a lie; right now I was very interested. "I'm thinking of taking lessons. My birthday's in June." One of those was true.

"Well then, this is a good start." Zach pushed into Michael's room with familiarity and grabbed his guitar from the bed. In my fantasies, if I had them, he would have sat down there with me next to him, but that did not happen. We went into the kitchen and pulled out chairs, side by side.

"So let's say you want to play a song in G 'cause the chords are easy, but G's too low for your voice." He strummed a chord. "So you slap this baby on, a couple of frets up"—he clamped the capo—"and voilá, now you can play those same easy G chords in the right key for you." His fingernails were neatly trimmed. "Wanna try?"

The guitar felt awkward in my arms, but the rest of it, Zach leaning over to position my left hand, felt totally right. Except to my stupid brain, which kept up a running argument. *He's eighteen! He thinks you're a twerp!* Then why is he being so nice to me? *Duh, he thinks you might pay him for lessons later on.* But look at him. He doesn't have to smile like that. Or take my hand to show me—

"Wow, those are some calluses," I said. Up close in the warm kitchen, Zach smelled different from Nate, or Michael, or Dad. Kind of spicy. Suddenly it was really, really hard not to giggle.

"You'll get 'em too, if you start to play," Zach said.

I looked up from my hand and for a second we were looking right at each other. His eyes were really more gold than brown, and his expression was perfectly earnest. He was not flirting with me or treating me like a kid. He was taking me seriously, one musician to another.

I was glad to be sitting down, because my knees really did feel weak.

"Show me another chord," I said, trying to match my voice to his expression.

"So okay, let's try a D," Zach said, leaning in again, and that's when Michael barged into the kitchen.

"Wow, Joss." That's all he said, but I got the message. He meant, "how dare you go in my room and help yourself to the one thing I'm good at, the thing which defines me." He meant, "you're lucky Zach's here or I might actually hit you."

But he meant something else too, which I didn't pick up on until after Zach had handed back the guitar, flashed me another smile, and left our kitchen, taking his capo and all the warmth with him. Michael turned back to me, clenching his guitar's neck like he probably wanted to clench mine. "So flying's not enough, huh," he said. "You selfish little bitch. You gotta take my friends too."

"I'm not—" I tried to respond, but Michael's door was already slamming. After a moment I wandered outside and plonked myself down on the picnic table, his accusation spinning in my head.

The Standers were wrong—the flying power wasn't turning me into a selfish person; it didn't need to. I was already there. All this time Lorraine and I'd been taking for granted that the Standers weren't "ye goode" people, the Flyers were. Nonconformist and free. What if we were wrong too?

"No," I said out loud. "They burned people alive. They send horrible letters. They're not ye goode. *I'm* ye goode." *Then you'd better start acting like it*. But I took Louis flying with me, right? *Yeah, and then what happened? Selfish, selfish.*

"Gosh, I'm glad I'm not the only one who talks to himself in this family," said Dad's cheerful voice behind me. He and Lorraine were walking across the yard arm in arm.

I must have jumped, because they laughed. "What're you doing here? Who's running the store?"

"That's the problem with youth today." Dad shook his head at Lorraine. "Responsibility, that's all they think about. Can't a man go for a walk on a beautiful day, and the start of fishing season? I closed up for an hour so we could go watch the boats."

"You sound like Thoreau," I grumbled.

"Wow, English Major," Dad said, looking impressed, and I felt like yelling, *Don't listen to me! I got a B- on my paper and I'm a selfish bitch*. I should have said something comforting like, "Don't worry, Dad, someday you'll get a boat again and go out there on the water."

"Jocelyn," Lorraine put in, "we should talk. I have a new theory." *Oh, wonderful. Just what I need—something else unprovable.*

"Ah, yes." Dad smiled. "The Top Secret Research. The scary old books. One of these days the women in my life are going to turn me back into a toad, is that it? You'll have to excuse me, but I hear the store calling."

I was all ready to be nice. But then Lorraine said, "Listen, Joss. I think the Stander could be Reverend Paula."

"Are you kidding me? That lady? Printing out letters and stabbing dolls?" *Whoa—isn't that what Louis had said?* Only not as sneery. So much for being nice.

"Hear me out," Lorraine said, but I clamped my hands over my ears.

"No. No. I'm *done*. The whole Stander thing is stupid. I don't believe it anymore. I just want to be left alone, okay? I just want to be left alone to fly."

She should have slapped me. Or sent me to my room like a little kid. But instead my stepmother sighed and shook her head and went into the house.

Leaving the little kid to follow. *Selfish, selfish, selfish.*

"I have a monetary opportunity to share with you people today," Mr. Evans announced next day. "Monetary means moolah," he explained to our blank silence. "Bank. Benjamins."

Everyone sat up at that.

"The Kiwanis Club is sponsoring an essay contest for Fourth of July. The theme is, 'What Does it Mean to Be a Citizen?'" Whispering broke out—"*Wow, Mr. Evans, could you be more boring?*"—until he added, "And there's a five hundred dollar prize."

"*What???*" "And I'm thinking that, even though we've left the Transcendentalists behind, *some* of you"—he looked right at me—"might like to rewrite your essay and submit it to the contest. *Some* of you have themes that fit perfectly." More furious whispering—"*As if! That was the worst thing I've ever had to write!*"

"Yes, I know that essay did a job on your confidence," he continued, still looking at me. "But remember what Emerson said: '*Trust thyself.*' Here's your chance: trust thyself, have a little faith in thy writing ability, put thy back into it. And who knows? Maybe win five hundred bucks. Contest deadline's in three weeks."

He offered to help any of us who wanted, on our own, to tweak our old essays and go for the money. Then he moved the class on to our current book, *Huckleberry Finn*. I like Huck, though I wish he didn't use the "n-word." But this time he sat unopened on my desk. That Emerson quote hovered over me like a cloud. I hadn't used it in my essay because I didn't get it. But suddenly I did.

"*Trust thyself,*" Emerson had said. "*Every heart vibrates to that iron string.*"

Like a guitar! Mr. Evans calls these "Aha Moments." Understanding plucked me, and I vibrated: *hummmm.* Has being a nonconformist Flyer really turned me into a selfish bitch? When I pay attention and Trust Myself, I feel the answer: Yes. I'm not doing any better than Mom at balancing flying and relationships.

Have I been blowing off Lorraine because I don't want her to be right about anything? *Trust thyself. Hummmm.* Ouch. Yeah. I have. But it's not her fault my real mom isn't…her.

Which brought me to the question: Are the Standers real, even if I don't want them to be? *Hummmm.* Why shouldn't they be? I've been ignoring them because they're in a crusty old book—but Mr. Emerson's pretty crusty himself, and look what he's doing to me!

One resolution after another rushed at me, like waves. Find Lorraine. Listen to her idea about the Reverend. Tell Mom. Put your heads together. Solve this. Take Michael flying. Apologize to…everybody. My essay wasn't the only thing that needed revision.

"Earth to Jocelyn. We're on page sixty-four." Unfortunately it was my turn to read aloud, so not only did I get laughed at for spacing out, I had to keep my brain on Huck and Jim for the rest of the period.

I couldn't wait to get home—not to fly, for once, but to take Mr. Emerson's advice.

CHAPTER THIRTEEN

SECRETS SUCK

Too bad rewriting something isn't as easy as deciding to. I KNEW what I wanted to say, but Mr. Emerson wasn't helping me say it. Two hours after the end of school I was still struggling with my conclusion when Michael came home and started banging around in his room again. So we had this conversation in his doorway:

ME: "Hey, you gotta be so loud? I'm trying to work here."

MICHAEL: "Well, so'm I. Wear headphones."

ME: "*You* wear headphones. What are you working on?"

MICHAEL: *(stuffing something under his bed)* "Stage props. It's a secret. For the Fourth of July concert. Zach's playing, and he asked me to make some stuff."

ME: "If it's a secret, how come you just told me? Do you get to be onstage with Zach? Can I see what you're making?"

MICHAEL: "No. Get out of here."

ME: "Hey. Want to go flying later?"

MICHAEL: *(looking suspicious)* "What is this, some kind of bribe?"

ME: "No, really. I've been thinking about this for a while. I wanna, you know, get back to where we used to be and stuff. It was fun."

MICHAEL: *(grunts)*

ME: "I kinda miss it."

MICHAEL: "Thought I was too heavy for you."

ME: "Yeah, well, remember how Louis sorta boosted your butt

that first time we tried it? We could bring him along again. And I've gotten stronger."

MICHAEL: "Uh-huh…But no, I'm good. I gotta work on these props. Maybe later."

ME: "Really?"

MICHAEL: "Yeah, but thanks for asking. Here, want my headphones?"

They were good headphones. No more distractions. Except… *Huh—so my bro doesn't need to fly with me.* He seems practically "chipper," as Dad would say. Making music with Zach must have taken his mind off his non-magic. *Well…yay. Cross Michael off my list of resolutions.* Three deleted paragraphs later I heard him leave the house. *Good idea—maybe I should go for a flight, focus my thoughts…*

"Honey?" Dad tapped at my door. "Can you come out a sec and stir this for me? I gotta zip into the store for more cheese."

I'll do anything for homemade mac and cheese, even without an essay I'm dying to ditch. I came straight out and hugged him.

Dad was still smiling as he returned with the cheese, his face wrinkled like a comfy coat. Did I mention my dad has the nicest face in the universe? He's not the handsomest guy, his nose is kind of crooked, but when he smiles, you feel totally loved.

Suddenly I wanted to tell him everything: the poison letters, the Standers, the whole sharing-the-spit idea. Why not? Lorraine didn't want to freak him out, but right now, grating the cheese, he looked so calm and steady, like he was still captain of his boat. *Trust thyself…Dad's ready for this.*

He wasn't ready for another hug, so my sleeve got grated and we both laughed. "Hey, Dad, you know those old books? Has Lorraine told you what we've found out from 'em?"

"Ah, no…guess she figures I'm not the most, ah, receptive audience in the world." He narrowed his eyes. "Why?"

"Well, it is pretty stupid, but maybe you can help us decide, like, who the bad guy is. We have to know before we can take him down, right? And she thinks it's Reverend Paula, but I think it might be Tyler Howe, because..." I stopped, since it's hard to talk when someone is staring at you with his eyebrows three feet up.

"'Bad guy?' 'Take him down?' Joss, what in the world are you getting yourselves into?"

Oh dear, maybe Lorraine was right not to tell... Too late now. "It's no big deal, Dad," I fibbed, dumping the cheese in. "We just think we've found a way to help Mom."

"Help your mother? What does she need help on?" Dad said. A year ago this would have made us both laugh, like, *What* doesn't *she need help on?* But Mom had been so cool since moving back to Dalby. *Yeah, till she got that horrible letter. And we still don't know who sent it.*

I closed my eyes for a second. *Trust thyself.* Yes, it *was* time to tell Dad. Mom needed *all* of our help.

"Oh, a while ago, she got this...letter." I stirred like crazy. *He's going to be mad at me for not telling him back in February. And at Lorraine!* I should've talked to her about this first.

"Letter? From who?" Sure enough, Dad was frowning. I took a deep breath to finish spilling the beans, when the kitchen door opened. *Oh, good—now Lorraine won't feel like I tattled behind her back.*

But it wasn't Lorraine. "Hey, sorry, should've knocked," said Zach's face, peering in. "Michael around?"

Dad's expression cleared. "Hey there, Zach! Come on in. Michael's not here, but hey, join us for dinner? There's plenty."

"Oh, no, thanks, don't want to intrude," Zach said, coming in. He was wearing a jeans jacket that made him look like a guy on an old movie poster. "Just dropping off this job application he asked me about."

"Michael's applying for a job? At Howe's? News to me," said Dad, but he looked pleased. "Good for him. And nice of you to bring it by. So, you're uncle's a good boss, then? Not a slave driver?"

Jeez, Dad, you should know, your ex-wife works for him, right? But Zach smiled. "No, Uncle Doug's great. And it'd be cool to have Michael in the stock room. I can introduce him to the wonderful world of inventory, and then he can take over my job when I leave."

"When are you leaving?" I blurted.

"Oh, not till summer. Gotta stay for Fourth of July, I hear that's a huge deal around here. I'm playing at the Festival, right? But after that—" Zach shrugged. "Time to head home, get ready to be a student again. Make nice with the family."

"Oh, right, you mentioned something about giving yourself distance," Dad said, leaning his butt on the edge of the stove as he settled in for a chat. I reached over and turned off the burner, trying not to call attention to myself, like Zach was some kind of wildlife I might scare off. "That work pretty well?"

"We'll see." Zach shrugged again. "My younger brother is going through a kind of alternative-lifestyle phase, I guess you could call it, and he was making life pretty miserable for me. My folks didn't want him going anywhere, and they wouldn't make him stop, so, yeah. I took it on myself to leave instead. See if maybe he'd grow up a little if I wasn't around to show off to."

"Being the bigger man," Dad nodded sympathetically. "Hey, you sure you don't want a seat? Cup of coffee?"

"No, really," Zach said, plunking some papers on the table. "Just wanted to deliver these." *Damn, Dad, he was just getting going!*

"Do you think I could get a job at Howe's?" I asked. It worked; Zach turned from the door. And there was that smile, just for me.

"Absolutely! In another year or two, kid. You do have to be sixteen. But I'll tell my uncle…oh, no, wait, he already knows you, right? How'd that go, the guest-speaker thing?"

"Really well," I gushed. "I'm so glad I asked him. He was a big hit. And I think he helped my grade." *Stop babbling.*

"Oh, I'll bet your grades don't need any help." There it was again, that taking-me-seriously expression. "Michael says you're a real smarty."

Michael *says?* "Oh, well," I faltered. "I'm okay, I'm just, like, totally stuck on this essay right now. My teacher doesn't think it's very smart, I guess."

"Want me to take a look at it?" Zach offered. "I took Advanced Placement last year, and I'm probably gonna major in English. I can totally un-stick you if you want." The smile *and* the serious look—oh, wow.

"Uh, sure," I said. Dad looked at me hard, but I sensed approval. Whatever Mom's problem was, we were not about to share it with outsiders, no matter how gorgeous. "Lemme go get it. My teacher said I used too many clichés, but I don't know how to fix it." I retrieved my poor old re-re-rewritten essay.

"Look, if you two are gonna get all literary, take it in the living room, okay?" Dad gave me a sideways smile. "That is real nice of Zach to help you. Did you tell him about the contest?"

So I did. Just me and Zach Howe, sitting on our couch. Yeah, he's leaving this summer. And yeah, he's eighteen. But I'm almost fifteen! And he's going to be an English major! I gave him a pen and we went through each of Mr. Evans's comments. Zach had this really nice way of showing me how Mr. Evans's critiques really were compliments. Somehow I believed it more coming from him. "He's challenging you," Zach said. "Not letting you get away with being ordinary. And you're not, are you? Ordinary?"

I shook my head, too happy to speak.

"So your thesis…Nonconformity is the best way to show you're being true to yourself. And that's what being a citizen is all about. Uh-huh. Example Number One, Colonial America standing up to England. Example Number Two, Thoreau living alone in the woods." He was totally concentrating, one hand pushed into his hair. "See, 'be all he can be' isn't original, it's a line from the Army, right? So how could you say that in *your* words? Trust your voice."

"What was your brother doing that was so bad?" It just popped out.

He looked up, showing a little crease between his eyes. "Rory decided he was gay."

I felt…disappointed? And it must have showed on my face, because Zach added, "No, I don't have a problem with that."

"Me neither," I put in. "It's totally cool."

"Right," Zach said, scratching his chin, looking kind of faraway. "But Rory was not totally cool. He wanted to rub it in my face all the time, like there was something wrong with me because I didn't want to hear about everything he was doing with his 'lover.' I mean—'*lover?*' He's, like, younger than Michael." Now Zach sounded younger himself—more like, you know, me. I found myself nodding.

"So he made you feel like it was *your* problem?"

"You got it." His eyes flashed. "Talk about nonconformity! Here I was, being the good kid, getting straight As, and my family seemed to think I was the weird one. They shut me down. If it hadn't been for my wrestling coach, I wouldn't have had anyone to talk to that last semester. Mr. Plonsky gets me. He's more like my dad than my dad."

"But you were just trying to stay true to yourself," I said. Totally cheesy, but it made him smile again.

"Yup. I got nothing against gays, but man, don't tell me I'm weird just because I'd rather have a girlfriend."

"So do you?" *Wow, can't believe I asked that.*

"Workin' on it," Zach said, "and speaking of working, if you fix this part like I said, and that other section on page two, hey, I think this essay could go somewhere. Let's just look at the ending, see if we can—"

But that's where Michael and Lorraine came in, and Zach remembered that he'd only stopped by for a moment. He refused dinner one last time, bumped fists with Michael, confirmed their lesson for next day, and took off. Leaving me on my own with my essay's conclusion, and the best-tasting mac and cheese on the planet.

"Don't you look pleased with yourself," Dad said, glopping big spoonfuls on our plates. "Zach came through, huh? Got your essay un-stuck?"

"*Zach* helped you with your essay?" Michael snorted. But he looked more skeptical than mad. That bugged me. Why couldn't Zach help me if he wanted?

"Yes, and we talked a lot," I said, super mature. "He is a very nice person."

"Beth says the same thing," Lorraine said. "He's unusually... clean-cut, I guess. Maybe his uncle was that way at his age."

"Well, the resht of his familysh not," I said with my mouth full. Swallowed. "He told me he had to leave 'cause his gay brother was all in his face about how he should be gay too, or something like that."

Michael frowned. "Yeah, there is that. Zach is totally homophobic. It's weird, 'cause he's so chill about everything else."

"Nuh-uh, he's not anti-gay, he told me. He just didn't like how nasty his brother was being."

Dad and Lorraine had stopped eating and were watching me and Michael like a tennis match.

"Oh, is that what he told you? Funny, that's not what I heard him say to Tyler. They were talking in Howe's yesterday when I went in for that Ace bandage, Dad. Talking about Zach's brother Rory." Michael's expression is always meanest when he's about to score some points. "You shoulda heard your boy, Joss. Whew. That was some of the filthiest language I've ever heard. I practically had to cover mine virgin ears."

"Michael, that's enough," Dad said. "We get it. Zach's being a typical guy. No big deal. Pass the salad dressing."

And that's what I tried to tell myself as I finished my dinner. *A typical guy. Probably just playing along to make his cousin feel good.*

So is that what Zach was doing with me?

Well, he'd given me great advice on my essay. And he'd called me extraordinary, or something like that. And shared his family's issues like I was an actual friend. Michael didn't know the real Zach, I decided. He just saw what he wanted to see. In fact, he probably made up the whole thing just to bug me. I felt sorry for him.

I wrote my conclusion and switched over to math before I started second-guessing my writing. Plenty of time before the contest deadline, right? It wasn't until I was in bed that I re-membered: I'd never talked to Lorraine about the Stander! Oh well—tomorrow, then. *I haven't forgotten, Louis, I'm workin' on it.*

Zach said he was "workin' on" having a girlfriend. What did *that* mean?

Next morning I ate my cereal super fast, and grabbed Lorraine when she came into the kitchen for her tea. She was wearing that silky kimono which used to annoy me, but now it looked kind of stately.

"Tell me what you figured out about Reverend Paula."

Lorraine raised her eyebrows, then nodded. "Okay." She sat down with me. "Well, we know she's Seen you, and possibly Beth too, so she's on my list of suspects. So I went to the church lobby and read her welcome letter that's on the bulletin board." *Huh—non-book research for Lorraine.* "Jocelyn, it was extraordi-nary: it read like a modern version of what those old books said about 'Standing for ye goode.'"

"Why? Was 'stand' capitalized?"

"Oh, I don't mean literally. Just the tone of it. It was very… righteous."

"Well, duh—she's a minister!" But I didn't say it rudely.

"This was more…specific. Maybe you should go have a look. Oh, I don't know." She sighed. "Do you have any ideas? Or do you still think this whole line of attack is a waste of time?"

Savannah's mom honked for carpool. "No," I said, stuffing an oatmeal cookie into a baggie. "I'm…you're right. I'm sorry," I made myself say. "But…she's such a nice lady."

Another honk. "We'll talk later, okay?" Lorraine said as I swung out the door.

"Reverend Paula, evil?" I muttered to Louis during lunch. Erin was sitting nearby, so I'd been filling him in on our anti-Stander breakthrough under my breath, between bites of baked potato. "Gimme a break. Plenty of people might've Seen me and Mom." *Yeah, like Nate.* He had passed me a note during math: "Hey I'm bored wanna kick it later?" And here's what I thought: *Yeah, right.* Nate Cowper and his notes seemed incredibly unimportant now.

"Depends on how you define 'evil,'" Louis muttered back. I was still getting used to this new Louis who didn't automatically agree with me. "Mean? There's tons of mean people." *Hmm, guess he would know.* "Hateful? Duh, Joss. Tyler Howe. Or do you mean more like scheming, plotting, heh-heh-heh evil?"

"Ooh, can I play?" Erin asked, scooting closer. "Is this like that game 'Taboo?'"

"Um, no," I said, but Louis jumped in.

"What's your definition of the word 'evil?'"

Erin put down her apple, concentrating. "Cold-hearted," she said finally. Did I mention Erin's really smart? "Un-empathetic. Thinking other people aren't worth anything, unless they think like I do. Self-centered, I guess, but in a really, well, evil way." I stared at her and she giggled self-consciously. *Not worth anything unless they think like I do. What did that remind me of?* "So did I win?"

"Yes," I said, handing her half my oatmeal cookie. "First prize. Good work." *Something someone had said, here at school.* Mr. Evans? There were sure times when he and his red pen seemed evil to me, but deep down I knew he respected me. *Something about… having too much freedom?*

"Joss, what?" Louis whispered to me as Erin happily snarfed my cookie. "Did you figure something out?"

"I dunno," I muttered. "But I could almost see how…Huh. Yeah. Maybe."

People around us were putting their trays away. "Can we play again tomorrow?" Erin asked. "C'mon, Louis, we get to dissect frogs today!"

Louis nodded, torn between the excitement of being liked and the unfolding news on my face. "Yeah," he said. "So…?"

"What about Mr. Howe," I hissed. "That talk he gave here… that sounded like what Erin said. He made island people seem kinda weird and out of touch. Not worth as much." I would never have called Mr. Howe evil, but un-whatever, like Erin said? Definitely. And he'd probably Seen Mom on the roof of his store.

Louis's eyes got big. "Plus he fathered Tyler," he whispered, making Mr. Howe sound like Darth Vader. But then Erin yanked on his backpack and we all headed off to class.

Savannah's mom had taken her to another appointment after school, so Dad closed the store for twenty minutes to drive over and let Michael drive us home. I had to work pretty hard to come up with answers to the Dad-questions about What I'd Learned At School, because I'd spent the last three periods in a debate with myself that went like this:

He looks down on Dalby people, and he's Tyler's dad. Yeah, but lots of people have jerky kids. He's way too dignified. *He might've Seen Mom on his roof, though. And he was totally muttering to himself that time—maybe saying a prayer!* Oh, come on, tons of people might've Seen her, tons of people mutter. Why him? Why *not*

Reverend Paula? *That's not the point: Mr. Howe thinks Dalbians are, like, backward. He practically said so to Mr. Evans.* So what? He didn't really mean we're worth less, like Erin said. Mr. Howe's too nice to be hateful. *Can't you be evil and nice at the same time?* Yeah, how's that work? And can you really see a guy like him pasting a poem onto construction paper?

"Um, before the Civil War people used to say 'The United States *are*,'" I told Dad, "but afterward they started saying 'The United States *is*.'" He waited for more, but my brain had been kind of occupied all afternoon.

And then, speak of the devil! I never understood that phrase before, but as Michael turned into the village center, there was Mr. Howe, walking toward the church. Dalby has several churches, but the one in town is the prettiest, old-fashioned and pointy.

Suddenly I wanted to test my idea. "Let me out here," I told Michael quickly, before I could change my mind.

"What in the world?" asked Dad as Michael carefully turned on his blinker and pulled over.

"Just gotta see something," I mumbled, and hopped out.

"Say hi to your mom for me," Dad called behind me, and I just had time to think, *Huh?* before Mom was saying hi to me herself. She was coming out of the little patch of woods across from the church, just behind our truck. There's a little trail in there, a "meditation path" the church put in, winding through the trees. I once tried flying along it, and it hid me real well, but I got a little scratched up. From the look on her face, Mom was in there to think about stuff, like the church intended.

"Hey, Eagle Eyes, did you spot me from the road? Nice," said Mom. *Oh shoot, she thinks I hopped out to see* her. I gave her a hug, glancing back; Mr. Howe was straightening the sign by the church's parking lot. "So how's my girl?"

I looked at her carefully; Mom doesn't say stuff like that. She seemed kind of bouncy, like the bark path we were standing on was pumping extra energy into her sneakers. "I'm good, Mom. What're you doing out here?" Mr. Howe was now entering the church, and I really wanted to rush up to him and, I don't know, start a conversation just to shut off my silly idea. But I wasn't about to ditch my mom. Been there, done that, and—*Oh jeez. He's her boss. She sees him thirty hours a week! Mom's smart; wouldn't she know if her own boss was evil? Besides, why would he need to send her letters? He could have tricked her into flying by now and stood beneath her, if he really knew.* Maybe I should just ask Mom! She didn't seem to notice how distracted I was.

"Just out for a walk before work," Mom smiled, all peppy, like the opposite of the dark clouds growing over the village. "Soaking up the beauties of nature. Keeping my feet on the ground."

That was such an un-Mom thing to say, I almost thought she was talking in some kind of Flyer code. Except Mom wasn't a Flyer these days. I felt a sudden rush of anger. Out for a walk? She should be up in the sky where she belonged! *What if Mr. Howe did send those letters? Hey, maybe he's having a cup of coffee in the church! I could rush over there, talk with him, sneak a sip when he wasn't looking...*No, wait. Lorraine said we have to *know* first, or it won't work. And I'd give myself away.

"Huh?" Mom had asked me something, but she didn't look pissed at me for not paying attention. "Sorry."

"I said, Why don't you join me and we'll walk back through the path? It's so pretty in there right now."

Mom was right, it was prettier than I remembered. The salmonberry bushes were green again, decorated with bright pink blossoms, and some dandelions sparkled in the grassy parts. Dark cedar branches arched over our heads, keeping out the rest of the world. It did feel kind of churchy.

She started asking me school-questions like Dad, and I pulled a few more Civil War facts out of my brain while preparing a careful list of everything I'd saved up. *We almost have a plan, Mom.*

I might even know who our enemy is. You need to help. We're doing this for you, you know... Okay, maybe not that last part. "And Lincoln was totally against it the whole time," my mouth said. "He didn't want to fight." *Like you don't. But you will!*

Mom watched me closely while I babbled, like she was telling herself what a good parent she was, so interested in her kid's schooling. This fakey mom was not the one I wanted to be recruiting in a fight against Standers.

"I'm so happy to hear how well you're doing, babe," she purred. "That is a Step Forward. We'll have to celebrate this."

"Yeah, you should definitely tell your therapist," I said cautiously. Didn't want to make it sound like I was making fun of her little Step Forward/Step Backward therapy chart.

"Oh, I've stopped seeing her," Mom said airily.

We had come to the end of the path, and Mom turned like she wanted to walk it back again, but I stopped. "Really? When? Why? Mom, is that a good idea?"

She laughed. "In reverse order: yes, it's an excellent idea, in fact I call it a Step Forward. And why? I'm doing really, really well just being a normal woman for a change, that's why. As for when... Oh, a couple of months now. And yes. Really."

Maybe she's taking pills again. There is a kind that could make her all happy like this, right? And make her do stupid things like stop seeing the therapist she's been working with since she got her life back together? Last time Mom said she was doing really, really well was about a week before she tried to kill herself. *I should tell Dad.*

But Mom snagged that thought right off my face. "And babe," she added seriously, Normal Woman to Normal Woman, "I would appreciate your trust here, okay? That piece of information is just between us." She looked like her old self for a second, fierce and proud, and I felt totally...

"Sure, Mom. Of course I won't tell."

...torn. Like two different moms had hold of each arm and were pulling in opposite directions. New Happy Mom shared her secret: *I quit therapy, and I love you so much that you're the only one I'm telling.* Old Independent Mom flashed me a warning: *you've violated my trust before, and if you do it again I'll shut you out for good.*

New Happy Mom's path was bright and full of flowers. Old Independent Mom's path was dark and scratchy. Problem was, I liked that mom better.

Ever have that feeling when you get a hangnail and all you want to do is rip it off? You know if you do, it'll probably get infected. But another part of you is just as sure that ripping will heal it faster, plus then you won't have to keep seeing that stupid hangnail just asking to be ripped. That's how I feel about keeping secrets.

But if I thought keeping Mom's was hard, that was nothing compared to Savannah's.

CHAPTER FOURTEEN

REALLY UGLY LIPSTICK

Savannah called later that afternoon, as I was playing Solitaire in the kitchen, too distracted for reading.

"Joss, I need you to come over. Now." This was not her hang-out voice. I set my cards down.

"What's up? What's wrong? Dad's working, so I'll have to ride my bike, all right?"

She didn't answer. "Savannah? You okay?"

She gave a little sob. Definitely not okay. Then a deep breath. "No, don't ride, that'll take too long. I just need to…" She blew her nose.

"Is it Tyler?" I asked grimly. *I knew it.* Sooner or later that jerk was going to say something horrible, no matter how sweet she thought he was. Maybe he'd hit her!

Savannah gave a kind of snort-laugh, a little explosion in my ear. "Yeah, half of it is." I was still working on this when she spelled it out for me. "I'm pregnant, Joss."

I've watched this scene in movies or read it in books so many times, I knew exactly how it should go: lots of "omi*god!*" and crying and gripping the phone with tears on our eyelashes and proud little smiles on our lips. Our scene wasn't like that.

ME: "Oh."

SAVANNAH: *(still a little shaky-voiced)* "I know, right?"

ME: "So, wow. Man."

SAVANNAH: "That's what my appointment was for today."

ME: "Right. Right."

SAVANNAH: "Aren't you supposed to ask me how I'm feeling and stuff?"

ME: "Oh wow, I'm sorry. How're you—"

SAVANNAH: "How do you think? I'm freakin' out here. This was *not* supposed to happen. We were being all careful and everything. Joss, what'm I gonna DO?"

ME: *(wanting so badly to say, "You're asking ME?")* "Um, your parents know, right?"

SAVANNAH: "Yeah, they had to be told 'cause I'm a minor. They screamed at me. Then they screamed at each other. Dad went out. Mom's not talking to me right now."

ME: "Whoa. So, um…how far along are you?"

SAVANNAH: "They said seven weeks."

ME: "!!!"

SAVANNAH: "You still there?"

ME: "Seven weeks? Are you crazy? How come you didn't figure it out when you didn't get your period?"

SAVANNAH: *(sounding very un-Savannah-ish)* "Don't yell at me. That's what Mom said. I just…I kept hoping I'd, like, counted wrong. I didn't think this could really happen to *me*."

ME: "Seven weeks. Jeez, Savannah. You haven't given yourself all that much time to…you know. Make a decision, right? What're you gonna do?"

SAVANNAH: *(nicely not pointing out she'd already asked that same question)* "I don't know. I don't know. I wish there was someone I could talk to about this!"

ME: "There is! You know those posters at school, with the phone number? They're pink, and there's, like, a picture of a pregnant girl…"

SAVANNAH: *(stony)* "Joss, those are for if you want an abortion. Are you saying I should have an abortion?"

ME: "I'm not saying anything! It's your b—your decision, okay? I just want you to talk to somebody who can help you. You really can't talk to your mom?"

SAVANNAH: "No. No. Not right now. She's…no." *(ridiculously long, uncomfortable silence)* "Joss—I know. Let's go to church."

ME: "What?"

SAVANNAH: "That's what I need to do. I need to pray on it. And maybe I can talk to Reverend Paula. She's really Wise."

ME: "That's great, but, Savannah. You need to talk to, like, a health person too. And you have to do it *soon*."

SAVANNAH: "Yeah, okay, I will. So will you come to church with me?"

ME: "Me? Why do you need me?"

SAVANNAH: "You're my best friend, idiot. And, oh. Joss, remember. This is total, top, top secret. You can't tell ANYONE."

ME: "Who would I tell?"

The conversation went on for a while, looping back over the same topics until it felt like déjà vu. But I learned a couple of things. One: I guess I am an okay friend, because I agreed to go to church with Savannah even though I'm not a church person (and reading about all those burned witches sure hadn't helped). And two: turns out I wanted to tell a ton of people about Savannah's pregnancy. Nothing like feeling completely helpless to make you want to talk to everyone and get their advice.

Guess that's a third thing I learned: we may both be Flyers, but I'm nothing like my mom. Not that the Standers cared.

I wasn't lying when I agreed to go to church with Savannah. I just wasn't real specific about when. I meant to go that Sunday, until Nate called. But it wasn't what you'd think.

"The BABY GOATS. They've been BORN!" He sounded like Louis.

"When?"

"Last night! Ms. Schneider's son called me—he was spending the night out there 'cause animals like to give birth in the middle of the night, and…" He went on for a while. It was so weird to hear his voice so excited and not feel…anything. "So, wanna bike over and see?"

There's no cuter newborn animal than a goat—puppies aren't even close until their eyes open. But goats—kids—look right at you from the get-go, so smart and perky, and their little lips are so soft, and their ears!!! Anyway. I went.

We spent about half an hour watching the little twins stagger around Pansy, getting used to their legs and nursing with fierce little butting motions. During that whole time we talked about nothing but goats. There were other people there, yeah. But it also felt like just the right topic.

On our ride home, Nate yelled over his shoulder, "How come you never want to hang out anymore?" Then he sped up.

I bore down on the pedals to catch up. "What about Savannah?" Man, it's weird to yell a conversation like that, especially out of breath.

"Yeah, that's not happening," said my Once-Upon-a-Time-Almost-Boyfriend. "She's outta my league."

The strange thing was, I agreed. "Well," I said, trying out my feelings. Not hurt. Not even insulted. Relieved to be done with this whole Freshman Romance thing? *Yup. I got more important things to worry about. So does Savannah.* "She is kinda out there. But we can still hang out."

Nate gave me a smile that would've stopped my heart six weeks earlier. "F'shizzle, Burger."

I smiled back, thinking, *Savannah's right, I must be totally immature because watching my crush turn into a plain old friend is making me happy.* And then I remembered—*Oh, shoot, Savannah's probably been trying to call about church.*

But then Nate said, "Hey. Your boy Louis doesn't have a phone, right? Let's go tell him about the goats."

All I thought then was, *Cool*.

The following week at school was the best week of the year. With only two to go—about time!

First of all Dora, the other goat, decided to have her babies during school, so we got to postpone our Civil War test and go watch. She had 'em right next to the fence post that I had personally planted! They were just as cute as Pansy's kids, only floppier.

Also, I'd buried my unfinished (but almost awesome) Transcendentalism essay under my science lab folder (all As!), so it wasn't bugging me. I had another week till the contest deadline.

But that's not the best part. Suddenly Nate was talking to me more than he ever did when I thought he might like me. He pulled Louis and Erin into our lunch circle, like one big happy family, even with Tyler. Savannah's quieter these days, and even though she still let Tyler put his hands all over her, she didn't make a big deal of it anymore. She hadn't told him yet about... you know. It still killed me to keep her secret, but the little looks she tossed over now and then made me feel warm and needed, and when I promised her I'd go to church next weekend, I knew I'd keep that promise.

To me, church smells like a dressed-up library. I mean, it's mostly books and not-completely-vacuumed dust, but there's also perfume and cologne, the smell of people trying to look their best. It's one of the only places on Dalby I've seen neckties.

Reverend Paula wasn't wearing a necktie, of course, but she had one of those stiff little white collars around her neck, above a plain brown dress with shiny buttons: very serious. Her dress matched her tone, and that nasal voice of hers made her sound kind of drone-y.

Gotta be honest: church is so distracting to me, with all the standing up, and sitting down, and the stained glass windows, that I barely paid attention to anything but scenery and people, especially Savannah. After all, I was there for her, so I kept checking in to see if she needed me to put my arm around her or something. Mostly she kept her eyes closed, and I wondered if she was praying, and what that felt like, since I wasn't raised that way. Not until she lifted her head and looked hard at Reverend Paula did I finally start listening.

"…but what do we do when the right choice isn't obvious?" The reverend had been talking for a while, so this was the main sermon. "What do we do when faced with two paths, neither of which is posted with a lighted sign saying, 'This is the road that will lead you to purity!' In fact, many times, isn't it just the opposite? The path we're considering will advertise itself as the path of ease, of freedom. It'll say, 'Go this way because it *feels* right. Trust your *feelings*.'"

A flicker of recognition passed through me. She sounded a little like ol' Ralph Waldo.

"But there is such a thing as too much freedom. This we know. Sometimes doing what feels right means giving in, allowing ourselves to fly away on the winds of self-delusion when we should be standing firmly on the ground of discipline. Sometimes the path we should be choosing is the harder path, because, you know, standing for the right thing won't win you as many friends as gliding along through the flowers of self-indulgence." *Man, now she sounds like Mr. Howe!* "My friends, bottom line: beware of false gut feelings. Pray hard and you will know the truth, and know which path to take. You will do what is right because it is right, because God is telling you it is right, and not because you yourself have decided it *feels* right. When you pray, you come down to earth and you *know*. And then you walk that difficult path without doubt, and say good-bye to the promises of false freedom."

She said a few more things after that, but Savannah turned to me and whispered, "Did you see that? She looked right at me. She's talking to *me*, Joss."

Which was weird, because I could have sworn Reverend Paula was looking at me when she said that stuff about false gut feelings. Only that made no sense. I wasn't the one making a difficult choice.

I sort of fake-sang along on one more hymn, and when the people on the bench in front of us reached back to shake hands, I realized it was over. My head felt weirdly full; I wanted to get out and fly and think things over up where the air is clear and smells like real lilies, not sprayed-on ones. But Savannah was clutching my hand and going on about Reverend Paula sending her a message.

"So..." I finally said, wishing I could just dive right in and ask, "You gonna have an abortion or not?" I shifted my poor butt—man, those benches are hard. "You, uh, feel like you know what to do now?"

Savannah frowned at me. "Joss, weren't you listening? It's not how I *feel*. I have to keep praying until I *know*."

"Well, somebody sure got the word today," said Zach Howe, who was suddenly beside us. He wasn't wearing a tie, but his button-down shirt and khakis made him look older, and so did the smile he was giving Savannah. "So you got her to come today. Good job. How'd you like the sermon, kid?"

I recovered myself. Of course Zach would attend this church; his uncle did, and he was that kind of guy, wasn't he? Clean-cut, like Lorraine said. More like Mr. Howe's son than Tyler, that's for sure. "I thought it was very interesting," I said solemnly. From the corner of my eye I noticed Mr. Howe, handshaking his way toward us. "Reverend Paula kind of reminds me of your uncle," I added.

Zach turned his smile full blast on me. "Doesn't she? Same

message, right? Take it slow and steady, don't rush down a new path just because you think it's cool. Wish my brother would hear that."

"Hear what, now?" Mr. Howe joined us. "Our minister? Well, son, if your brother had been listening to ministers in the first place…life would have worked out a bit differently, wouldn't it? But the road to hell is always 'cool,' isn't it? Good morning, young ladies. So nice to see you here."

Oh, wow, it was weird to stand next to him and say polite things with my mental debate whirring back to life. *Standers always follow their church, that's what the books said*. Oh, come on, everyone listens to the minister. Does that make them evil? *But listen, he's taking Reverend Paula's words and twisting them—she never said anything about hell!* Yeah, but she used the word "stand" a couple of times, didn't she?

I wanted so badly to ask Mr. Howe straight out, but—what would I ask? *Excuse me, do you hate flying people?* If he was the one, I couldn't risk letting him know I suspected him.

But I could find out from Zach. As soon as Mr. Howe made his good-byes and went to drink coffee in the church's meeting room, I did just that, before I could chicken out. "Hey. Does your uncle hate, like…different-type people?" *Jeez, that sounded stupid.* "I mean, like, does he hate your brother because he's gay?"

Savannah looked startled; she hadn't been part of this earlier discussion, and I felt a little pride about that before I kicked myself. This was *not* a competition.

Zach shook his head. "No, Uncle Doug doesn't hate Rory. He just agrees with me that Rory's taking advantage of people not wanting to seem anti-gay, that he's pushing things too far. Like the rev said, too much freedom."

"You think that too? That there's too much freedom here?" The more I thought about it, the more Reverend Paula's sermon reminded me of Mr. Howe's speech to my class. I remembered

Mr. Evans arguing with him. He'd figured out Mr. Howe from the beginning. *But Zach's not like that.*

"Oh, I don't know about Dalby," Zach shrugged. "I haven't been here all that long. I do know Uncle Doug's pretty old-fashioned. He has issues with modern stuff like kids talking back to their parents."

"Oh, I know, Tyler gets in trouble for that all the time," Savannah said, with her little head-toss.

"What about gays?" I couldn't ask about Flyers, but gay people seemed to be working as a substitute here. "I mean, Rory's lifestyle bugs him, right? What if he had gay customers? Would he still sell stuff to them?"

"Joss, what are you talking about?" Savannah frowned. But I wasn't done.

"Would he, like, try to stop them from being gay if he could? Or stop anybody from being a certain way if he thought they shouldn't be?"

Zach looked at me curiously, like there was more to me than he'd noticed before. It felt amazing, having those golden eyes fixed on me like that, and I had to bite my inner cheek to keep from smiling. "You sound like this is kind of personal. But you don't have anyone in your family who...do you?"

"Not in my family. But my friend's mom."

"Not me," said Savannah quickly. "She means Louis."

"And I don't want him to get picked on," I added. "Your cousin Tyler was picking on him, so I'm wondering if, like, he gets it from his dad." *Or you? Michael said he'd heard you talking crap about Rory...but Michael was just trying to provoke me.*

"But Ty apologized that time." Savannah looked annoyed. "And he's been really nice ever since."

"Oh, back in February? I remember," said Zach. "A teacher called home and my uncle and Tyler had a talk, I think. So that was your friend, huh? The kid with two moms?"

"Janice isn't his mom, she's just his mom's girlfriend," I explained. "But Louis is way happier with her than he ever was with any of Shasta's boyfriends. So it's good. But what I'm trying to say is…" *What was I trying to say?* "Does Mr. Howe think that's too much freedom?"

"I wouldn't worry about Uncle Doug," Zach said easily. "Like I said, he's just kinda old-fashioned. You respect him, he'll respect you. You tell your friend his moms can keep shopping at Howe's."

Well, that didn't sound like much of a Stander. *But what does that prove? Zach doesn't know about any of this. What exactly did I hope to learn from him?* I still felt vaguely reassured.

"So, you two coming back next week?" he added, and I realized, wow, the church had emptied out and he'd stayed to talk with just us. And Savannah hadn't flirted at all.

"Definitely," she said. "Reverend Paula is so Wise." She hooked my arm. "And Joss'll come back too, right?"

I didn't want to. I didn't like the stand-up-sit-down, didn't like Reverend Paula's droning voice, and most of all I didn't like feeling so confused about Mr. Howe. *Was he or wasn't he?*

But Savannah was my friend and she needed me. And Zach would be there, and he seemed to like talking to us. To me. "Yeah," I said. "Prob'ly."

"Reverend Paula said what?" Lorraine asked sharply at dinner when I explained about my church adventure.

"I don't remember exactly, I didn't bring a tape recorder," I grumbled. Mom had refused my dinner offer for the millionth time, but in that same, happy-perky way that creeped me out and reminded me that I'd promised not to tell about her quitting therapy. "She said, like, standing for the right thing is hard but you have to do it anyway."

Dad and Michael looked blank, but Lorraine narrowed her eyes at me. "Those exact words?" she asked quietly. "Joss, this is important."

"I think so." I remembered more about Zach than Reverend Paula, but I couldn't tell her that. Of course she would focus in on the rev.

"Right," my stepmother said firmly. "Next week, I'm coming with you."

"Oh, great!" I said. But I thought, *Oh, great. Then Zach probably won't talk to me.*

By the time next Sunday rolled around, though, I was as ready as she was. Something else happened. And now, like Reverend Paula said, I didn't just feel, I *knew* who it was—and how to take him down.

Louis and Shasta have no phone, right? So when it happened, Shasta had to run back around her house to unlock the Co-op before she could call Sheriff Gil. Then she called my dad. Half an hour later, we were standing around watching Sheriff Gil photographing the damage.

My shock had turned into a lump of anger burning in my stomach. Louis and I had walked home from Nate's, where we'd spent a hilarious afternoon helping his mom wax floors and skating around on towel-wrapped feet. Nate had started calling Louis "Red," his best nickname ever. But then "Red" came home and ran smack into that horrible word painted huge and ugly over his front door: WHORES. And found his mom crying in her bedroom, surrounded by scrawled messages, on the walls, the mirror, even the ceiling. STRAIGHT IS THE PATH, YOU…and then some words that I don't want to write, or even think about.

Louis's face clamped into a hard mask that said, *Don't even think of asking me how I feel.* I knew what I felt, though: the same thing I felt about the poison letters, now I was making myself think about them. *Who do you think you are? How dare you???!*

"I just don't understand how I didn't hear it," Shasta moaned for the tenth time. Louis hadn't moved from her side since he got home, his arm around her shoulder, but she couldn't stop crying. "I was right next door the whole time. The whole time."

"Well, I'd call that a blessing," Sheriff Gil said. He was leaning on the hood of his car, filling out some forms. "Whoever did this wanted to stay quiet. Otherwise who knows what kind of mess they'd've made?"

"Huh," Louis snorted, but I thought the sheriff had a point; nothing was smashed. The horrible work had been quick and silent. And targeted. Louis's room was untouched.

"I did hear the goats," Shasta sniffled. "But I thought they were just talking to each other. Oh, and you guys were trying to warn me, weren't you?" She gave a little sob and pulled away from Louis to go caress their knobby heads. Louis stared at the ground.

"You think it's Tyler, huh," I told him, very low.

"Yeah, ya think?" Louis didn't bother to keep his voice down. "Who else? He's been nice for two whole weeks, guess it must've been killing him."

"You kids have something to tell me about this?" Sheriff Gil said.

"No sir." I shook my head vigorously. "We were talking about something else." I had absolutely no proof, and the last thing I wanted was to put the Howes on their guard. "C'mere." I pulled Louis over to the far end of the yard to sit on some boulders. Across the way I could see Dad coming from our house with a bucket full of something. "Look. What if Tyler wrote the stuff, but he got the idea from his dad? Mr. Howe."

Louis looked scornful. "You thinking about that Stander thing? What's that got to do with it? Tyler hates queers. He doesn't need any help with that."

"I know, I know. But…" I took a deep breath, trying to focus all the stray "ahas," about Mr. Howe and Reverend Paula, and the letters, and being Seen, into one bright spotlight of accusation. "'Straight is the path…'" It sounds like that letter my mom got. Maybe Tyler—"

Louis interrupted. "That's dumb, Joss. Tyler hates me, I don't care if Nate's making him act nice. What's this got to do with your mom?"

"Well, I dunno." But then Dad was there.

"Hey, son," he said to Louis, squeezing his shoulder. "I got the best possible cure for ugliness here in my hand. Gil's done taking pictures. So get your mom and let's scrub your place down so the jerks who did this will know you guys aren't rolling over. Make it all go away before Janice gets home."

His bucket was full of cleaning stuff and, for some reason, makeup remover. I understood why when I got nose to nose with the nasty words smeared all over Shasta's room: they were written in lipstick.

"This much lipstick?" I panted, watching the wall return to normal under my scrubbing. "Where would Tyler get that? From his dad's store, that's where. I'm telling you, he couldn't have done this on his own." My own dad was outside, working on the front door. I couldn't share my theory with him, since he didn't know about the poison letters. I needed Lorraine.

"Savannah gave it to him," Louis said darkly. He hadn't agreed with a single thing I'd said since we got here, but Dad was right, the scrubbing seemed to be helping his spirit. Shasta came in then with tea for us, so we stopped arguing and went over to give her hugs and tell her one more time that everything was okay.

Everything wasn't, of course. But as we erased the last of those filthy words, my theory hardened, and it felt good. Tyler wasn't just a homophobic jerk. He was his evil dad's evil little puppet. Sooner or later I'd make Louis see that.

But Savannah blasted my theory out of the water. I called her that night, with the excuse of seeing how she was doing, and before I could even ask, she had given Tyler a...what're those things they're always talking about in crime shows? An alibi.

"Omigod, it was so romantic, Joss," she sighed, like I was interviewing her for *People* magazine instead of asking how her afternoon was. "Ty said he'd noticed I seemed kind of down and he wanted to do something special. So he took me out for ice cream, and he got them to put, like, a rose on our table ahead of time. And then we went over to Island Styles and he let me pick out the most beautiful scarf! And then his mom took us to his house and made us little sandwiches. And then we went into his room…"

I had to stop her there. "Okay, yeah, got it. Romantic."

"SO romantic. I wish you could see that side of him, Joss."

And I wished she hadn't proved that Tyler hadn't lipsticked my friend's house.

So it was Mr. Howe alone. With a shock, I realized my first instinct had been right. Zach said he was old-fashioned, but it was more than that: Mr. Howe hated anything nonconformist. That's why he opened his store here, to get people to buy "normal" cards and pottery and jewelry and marshmallow Peeps, instead of handmade beaded stuff and flax cookies. Straight is the path.

Should've trusted myself, I thought bitterly. *I could've drunk out of his cup at church yesterday.*

I remembered those old drawings of ministers in Lorraine's books, hyped up on righteous anger. I'd pictured Tyler slashing the lipstick around with a big grin on his face, but in my new image, Mr. Howe was glaring, his jaw set. He was wearing his tie.

"So have you told Tyler about the baby yet?" I said brutally. "It's his too, you know."

"Shhh!" Savannah hissed through the phone, not knowing I was alone in my kitchen. Then she returned her voice to its usual sad dignity for this topic. "I'm going to pray on it one more time this Sunday, and talk to Reverend Paula. I need to prepare myself, Joss. Ty will respect my decision, but it needs to be mine. He's still such a boy in so many ways."

Right, and you're such a woman. But my heart ached for my sad-sounding friend. Her boyfriend was a jerk with an evil father. "You know I'll be there for you," I said. "But your mom, how is…"

"We talked," Savannah said, "but she couldn't stop crying, so… Yeah. Reverend Paula will help. So how was your afternoon?" she added politely. Done with that topic. She said all the right, horrified things when I told her about the attack on Louis's house. I wished Louis could have heard her. I wished there were no ugliness in the world.

The sky was still bright at eight-thirty, plenty of time for a flight before bed, but I felt too heavy now. I tried to study for my math test, but the equations I'd understood last week kept sliding past my brain. *Forget it, I'll study before school.* So I said my good nights, brushed my teeth and crawled into bed, staring at my old poster of Harry Potter. He's covered in grime and blood, facing a monster.

So am I, I thought. *He may not want to kill me, or Mom, or Shasta and Janice. But he wants to stop us being who we are. So, really…he kind of does.*

It was an Aha Moment. *I may know only one other Flyer in the world, but we are part of a bigger group—a huge group. Our name is Anyone Who's Different.* Gays, Flyers, weirdos. Perfectly nice-seeming people like Mr. Howe wanted to blot us out, using the wise words of perfectly nice ministers to inspire their hatefulness.

I didn't feel brave and strong like Harry. I felt angry.

After an hour of tossing and turning, I got out of bed and finished the conclusion of my re-re-rewritten essay. "Live and let live." I knew it was a cliché and I didn't care: *that's* what the Transcendentalists were trying to say about Nonconformity! Not just "Be Different," but "Respect Difference." You don't have to love thy neighbor, but you do have to try to get along, no matter how weird she is. *That's* what it means to be a citizen.

By the time I finished it was midnight, and I was completely revved. I snuck out the back door in my nightgown, leapt off the steps and did two huge laps above the village, a breeze sighing gently around me. Oh, that summer air! Wild roses and tidal mud blended with the lily-smell, and the rigging of sailboats tinkled from the harbor. My nightgown fluttered and I nearly laughed out loud: if Reverend Paula saw me now, she really would think I was an angel.

But I was a Flyer and I knew what to do. I would give my essay to Mr. Evans in the morning, go to church with Savannah next week, and find a way to drink out of Mr. Howe's coffee cup without him noticing. I would live and let him live, but I would not let him stop me. Or Shasta, or Mom, or anyone who wanted to feel the way I felt at midnight in the sky.

CHAPTER FIFTEEN

PEWS AND PARTY-CRASHING

Turns out there's a fancy word for Aha Moment: "Epiphany." Mr. Evans explained the word, right after telling me my essay had "legs." I didn't need a translation to know that was good. Finally! Somehow, last night's epiphany, on top of Zach's help on the purple part, had created "your best work, Jocelyn—what I knew you'd tap into if you tried hard enough."

He especially liked the ending. "Yes, Live and Let Live is a cliché, but you've given it your own twist. This is *writing*. I'll be proud to enter it in the contest."

Mr. Evans said that!

Then I had another epiphany. I was on a roll. For my birthday next week, I decided to invite everybody I know. If Respecting Differences was what Flyers stood for, I was going to go one better: I was going to Celebrate 'em. *A cookie party!* Everyone could make one, and decorate it to represent themselves. Savannah's would be her horse-with-a-rose logo, of course. *Oh! I should have my party at Savannah's, her kitchen is twice as big as ours.* Which meant I'd have to invite Tyler. Well, I would. *Yup, even Tyler—now that he's not an evil puppet after all.* It'd be interesting to see what kind of a cookie he'd make.

And maybe Tyler would go home and teach his dad about getting along with people you don't approve of. Maybe Mr. Howe would have an Epiphany of his own, and I wouldn't have to figure out a way to snag his coffee cup. *Yeah, right.*

So what. I could totally do this.

And, oh yeah—I did pass that math test…just barely.

I forgot to have an "Aha" about Lorraine, though. The Sunday before my party, she joined me and Savannah at church.

After the usual standing and singing and sitting, Reverend Paula got up for her sermon. Her dress was dark blue today. I sat on that hard bench sandwiched between Savannah and Lorraine, but super aware of Zach a few rows behind us. I felt like a rubber band being stretched in four different directions, but at least one of them was the sermon. Right away she started talking about the attack on Louis's house, which by now everyone knew about.

"There is no room for hate in our community, or in our world," preached the rev. "What happened in our midst is reprehensible, and we all need to pray for the cleansing of that angry spirit that was unleashed last week onto members of our Dalby family." I felt people nodding around me. "We need to pray for harmony."

Harmony. My mind wandered at that word, imagining each of us vibrating to our own little iron strings, and all those strings humming together like a choir. When Reverend Paula said, "But sometimes harmony is hard to come by when we all start playing different tunes," I felt a little jolted, like she'd read my mind. She went on: "The opposite of harmony is discord, and some people say discord is the same thing as hatred. But my friends, sometimes anger and hate are called forth *from* discord, created by the willful choices of individuals. When this happens, we need to look deeper at our own choices, our own actions, to see how we may be creating discord and calling forth anger and hate."

I heard shifting sounds around the congregation. On either side of me, Lorraine and Savannah stiffened. *Wait, what did she just say?* I concentrated so hard, trying to roll the words back through my mind, that I almost missed the next part.

"…people choosing actions or behaviors that go against our deepest moral core, then discord is created. People sacrificing what is right and good for what satisfies them: discord is created. And people putting their own souls at risk in full view of their neighbors who care for them: discord is created."

Savannah gave a little shiver. On the other side of me, Lorraine seemed to radiate cold, and I shivered too. *Is she saying… it was Shasta's fault for making someone angry enough to attack her?* That could not be right.

But before I could get a handle on this, Reverend Paula switched gears and started talking about forgiveness, and the possibility of redemption. I didn't understand, but it sounded a lot nicer, and the congregation seemed to relax along with Reverend Paula's voice. Not Lorraine. And at the end of the sermon, when we were supposed to stand up and sing a hymn, she stayed sitting. It was a little embarrassing, but I reminded myself to Live and Let Live.

People were still shaking hands when Savannah squeezed past us into the aisle and headed straight for Reverend Paula. Her eyes were red—was she upset about Shasta too? I wanted to get off that pew, but Lorraine stayed sitting. She looked grim.

"I think that answers our question," she said.

"What question?"

"Whose cup to drink out of. You heard that sermon, didn't you? She thinks your soul's at risk."

"*My* soul? But I thought she was talking about—"

Lorraine put her hand on my leg to shush me; Zach was standing in the aisle.

"G'morning," he said, smiling in a way that looked a little pained. Did he feel bad about the sermon too?

"What'd you think about that?" I asked, leaning across Lorraine, who was shaking her head.

Zach raised his eyebrows. "Harsh," he said. "Definitely gonna be some people feeling uncomfortable this morning."

"I know, right? But I'll bet your uncle liked what she said. Don't you think?" I looked at Lorraine for her reaction. She was frowning. Didn't she get it? Reverend Paula wasn't the Stander. *What, did she think Reverend Paula went running through Louis's house last week smearing lipstick on the walls? She hadn't even used the word "stand" today, not that I'd heard.*

"He's home today, not feeling well," Zach said, "so I—"

My stepmother interrupted. "Jocelyn. We need to go. It's time for coffee."

I shook my head. "You go ahead, you know I don't like coffee. I'll just hang out here and wait for you."

Lorraine turned so pale her freckles suddenly looked bright. "I'm sure they have cocoa or something. It's *time*," she repeated, standing up.

I'm not stupid, okay? I knew exactly what she wanted me to do. And I wasn't doing it. She was wrong. Mr. Howe was the Stander, not the rev, and since he wasn't here today I was going to sit and talk to Zach about that weird sermon. Maybe he could help me make sense of it, since Lorraine and Savannah were freaking out on me. I crossed my arms.

"I'm fine right here," I said. With a backward glare, Lorraine marched up the aisle, following the last of the congregation.

"Huh. Guess someone doesn't approve of me," Zach smiled. He sat himself in Lorraine's spot in the pew. "Don't worry, my intentions are pure. We're talking about church stuff, right?"

"Right," I said, and oh, it felt so adult, so *good* to sit there with him. "So…you heard about what happened to my friend's house, right? You think Reverend Paula's saying it was my friend's mom's fault for being attacked because her…lifestyle…is, like, weird?"

Zach looked at me sadly. "I don't know, kid. It did sound like your friend's mom…well, maybe she's a little bit like my brother?

Not saying she meant to rub people's noses in her…lifestyle, like Rory does, but…maybe, without meaning to? She kinda stirred somebody up?"

"But how is that her fault?" I demanded. "If that was true, then shouldn't we blame lots of people for getting hurt?" *Wouldn't it be my mom's fault for nearly getting raped last year when she was drunk and made those guys mad? Make sense of this,* I thought at him.

"Well, let me ask you a question," Zach said, widening those golden eyes, and I thought, ridiculously, *This time next week I'll be fifteen.* "Have you ever known something, really *known* it, but you knew nobody would believe you if you told them? I had this vision of my little brother…" He looked away. "I can't even tell you about it, you'd think I was crazy. But when I tried to tell Rory about it, what I'd seen and how it related to, like, his making out with his boyfriend in the parking lot at school, well…he shut me out. And I was angry, yeah. Not 'cause I hate gays, but 'cause I love him. And I don't want him to…end up like in my vision."

I should have asked him to clarify. I couldn't tell if he was saying whoever had attacked Louis's house had done it for noble reasons, or that he'd had a vision of his brother in Hell, or both. I should've asked, and argued. But Zach looked so vulnerable all of a sudden. *Have you ever known something, really* known *it?* Are you kidding me? My thoughts went straight to my mom.

I was lucky, I had five people who knew I could fly. So did Mom. But she was so messed up about whether or not flying was right, she was willing to let one mean, anonymous person scare her out of it.

Oh jeez. I stopped in midthought. *Mr. Howe's her boss. If he can send her letters like that, what could he be saying to her at work? Carefully, sneakily, masking his words so they sounded nice when really he was telling her over and over, Don't you dare be wild and free.* And she doesn't know about Standers, and she's not thinking clearly anyway. She has no way to protect herself.

Maybe Zach could help her. *He works at Howe's too, right? He wouldn't need to know all that mess about Flyers and Standers—just that Mom was going through a bad time, and needed someone to, like, shield her a little from the boss.*

"I know what you mean," I said slowly. "I have somebody I love who's maybe gonna end up really bad, like Rory, but I feel like I can't do anything about it."

Zach nodded.

"You actually know this person too," I went on. "And, this person's problem, well…what you said about knowing something that no one would believe? It's like that. It's…" His eyes, I swear, were throwing out a beam of light like a rope I could grab onto. *I could tell Zach. I could show him, even.* He'd understand. He loves his brother and wants to help him. He could help me help my mom. He lives with our enemy—maybe he could even get his uncle's cup for us!

I listened to my gut, my iron string. *Hummmmmm.* Yes. "If I tell you something crazy, will you promise not to tell anyone?" It sounded babyish, but Zach nodded again, still serious.

"Of course I promise."

I took a deep breath. And that's when Lorraine came swooping back in.

She couldn't exactly grab me by my scruff and drag me home. I could have stayed if I wanted. But our moment was broken. Zach dropped his rope-gaze—"Hey, we'll talk later, okay? I better get going"—and took off. And of course Lorraine asked me what he was promising and I said "Nothing" and I knew she knew, and it made me furious, but before I had a chance to chew her out she beat me to it.

"Reverend Paula was talking to Savannah," she whispered as we pushed through the church doors and into the sunshine. "Her cup was *right there*, Joss. It would have been so easy. Why didn't you come with me?"

"Because it's stupid," I said, trying to smile at my fellow churchgoers and still keep my voice harsh. "She's not the one, it's Mr. Howe, and you know it, you just didn't want me talking to Zach, because—"

"Yes, why? Because you were about to share something that isn't only yours to share, Jocelyn." Lorraine stopped at the parking sign and faced me. Her freckles looked painted on; I had never seen her so angry. "I haven't convinced you about Reverend Paula yet—fine. We'll go back next week and hear another sermon, and you tell *me* she's not the one, preaching about people's differences causing discord in the world. Dalby folks don't believe that." She dropped her voice even lower. "But let's imagine for a moment you're right about Mr. Howe. Do you really think his nephew wouldn't tell him you can fly? And that somebody's trying to stop you?"

"Zach promised," I said stubbornly. "And Mr. Howe knows about Flyers already. That's why he sent the letters."

"But he doesn't know *you* know about Standers! And neither does Reverend Paula. Our only weapon is to take her by surprise—like we could have done today," she added bitterly.

"But—" I sputtered. "You can't have it both ways! If Reverend Paula's the Stander—" Lorraine motioned my voice down, I was starting to shout—"then who cares if I tell Zach and he tells his uncle! You must think I'm right after all!"

She flushed. "She's their minister, Jocelyn. You can't take the chance they wouldn't tell her…or tell somebody, the media even. Reverend Paula would find out that we know. And then we'll have no hope of disempowering her."

"Let's just go tell her then," I hissed. "Right now. Who needs a cup? If she knows we know, then it's a standoff: she'll have to quit harassing people like me and Mom and Shasta—which is stupid, 'cause she never did, but whatever. Go tell her. Watch. Nothing's gonna happen!"

"You're right there," said my stepmom. Her narrowed eyes

flashed. "Not a thing is what would happen: not another flight is what would happen. Because you'd never know when she was underneath you, praying. She's already stopped your mom, just out of fear. She's working on Shasta and Janice now. Do you really want her to stop you too?"

Savannah joined us then, so I had no chance to tell Lorraine how wrong she was. "Never mind. I'll see you at home," Lorraine said, turning away.

My best friend was smiling as bright as the morning, and her eyes were clear again as we walked back to my house. "She gave me great advice, Joss," is all she would tell me about her talk with the reverend, but I noticed she kept touching her stomach. Still, all Savannah wanted to discuss was decorating her house for my cookie-party.

But underneath the happy talk about streamers and balloons, I felt shaken by Lorraine's anger. It had poured out of her like a spring, cold and pure...and certain. I gripped my image of Mr. Howe scrawling the lipstick, Mr. Howe sneering politely at my teacher, Mr. Howe muttering as he peered up at my mom's foot on his roof. Lorraine was wrong, she had to be wrong. But she was trusting herself, I had to admit. I wouldn't apologize for arguing, but fine, I would go back to church with her one more time, just to show her.

Except we were all kind of busy that next Sunday.

Everyone's always in a fantastic mood for my birthday, since it falls right at the end of school. We were officially done being freshmen. "Woot-woooot!" Tyler yelled, racing out of the building, and we all joined in.

Even the weather got into it! Four days of sun in a row, and my birthday was the nicest of all. The harbor looked like a postcard, all the sailboats mirrored in the water. Wild roses were nearly done, but the garden ones were taking over, red and yellow and pink, and the village was filling up with tourists in bike shorts. It was SUMMER. Less than two weeks to Fourth of July! Fireworks, Citizen Celebration—a little heart-leap, thinking about my essay…Zach playing in the concert—another heart-leap…

Lorraine and I made it through the week being polite to each other. And she and Dad ordered me the last Harry Potter book…*three more weeks till it comes!!!!!!!!!*

Even Michael added to my sparkly mood, acting as pumped about my birthday as I was. "So, is your party, like, at the exact moment of Summer Solstice?" he asked. "When is that, anyhow?" I had no idea, but I was so psyched to have an un-snotty brother for a change, I didn't even mind when he gave me cheap dangly earrings from Howe's for my birthday. He didn't know how I felt about Howe's.

"Dang, girl, you keep on eating cookie dough, you're gonna end up like me," Heather told Savannah, patting her stomach.

I pooched my belly out and turned to Savannah. "Yeah, girlfriend, gimme some," I said, trying to belly-bump her like basketball players do with their chests.

"No thank you," Savannah said, turning abruptly. *Holy shih tzu, I actually forgot…* Her belly was full of more than cookie dough. "Sorry," I muttered, but Savannah grinned and did a fake hula instead of getting mad. She was still keeping her secret from everybody but me, which is pretty incredible if you know Savannah.

Tyler came up behind her and put his hands on her wiggling hips. "Hey, Hawaii-girl, wanna get lei'd?"

We rolled our eyes. Nate was always telling me, "Dude, Tyler's an idiot, but he's a good guy," and every now and then I'd see it, like when Tyler repaired Erin's hot air balloon-cookie with frosting after it fell off the table. He was my BFF's BF, after all, and it wasn't his fault his dad was evil. Plus, get this: Tyler made a rainbow cookie! I am not joking. "Dude, that is so g—" Nate started to say when Tyler was adding the colored sprinkles, but then he saw my face and changed to "—cool," and it was! Louis was keeping his distance from Tyler, but Nate was hanging with him, and I heard him call Louis's eagle-cookie "legit." I'm telling you, it was this crazy mix of people and sugar and happiness, all on my magic day. Then the phone rang.

A few seconds later, Savannah's mom appeared, with the telephone instead of the sprinkles and jellybeans she'd been supplying. "Jocelyn, it's for you," she said. "It's your dad."

"Dad! Thank you for my party!" I screamed into the receiver, watching Louis dab frosting on Nate's nose. Dad was paying for all the food, and I wanted him to know how wonderful it was. "We're having an amazing time!"

He cut me off. "Hon, listen to me. Your brother's hurt. They're airlifting him to the mainland right now. Gil's flying me over in his plane. Your moms are coming to get you. You can make the five o'clock ferry and meet me there."

He sounded like a robot, pitching those short, ugly sentences at me in rhythm. I didn't know what to do with them.

"Jocelyn?"

I cleared my throat. "Hurt how?"

"They don't know all of it, but it's bad. He was unconscious. They found him…" The phone went quiet and I was frozen by an image of my big, strong father holding his hand over the receiver, doubled over while the tears attacked. "…Sorry. They found him at the bottom of the cliff. At Whittier's Bluff."

"Oh my god."

"He had some kind of canvas wings strapped on…"

"Oh, god."

"Jocelyn. It's not your fault, hon. But it looks like your brother was trying to fly."

CHAPTER SIXTEEN

LUCKY ICARUS

Not your fault. Not your fault. Of course not, if you were Dad, trying to make sure his daughter didn't blame herself for the magic which somehow came to her and not his firstborn. But if you were me, and knew what I knew—Michael's first attempt off the Toad, his talk about the Solstice, his latest "project" in his room—and kept your mouth shut, well. Who else's fault could it be?

Getting older sucks. A year ago, I would have loved the drama: all those people gathered around, Nate Cowper asking, "Joss, what's wrong?" The shock, the hugs, the awed silence as I slipped away from the crowded house to climb into the truck. Not now. I was rigid with guilt and fear.

Halfway to the ferry, Lorraine tried to lighten the mood: "Michael strikes again, huh? He sure has a thing about your birthday." She meant last year, when Michael stole the truck and tried to drive off-island, ruining my party. But Mom and I kept silent. I wish I could say we were suddenly connected, two Flyers squished together in the front seat, flooded by the same raw tide of feeling. But I had no idea what she was thinking.

When we got on the boat, I let the two of them go upstairs to the seating area, and I sat in the truck by myself and cried.

Michael was a mess, the doctor in charge said. But she said it with a smile. He was a mess who would live to walk and talk again, "Which is more than Icarus could say," and by then my brain had woken up enough to recognize the reference to the

Greek myth Mrs. Mac taught us. Part of Michael's fake wings were still clinging to him even after the medics had cut them away, and everyone in the hospital seemed to know the story of the Flying Boy. At least they didn't think he'd tried to kill himself. "Punctured lung, four broken ribs, broken arm, broken leg, concussion." The doctor rattled off Michael's injuries, then shook her head. "And we need to thank the good Lord, or your son's engineering skills, that this is all. No internal injuries—and that, folks, is a flat-out miracle."

"Engineering skills?" Dad repeated. Since we'd caught up with him after his flight in Gil's plane, he'd refused the muffins Lorraine had picked up from the hospital cafeteria, and his coffee looked untouched.

"The wings," the doctor said. She was tall and dark and beautiful like a TV surgeon. "He used PVC pipe, so he must've managed to soar a little before he crashed, and that gave him a lighter landing. Boy, I've been up on that cliff, what is that—four hundred feet? Anyway, he didn't drop like a rock, and that's what saved his insides. Just his outsides got pretty banged up. Nothing we can't fix, though." She shook her head again. "Teenagers."

The next hours are kind of a blur. I ate some soup and a candy bar. I remember trying to sleep on the brown plastic chairs in the hospital waiting room, draped over the metal armrest. I woke up once to find Mom's sweatshirt covering me, and Mom hugging herself in the next seat.

"Kid wanted to fly," she murmured, but when I said, "Huh?" she just patted me and I went back to sleep, numbed by the vibrations from the giant, silent TV.

Later I woke from another half-nap to see my moms and Dad clustered with their heads together. I heard the words "helicopter" and something-"thousand," and then Mom, very clearly,

"Well, what good is f----- insurance if it doesn't pay for *that*?"
But Dad noticed me and shushed her.

Great. So now they're worried about money, too. I tried to fall back
asleep, but now this thought kept getting in the way: If I won
the essay contest, I could help pay for the damage I hadn't kept
Michael from causing.

But somewhere in that blurry time while Dad was out getting sandwiches, Lorraine and I started talking about Standers
again and Mom listened, like, *of course we have an enemy, no biggie.*
"Mr. Howe, huh? Makes sense," she said, and she didn't say anything about Reverend Paula, but I didn't rub that in Lorraine's
face. "Told Ron your theory yet?" Mom asked us, then shook
her head, "No, better wait a while. We've all got our hands full."
It was weird to see my family coming together over Michael's
crash. Until it nearly fell apart again.

Saturday, after that groggy night, we all came home except
Mom, who begged an extra day off work from Mr. Howe and
stayed to visit Michael between surgeries. I begged to stay too,
but Dad had to reopen the store, so he needed me to cook, and
turn Michael's room—which probably hadn't been cleaned in
a year—into a hospital room. My unshared guilt helped me do
what Dad said without arguing.

I got to skip the cooking, turns out; people kept stopping by
with casseroles and pie. And of course they wanted to know
exactly what had happened. Our story was, Michael had been
experimenting with some homemade climbing gear, and any
"Flying Boy" stories they might hear were silly rumors. I was
working off my guilt, dusting and scrubbing, when Dad announced he was going over to Mom's to feed the cat.

He took long enough. Only when I heard the door slam a
half-hour later did I realize he'd been gone all that time.

Reading poison letters. The ones he'd found underneath the
bag of cat food in the pantry.

He had them spread over our kitchen table by the time I came out of my room to see why he was so quiet. I recognized them instantly, typed in big font like the first one. There were so many.

My guilt washed back in like a tsunami. She'd had more. She'd kept them and never said. And I'd never asked.

"What are those?" *Like you don't know.*

"Filth." Dad looked pale, but his voice was boiling. "Anonymous, creepy, crazy, stalker filth. Someone *knows,* Joss. Someone's *been* knowing a long time. And they've been working on your mom like water dripping on a stone."

I picked one up and read it, the same way you can't make yourself look away from a traffic accident.

> Good girl, Flyer.
> You've been keeping your feet on the ground. Notice how much smoother your life is flowing now?
> Notice how well your kids are doing?
> Keep it up and someday you'll have a normal life again,
> with a husband to take care of you instead of just a cat.
> Sing in tune and join the choir.

I shivered and dropped the thing back on the table. "How many are there?" I didn't know what else to say.

"Sixteen. I read 'em all. They're not dated, but something tells me they didn't all show up in the mailbox on the same day. She could have been receiving one a week for the past…"

"Four months," I said, "because after Valentine's Day she—"
Shut up, idiot.

"Because what?" Dad's eyes lasered into me. "What about Valentine's? What do you know about this, Jocelyn?"

I've lied to my dad before, lots of times, but always over the phone, or looking at the floor. No way could I stand up to those eyes. I told him everything.

Maybe it was the stress of almost losing his son off a cliff, or the shock of finding out his nightmare had come true and our family secret had leaked to the worst possible person. Because even after I broke down, Dad did not hold out the warm, life-ring arms I had always counted on to rescue me in my crying-storms. His voice had gone icy.

"You knew. For four months. You knew some kook had Seen your mom and was harassing her. Stopped her cold. That's why all the research with Lorraine? She knew too? And you kept this from me?"

"No, she…" What could I say? I didn't want to get Lorraine in trouble. Was it her fault if she'd kept Mom's secret better than I had?

"Yes, I knew," said Lorraine from the store curtain behind us. I have no idea how Lorraine figured out what Dad and I were discussing in the kitchen. Maybe, sitting at the cash register, she could smell the ugliness the way she smells the sweetness of flying. She was staring at the letters, gripping the curtain like a support. "Ron, I'm sorry. Beth made her promise. Joss did the right thing to tell me anyway, but it was my choice to leave you in the dark. Oh, honey," and my quiet librarian stepmother flung her arms around Dad's neck and sobbed. "Please, please forgive me. I thought we could solve it with our research, I thought we were getting somewhere, but all this time…oh, poor Beth. Poor Beth. I called it so wrong, and look how much she's had to carry, all alone."

This time Dad's arms did their work. "It's okay, it's okay, hon," he muttered, stroking her hair till it started escaping its braid. Who knows when Lorraine cried last? I looked down, trying to breathe away my own sob-shivers. The kitchen air felt soggy with emotion. "Thank God for therapists," Dad added, "or Beth would be a total nut case by now…again."

Tears burst back out of me. Now I was going to have to spill Mom's secret about that too. *He's going to hate me forever.*

Dad's hand appeared on my shoulder. "What is it," he said, so gently that I cried harder. "Something about Beth's therapy?" I nodded with my eyes squeezed tight. "Let me guess…your mom made you promise not to tell," he sighed. *Snuffle-sob-snort.* "Don't worry, babe. I think I can figure this one out." His warm, heavy arms came around my neck from above. "Holy cow," Dad said to the ceiling. "We're all going to need therapy after this."

"Will sandwiches do?" Lorraine asked, wiping her eyes. "Let me redeem myself with some grilled cheese."

The grilled cheese must've dissolved Dad's shock, 'cause he started firing questions even before he finished chewing.

"So you think these Standards—"

"Standers."

"—are a kind of moral police, enforcing proper behavior on everyone? Then there must be millions of them! I mean, what about all these politicians and preachers who like to tell people how to live? What about the Taliban? What about my grandmother? Aren't they all Standers?"

I let Lorraine do the talking while I stacked the nasty letters and shoved the pile behind the vase of my fading birthday bouquet. I still felt quivery from totally losing it, but her voice sounded steady, and believable.

"Not every self-righteous person is a Stander. We think they're nearly as rare as Flyers. Here and there, in no logical pattern I

can find, up pops a person who perceives the magic of Flyers—
maybe through smell, maybe some deeper magical knowledge.
They don't waste their time questioning the magic, or marveling
over it and publicizing it like any ordinary person. They instantly
feel its threat, and they wish to destroy it. In the olden days, when
everyone believed in magic and witches, it was easy to do that
publicly: make an accusation, destroy the Flyer. Today, in our cul-
ture, that would be impossible."

"Yeah, today they'd give a Flyer her own reality show," I
chimed in. Not because I've thought about this or anything.
"Standers would hate that."

"That's how we know whoever took that video of Beth wasn't
a Stander, just an onlooker," Lorraine added. She started repair-
ing her braid as it hung over her shoulder.

"Because he didn't pray underneath while she was flying over?
That's really all they have to do? And you can't fly anymore?"
Only took a year, but Dad had finally gotten comfy with the
Burgowski f-word.

"That's what we've gathered from our research." Braid fixed,
she refastened the elastic.

"But all *you* have to do is…"

"Drink out of their cup, yeah," I said. It felt good to have Dad
look right at me. "And then have them drink again."

"Well, what are we waiting for, then?" He pushed up from the
table. "This is war."

"Well," said Lorraine at the same time that I said, "Um." Dad
waited.

"Your humble researchers have a difference of opinion here,"
Lorraine explained, with a polite glance at me. "I think Reverend Paula is the Stander. She thinks it's Douglas Howe."

Dad sat down again. "You have got to be kidding." We two
research experts stared at him. "Seriously? Howe and Paula?
The president of the Rotary Club and the leader of the big-

gest church? The two most influential people…ohhh." His frown changed, but it was still a frown. "I think I see what you mean. They're both used to making declarations about the right way to live. I could see 'em feeling threatened by magic. But these?" He flicked at the pile of letters. "They're so…slimy. I can't see that. Both the reverend and Doug seem like people who would tell you to your face if they didn't approve of you. Very politely, of course. Why be sneaky if you believe in your own authority?"

"Because sneakiness works," Lorraine said immediately. "You think Beth would have stopped flying because someone told her to? But take the time to learn her vulnerabilities, her self-doubt…work on that for a while…and voilá. One grounded Flyer."

"And don't forget about Louis's house," I said. "That's why I think it's Mr. Howe. Reverend Paula wouldn't sneak into a house and write stuff like that."

"It's what she believes," Lorraine argued. "You heard that sermon: '*people putting their own souls at risk in full view of their neighbors*'. She just uses nicer language on Sundays. And look at this letter." She fished through the pile. "Right here: '*Sing in tune and join the choir*.' Tell me that doesn't sound like what she said last week about harmony and discord, and being different means you stir up hatred!"

"But Mr. Howe said there's too much freedom, he said it way last February. And he has a store full of lipstick."

"Reverend Paula has her own lipstick, Joss."

"Okay, okay," Dad said, seeing we were just getting started. "Drink out of both their cups! How hard can that be?"

Lorraine and I started explaining the "*knowingly* drinke" part together, word for word. "Jinx!" she called. It made us both giggle, and giggles never felt so good.

Next Sunday, we decided. We'd *all* go to church, and we'd make our decision together. And then we'd act.

"But," Dad said, "'we' means Beth too. So somebody has to tell her about the plan when she gets home tomorrow. And about the letters."

They looked at me. It was weird: this wasn't like Dad making me clean out Michael's room. All of a sudden we'd turned into this three-person team. Was it being fifteen? I liked it. And I accepted my mission.

Mom came home next day, but she was so sleep-deprived from hanging out with Michael that Dad said I should wait a day or two and let her get back to normal. He didn't have to tell me how touchy our conversation was going to be when Mom found out we all knew how she'd been tortured by those letters for so long. She hates being pitied more than anything. I think I get that, even though I've never had anyone pity me.

Wow. Guess I'm kind of lucky that way.

I spent my first school-free, fifteen-year-old Monday biking down to Seal Rocks with Louis. We lounged on the sunny boulders above the channel, watching the seals doing the same thing across the water, listening to the gurgle of the tide as it rushed between. Between handfuls of potato chips, I filled him in on the truth of Michael's crash, Mom's new pile of poison letters, and our family plan to go to church next Sunday and defeat our enemy. It sounded too nasty and dramatic to be part of our normal old Dalby life of kelp bulbs glistening in the water and seals grunting from the rocks. But Mom's secrets were toast now, so I felt released from my promises, and even better when I saw how Louis liked the idea that our enemy—whoever it was—was also his.

"Did he write the letters in lipstick?" he asked hopefully. Louis agreed with me that Mr. Howe was the one, not Tyler, now that Tyler had started calling him "Red" like Nate did.

He also had a cool theory. "Michael didn't get any letters, did he? Telling him he should try flying? I mean, that would be a real good way to get to your mom, right? Show her what a bad influence she was."

Wow, I should have thought of that. But I shook my head. "No, I had to clean every square inch of Michael's room. Found a lot of disgusting crap, but no letters. Unless he burned them?" *Hmm.* "Guess we'll have to wait and ask him. They're supposed to send him home day after tomorrow. He's doing really well. Man, though, it's gonna be weird seeing him in casts. And I'll have to do all his chores."

Louis poured the last of our potato chips into his mouth. "It's gonna suck for him," he said, not in that macho way that boys do, but like he really meant it. And here I was feeling all sorry for myself. Louis may be a whole year younger, but he's a better person than I am. I don't know why that keeps surprising me.

Next day after breakfast I got a good-luck hug from Lorraine and went over to Mom's on my Mission. I found her still in bed. But not depressed this time.

"Wiped, babe," she croaked as I stood in the doorway. "I am SO out of shape."

"What are you talking about? Did you go jogging or something?"

"Can't you smell it?" She flashed me a grin that finally looked real on her face. "Lorraine would."

I sniffed. Nothing. "Come close," Mom ordered, and—

Sweetness. Lilies. "Mom! You FLEW!" I dived onto the bed and hugged her through the quilt while she chuckled. "I can't believe you! When? Where'd you go? How'd it feel? It felt great, right? Why'n't you TELL me? Wanna go again now?"

"Hoooo, boy. I knew I should've kept my little adventure to myself! Oof, get off me." But she was still chuckling. "Since you ask, however: I," she paused dramatically, "flew to the hospital. And back."

"No WAY. You flew to the mainland? Over all the ferries and cars and everything?" In the middle of my shocked admiration, I felt a stab of envy: why hadn't I thought of this? Because Dad would've been furious with me, that's why. But he couldn't chew out the mother of his son for wanting to be with him. "You *go*, Mom."

"Yes, I do," she admitted, smiling. "But man, I'm weak. Thought I was going to have to ditch over Santos Island on the way home. Made it to Dalby and actually had to walk the last couple of miles."

"Did anybody See you?" I asked hesitantly. I knew it wasn't the point—I mean, my mom had finally gotten out from under the poison-pen fear after four months!—but still. The Stander was out there. The last thing Mom needed now was another letter. Maybe I shouldn't even bring up the letters now. I could tell her next week...

"No," she said, but her voice got hard. "But even if they did, you know what? Screw 'em. That's what I decided. Not gonna let those a--holes be in charge of me."

Wow. Not sure which was better, Mom fighting back or Mom cussing in front of me like we were the same age.

"Oh, but speaking of being Seen, I figured out something about that video of me," she added casually.

"What?!"

"Yeah, I watched it a few more times down in the waiting lounge when Michael was asleep. The hospital has a computer you can use, right? And I think I recognize the voice of the guy who's filming."

"You're kidding! Is it Mr. Howe?"

She smiled. "No, babe, Mr. Howe didn't live on Dalby back then, remember? But I think it was the old minister, the one

Reverend Paula's church had forever. Oh, what was his name? Fish-something? Fishberg? I never knew him personally. But he seemed pretty straight-laced. He saw me breast-feeding baby Michael one time at the Saturday Market and said something really snotty to me."

"Omigod, Mom, why didn't you tell us before?" I didn't stop to think how that "us" might annoy her. "If Reverend Fish-something showed his video to someone who was a Stander—"

"The good Reverend Fish-something's dead, Joss," Mom interrupted. "That's why Paula came. Back in the '90s, before her hair was gray. She was the cool new minister. I think a bunch of people left the church 'cause they thought she wouldn't be conservative enough, but the joke's on them. Paula's almost as old-fashioned as Reverend Fishy, what I hear."

"Yeah, that's why Lorraine thinks it's her," I said, to be fair. "But Mom. Mr. Howe goes to that church. He's, like, a real upstanding member. Maybe Reverend Fishy passed his video on to Mr. Howe? And since Mr. Howe's a Stander, he thinks it's evil, he just doesn't know who the "Dalby Ghost" is. So he sends it to the nearest TV station—yeah, didn't it air around the time the Howes moved to Dalby, when I was like, nine? He wants to see if anyone comes forward—"

"And identifies me?" Mom nodded thoughtfully. Wow, I could not believe we were having this nice, rational conversation after all these weeks.

"And then when they invent YouTube, he puts it on there, still fishing for you!"

Mom nodded again. "Nice deduction, Sherlock. I think you got something there. So when I moved back here and started working for him...ugh." She shuddered. "And when he Saw me on the roof..."

"That's when he figured it out." We looked at each other, imagining that moment of triumph for our enemy. Then she added, "We should tell Lorraine."

Wow, Mom. Way to open the door for me and my mission! So I told her everything: finding the rest of the poison letters. Declaring a family war on the Stander—either Mr. Howe or the reverend (except now it *had* to be Mr. Howe!). And the Big Church Plan for next Sunday which would decide once and for all and then send me to drinke knowingly from somebody's cuppe during coffee time. "Hope Mr. Howe puts lots of sugar in his, I hate coffee," I said, trying to sound confident.

Then I shut up and waited for her reaction. If she screamed at me again, I was out of there.

But the Flying Burgowski Mother sighed. "Ron read the letters, huh? And he didn't freak out? Man. Will miracles never cease." It was an awesome moment.

"He was pretty upset at first," I admitted, but Mom was already moving on.

"So. Church next Sunday? What're we gonna do, have a little huddle there on the pew to vote on whose cup we're attacking?"

"Umm…" I hadn't really thought this part through.

"You, me, Ron, Lorraine. What if there's a tie? They think it's one person, we think it's the other?" I loved how she assumed we'd be on the same side. "I think the Flyers' vote should count more, don't you? I mean, it is our power that's at stake."

"Yeah! Definitely." But in my mind I saw a horrible whispered standoff in the emptying church, while our target finished his coffee and got away. "Maybe we should run that by Lorraine, though."

And this is how cool Mom was: "Maybe we should."

There was only one way the day could have gone any better: me asking Mom for the hundredth time if she wanted to fly with me again, and her saying Yes. We even made a date for Saturday, after Michael got home and she didn't need to save all her energy to fly to the hospital.

YESSSSSSS!!!!

CHAPTER SEVENTEEN

GO AHEAD,
MAKE OUR DAY

G otta admit, I've had a little waver toward Lorraine's side. Something Savannah said about Reverend Paula's sermon last Sunday when we were off at the hospital.

She called to see how Michael was doing, which I thought was nice. I mean Savannah has her own health issues, right? And she's getting pretty close to the date where she HAS to make a decision. All I dared to ask was, "So...?"

A long sigh down the telephone line. "Reverend Paula said something that really made me think, Joss. Like, 'God sends us burdens for a reason, and it's our duty to bear them.'"

"You know she just means in general, right? Savannah, she's not talking to *you*."

"Well, but she kinda is," my best friend went on in her new, dreamy-mature way. "And she said something about the need to stay grounded in reality and not go flying away on possibilities which will only hurt us in the end. I think she meant, you know, don't rush into anything you'll regret later."

Like having sex at fifteen? I luckily didn't say aloud. Fine, Savannah was just going to hear what she wanted to hear at this point, so as long as it made her happy... "Wait, she said what? Stay grounded and...?"

"Not go flying off...something like that. It was some kind of metaphor. But I really felt it. Joss, I think," another long, dramatic sigh, "I think I'm going to have my baby."

I try to be a good friend, I really do. So I said all the right things about it being her decision and I'd be there for her no matter what.

But my brain was going, *Baby*??? *My bestie*???*!! A baby!*

But I don't know how "there for her" I'm going to be, because as soon as we hung up, my brain zipped right back to Reverend Paula. *She's got so much influence. She's the minister.* Reverend Fishguy might have died before he could share his video of my mom flying, but what if the next minister found it?

Lorraine hated my Flyers-get-two-votes idea. I found her at work and whispered my plan while she was reshelving. Being Lorraine, she didn't say "hate," but I know what "we need to keep an open mind about this" means. And when I brought it up at dinner, Dad hated it even more.

"But we're Flyers! We have gut instincts about these things!" I insisted.

"No offense, honey, but what's the track record of your gut instincts? Going to school in McClenton?"

"That was Michael's idea!"

"And your mom's instincts? No offense, but don't get me started."

I decided to take offense. It was a very grumpy evening.

Didn't help that Michael was gone. Now I know what a car's rear wheel feels like when the other one falls off: all the pressure's suddenly on you but you can't seem to keep on rolling straight. I don't know how Tyler Howe stands it; I hate being the only child.

So that night I went flying by myself, way down to the south end of the island where I hardly ever go. It was super late, but I didn't bother to leave a note; they could just trust my instincts, dammit. I plunged into a stiff breeze, swooping through its layers, and watched the nearly-full moon rise, big and yellow. I opened the collar of my fleece to let the sweet air rush through me, and I hovered upside-down for a while, alone in the dark, gazing up at the crystal sprinkling of stars. But my mind was in the church, its pews, its little coffee area. And I got an idea. Simple but bold. The Flying Burgowski Mother would approve!

I spent the whole flight home planning where she and I would fly on Saturday.

Mom did approve, when I called her next morning before work. "Like your style, babe," she said sleepily. "I used to get my best ideas on night flights too." I glowed. Then she added, "But good luck selling that one to your dad."

She called it. I told Dad on the way to the ferry, going to visit Michael.

"That's the craziest idea I've ever heard. Did your mom come up with that?"

So much for starry inspiration. I explained with dignity that it was my idea, and furthermore I thought Lorraine would agree with me.

"Well, we'll just talk about it at dinner then. We need to focus on your brother right now. Is his room clean?" he asked me for like the third time.

I HATE hospital rooms—they remind me of last fall, with Mom. I got the shivers, crowding in next to those horrible monitors, my big brother looking so small in that steely, starchy bed. This was the first time I'd seen him since the accident almost a week ago, and awake Michael looked even worse than unconscious Michael. And he was a lot more bummed.

"Dude, you gotta get me outta here," he croaked. "The food sucks."

"Two more days, son. Just hang in there. Fourth of July's right around the corner. We'll get you a wheelchair, you can watch the fireworks just like normal."

"Normal, hah." It was that kind of visit. All the things I wanted to say—*Michael, give it up, you're never going to fly, just don't stay all crumpled and bitter, I need you to come back and be my snotty, sarcastic brother, my other wheel, I'll take you flying any time you want*—just dried up in my mouth. I don't think I said anything besides, "Zach says hi," which he probably would have if I'd seen him. We stayed for an hour and a half, till the ferry schedule and Dad's store called us home. Our conversation remained focused on how we could help Michael adjust to a summer of recovery, and Dad asked me for the fourth time if his room was clean.

"Jocelyn, I didn't think I'd still need to say this at your age, but No means No," Dad said at dinner.

"I don't even know why I told you," I muttered. My spaghetti was getting cold, which tells you how furious I was. "I should've just done it. Then you'd see."

"What we'd see if you actually swooped through the church office? Pandemonium. The secret's out. That's it. Done. Call the news trucks. Call Oprah. Call—"

"Not to mention," Lorraine put in quietly, "how easily your plan could backfire. No matter who the Stander is, they'll be ready. You'd be handing them their perfect opportunity." And I'd thought she'd agree with me.

"I wouldn't stay up in the air long enough for them to pray! Just long enough for us to see their reaction, then Mom could grab the cup of whoever's looking less shocked—"

"Our-Father-who-art-in-Heaven-hallowed-be-thy-name! Thy-Kingdom-come-thy-will-be-done-on-earth-as-it-is-in-Heaven!" Dad rumbled, all in one breath. "See how fast? They'd pray your little butt right out of the air before you knew what hit you."

I didn't know he knew any prayers, but I was too mad to think about it. This was *my* power they were talking about! My future as a Flyer! Well, mine and Mom's. It wasn't even any of their business. I said so.

Dad didn't exactly send me to my room, but dinner became so unpleasant that I went there anyway. See what I mean about being an only child? Michael would have backed me up, I know. Someone put my spaghetti in the fridge and I ate it later, cold, when the two front wheels had gone to bed.

By Thursday evening Dad refused to talk about our church mission anymore. We were going to sit, listen to the sermon, and make up our minds then. Period.

I went into a cold simmer, and this is the thought that bubbled through me all night: *I don't have to ask their permission. I'll fly, and they'll see.* I woke up Friday morning planning to warn Mom to be ready to "drinke knowingly."

When I visited her at work to share the plan, Mom was excited, and finally not in the fake-chirpy way. And when Mr. Howe walked past and said Hi, we both got the giggles like bad kids in class. Mom whispered to me that she'd deliberately asked Mr. Howe if he'd seen this kitten video on YouTube, kind of testing him out, and he'd asked what YouTube was. "Of course he'd say that, right?" Oh, it felt good, plotting together right under his nose. But she wasn't so hot on me flying in church if Lorraine and Dad didn't want me to, which surprised me. "I kind of like this team effort thing, babe," she whispered. "But I'll be there for you if you need me, don't worry."

I'm pretty sure that's the first time Mom's ever said that, and absolutely sure it's the first time I've believed her. When Mr. Howe came by again smiling, saying, "What kind of mischief are you ladies getting into?" Mom said innocently, "Girl stuff, Mr. H," and wow, it hit me like a little shock of joy. I walked home all

jazzed up, ready to be sweet as pie to Lorraine and let her think
I'd given up the whole swooping-in-church plan.

Turns out I didn't have to bother. There was Dad's truck
in the driveway, and there, being gently unfolded into a shiny
wheelchair, was Michael, casts and all. I rushed to help set up the
temporary ramp. I fluffed my brother's pillows and brought him
lemonade to soothe his creaky throat. And I stopped thinking
about Sunday and Standers for a change. If Michael got himself
nearly killed trying to be like me, the least I could do was spoil
him a little.

Word spread fast that Michael was home, and all his bud-
dies started calling, but Dad put them off, since the doctor had
warned about avoiding an infection in the lung. Plus, even after
they take that tube out of your throat, I guess you don't feel real
social. Michael did let Savannah stick her head in to say hi, and
being Savannah she waltzed right up and drew her horsehead
logo on both of his casts.

"You have to be Gatekeeper, okay, Joss?" Dad finally said, looking at his watch. "I have to reopen."

"Why don't you just hire someone to come in like you used
to, instead of closing the store all the time?"

"Can't afford it," he said briefly. "So you just hang out, okay?
Keep your brother happy. Call me if you need anything."

Happy, right. I tried my best with more lemonade and some
videos Lorraine had brought home, but Michael kept sliding back into a glum heap. Nicholas Cage sucked. Broken ribs
sucked. This summer *sucked*. You get the idea.

So when Zach Howe knocked on the kitchen door, I should
have been a good little Gatekeeper and sent him on his way like
the rest of Michael's friends. But I was running out of ideas for
spoiling my brother all by myself.

"Just, like, wash your hands and face, okay?" I inspected him:

jeans, Nike T-shirt, flip-flops. "You look good to me. I mean clean." Zach made an ironic bow, and I blushed, dammit. "Go on in."

I surfed around on the computer while Zach visited, but he didn't stay very long.

"That is one seriously banged-up guy," he said, shaking his head as he closed Michael's door behind him. "Is it time for his meds yet? Seemed like he's in pain."

"Oh, the meds don't help with that, that's just Michael," I said. "I mean he's depressed."

"Hm, depressed brother? Right there with ya," Zach said, and fist-bumped me.

Wow. It took my mouth a second to form words. "De... pressed? I thought you said Rory was just, you know."

"Oh, heck yeah, but it all started with depression when he was, like, your age. But he refused to see a shrink anymore, and that's when all the weirdness started." Zach perched on the arm of our couch. He was actually hanging out with me! Maybe I could ask him about...what, exactly? My thoughts would not hold still.

"Speaking of weirdness," Zach went on, "last time we talked, seemed like you were about to tell me something. You remember?" He raised his eyes to mine and there it was again, that light-beam tossed over for me to grab onto. "Wanna talk about it?"

I blanked for a second and then it came back to me. Oh yeah...last time I went to church with Savannah. Nearly two weeks ago, but it felt like two years. My standoff with Lorraine, when she wanted me to drink from the reverend's cup. Zach's face, remembering his vision of Rory. *I was about to tell him about Mom,* I remembered with awe, *and Lorraine stopped me.*

I still could. He's the only one who would get what it means to watch someone so close fall apart. I have my own visions of Mom, but they're real. And I've never talked about them with anybody, not even Michael, and I'll bet he has the same nightmare about that night in McClenton. Her sleeping-doll's face under the streetlight. But I don't even like writing that down, let alone talking about it.

"She's much better now," I said.

"Who is?" Zach's voice was gentle, almost like Lorraine's.

"Oh…the person I was gonna tell you about. That I'm close to, that I was worried about. I'm…I guess I'm not real worried anymore. 'Cause she's doing so much better." *Why not tell him? He'd believe you.* My iron string was vibrating like crazy: *Hummmmmmmmmm!!!* But I'm a chicken, okay? *"So, yeah, my mom and I can fly."* I couldn't stand it if that serious, open face scrunched into laughter right now.

"This person," Zach said, and his face stayed open, "you said we both know her, right?"

I nodded.

"And you were worried about her, but now you're not?"

I nodded again.

"So it's not like with my brother, you don't see her going down the wrong path, nothing you can do…not like that anymore?" The eye-ropes pulled me in.

"No, it's pretty awesome now, Zach!" I've never said his name before; it kind of freed me up. "Things have gotten so much better. It's like, ever since Michael got hurt, she and I have come together, you know? And the thing that I was worried about, she kind of got past that, I think. We…we're gonna get together today and, like…" *Fly! FLY!* "…celebrate."

Zach smiled his beautiful, golden smile. "That is awesome, kid. Sounds like you should give yourself some credit, though. I mean you probably helped your mom a lot—oops! I mean 'this person.'" Did he just wink? I didn't care. He wasn't making fun of me.

"Yes!" I scooted a little closer on the couch. "I know I did. 'Cause I didn't give up on her, and I kept bugging her, and I guess she kinda, I don't know, used me as her inspiration, sort of, to get better." This sounded awfully pompous, and I wasn't even sure it was true. But Zach understood.

"Well, right on. She's lucky to have you. Everyone needs an inspiration, like I had Mr. Plonsky, my wrestling coach. That's what I'm trying to be for Rory. He's got to know I won't give up on him, even if he doesn't like being bugged. That's the real reason why I need to get on back to Seattle and man up, instead of hiding out here. So, thanks for the reminder."

"You're welcome," I said automatically. My brain did that splitting thing again. One side: *Wait. My mom flies; your brother's just gay. Why's that a problem again?* The other side: *Wait. You really have to go?* I don't know which question would have made it out first if the timer on the stove hadn't gone off. "Oh shoot, that's for Michael's meds, so I wouldn't forget." *Oh, but if I get off the couch, this moment is over. And you're going back to Seattle.*

"Yeah, dope that poor guy up." Zach slapped his thighs and stood up, so I did too. The moment was over. "And keep on being an inspiration, okay? He's lucky to have you too."

Or was it? I zipped into the kitchen to turn off the timer and get Michael more lemonade to go with his pills. With my back to Zach's brightness I found the nerve to say, "Hey. When you're, like, in college, you can email me and tell me how it's going with your brother, okay?"

"Absolutely." He stood in the doorway, and there was an awkward moment till he realized he needed to move so I could go to Michael. We did that little dance of who goes which direction, then we both laughed, and I thought, *Wow. It's really happening. First Nate, and now Zach.*

"But I'm not leaving till after the Fourth, I'll see you before then," Zach said. "Gonna come hear me play?"

"Course I am!" Behind the door, I heard Michael's hoarse grumbling. "But, hey. I'm coming to church on Sunday, so I'll see you there, right?"

Zach's face switched to high beam. "Oh, right on! Savannah's got you hooked, huh? Or is it Reverend Paula? Man, you shoulda heard her last week. Now there's someone I wish I could get Rory to hear!"

"What do you mean?" I stopped with my hand on Michael's door. Sooner or later this conversation would have to end, but I wanted it to be later.

"Oh, just that whole staying grounded thing. Sticking with your fellow man, not thinking you're God's gift just because you're different." He shook his head. "That's my bro."

"So do you think Reverend Paula means—" A loud jangling cut me off. Michael was using the call-bell Dad had put on his night-table. "Oh shoot—I gotta go."

Zach gave me a little salute as I turned, fingers on his forehead. For the feeling it gave me, he might as well have put them on his lips.

Just five more hours to kill and I could fly with Mom. I made 'em pass by writing in here, then surfing the net. Michael fell asleep after his pills, no point in reading to him, and I was too hyped up to read to myself. Time CRAWLED. I ate the last of the spaghetti, thinking about email conversations I could have with Zach, when his face wasn't blinding me. I wondered how I was going to change Dad's old-fashioned mindset against underage girls on email. Facebook? Forget it. Maybe he'd believe me if I said I wanted to tour UW. Maybe I could talk Michael into asking, and then tag along, and get "lost" on campus, and find Zach's dorm…

The timer went off again, but I didn't want to wake Michael to give him pills. Then it hit me: how can I go flying with Mom when I'm supposed to be taking care of my brother?

I am such an idiot. How did I not think of that before? I tried cursing like Michael, but it didn't solve the problem. I would have to call Mom and postpone.

I reached for the phone and it rang, making me jump.

"Hey, babe."

"Mom! I was just gonna call you. You know our date?"

"Yeah, about that." Her voice creaked, but not with that horrible depression: this was anger. "Gonna need to postpone, I think. Don't worry, I'm not putting you off. I just…got a little problem here."

Now understand, I never saw all the duct tape. I had to stay with Michael, right? So I sat in the kitchen trying to absorb Mom's descriptions through the phone, into a brain that was already whirling with fantasy, disappointment, and now some serious self-doubt.

"*Duct* tape?"

"Everywhere. My whole living room, Jocelyn. They must have used, like, ten rolls."

"Used? How?"

She laughed bitterly. "What's duct tape for, babe? Grounding. Everything I own, furniture, TV, even my books for Chrissake, everything's taped down. Surprised they didn't tape the cat."

"Is Tion okay?" I imagined Mom's colorful living room, all her old-school movie posters on the walls. That old quilt. "Duct tape?" I repeated, stupidly. "The silver kind?"

"She's fine. Yes, the silver kind. *Duct* tape. I don't know how I'm gonna get it off my books without ripping them." Her voice seethed like a shaken-up bottle.

"Is there…Did they leave you a message?" I pictured Shasta's bedroom, all that horrible lipstick.

"Oh, they left a message all right. The duct tape IS the message. Stay grounded, right? But in case I'm too dumb to get that, yeah. There's another letter."

"Oh, Mom!" I felt stricken—that's the first time I've ever understood that word. "I can't come over, I have to be with Michael. Well, he's asleep right now, maybe I could—"

"No," she said sternly. "You stay there. I can deal with this. It's just gonna take me a while, that's all, and I knew you were looking forward to our date. So was I."

"We're just…postponing, right? Not cancelling?" I knew this wasn't the point right now, whether we flew or not. But it kind of was. Mr. Howe sure wanted us to cancel.

"That's for damn sure. They're not stopping me now." I pictured my bottled-up mom exploding all over that bland, silvery material Mr. Howe had tried to smother her bright little room with, her bright little self. Ripping that tape to shreds, swearing at the top of her lungs. Oh, I was proud of her.

"I wish I could be there to help you get it off! But Mom: what does he say in the letter?"

"He? Oh, Mr. Howe? Yeah, about that. It wasn't him."

I looked at the phone receiver like it was the one talking crazy. "What?"

"He's been in the store with me all morning, babe. He's there right now. It. Wasn't. Him."

"Oh," I breathed. *Damn. Reverend Paula after all?* "So Lorraine was right."

"Yeah, maybe."

"Whaddya mean, maybe? Who else is there? Plus—grounded, you said? That's exactly what Reverend Paula said in her sermon last week, Savannah told me, and so did Zach. They heard it. Grounded. Duct tape." I still couldn't wrap my brain around that prim lady breaking into my mom's house. Well, just walking in— it wasn't locked. But how twisted was that? *As twisted as the ministers in those old books lighting the pyre when they burned the witches,* my brain reminded me. *You just don't want Lorraine to be right.*

"Who else? I can think of someone, babe." But her voice sounded uneasy.

"Who, Tyler? Yeah, I thought so too, so did Louis. But Savannah alibi'd him when the thing with the lipstick happened. So it wouldn't make sense for him to do the duct tape. He hates gays, not Flyers." But something cold flickered in my stomach, and I started shaking my head even before Mom said,

"Not Tyler. Right family, wrong kid."

"Nuh-uh. No way, Mom."

The phone was silent for a moment, and I heard Tion meow plaintively. Then Mom sighed. "Look, I know you like him, babe." *You do?* "I like him too. Seems like a great guy. But think about it, okay? He's pretty straight-laced for a kid his age, isn't he? And he goes to Paula's church too."

"So does Savannah! So do tons of nice people!" I spluttered. "Mom, are you kidding me? Zach's, like, the most understanding person in the world! He's totally against, like, confronting people he doesn't agree with, that's why he came to live on Dalby! Like that thing with his brother? He loves Rory! Zach's not like his uncle at all!"

"Well, I don't know anything about his brother," Mom said. "Maybe you know Zach better than I thought." *That's right, I do.* "I'm just saying…whoever did this must've done it between eight-thirty and two-thirty, when I was at work. And Zach was not at work."

"And neither was Reverend Paula!" I said fiercely. "Whyn't you check on *her* movements? And anyway, Zach was at our house this morning, visiting Michael."

"Oh, yeah?" She sounded interested.

"Yeah. And we talked about…inspiring people."

"From eight-thirty till two-thirty?"

Now she was pissing me off. "No, course not. I'm just saying, Mom—he's not that kind of guy. You're being ridiculous." *Zach's on our side.* "Look, I'll prove it was Reverend Paula. Read me that letter."

She sighed again. "That is something I do not want to do. But fine, you're probably right. Paula makes more sense."

"Really, read it! I'll prove it to you!"

"No." Now she was angry again. "I'm not reading that filth any more. I'm going with you to church tomorrow and we're gonna end this s--- now."

Wow, it was cool to hear Mom talking like a movie hero. And cool to think I wouldn't have to fly in front of a whole roomful of people tomorrow. Our mission suddenly seemed so easy it was a little scary.

"Yeah, about tomorrow…you wanna meet me there? Where should we sit?"

"I don't know, Joss—right now I got this mess to deal with. We'll figure it out tomorrow."

And we would have, I know it. We were such a team! Even if she did have that silly idea about Zach—honestly, how much less Stander-y could you get? A guy trying so hard not to judge the one he loves, he moves away to an island! And those eyes, I know it sounds cheesy, but they're so full of caring. Not like Mr. Howe's hard, sharp ones. Or Reverend Paula: now that I think about it, her eyes are piercing like Mr. Howe's, not soft like Zach's. Kind of predatory.

So how come my gut instinct, my iron string, never warned me about Reverend Paula? Well, look at her. Those crazy, bouncy, curls. That drone-y voice. Harmless, right? Till you look at her eyes.

She Saw Mom on Howe's roof. And who knows where else. And she Saw me flying over her car.

So why did I just get a Cupid and a card, instead of poison letters? Easy: she thought the Flyer she saw was Mom, and she left that stuff to show the Flyer's family she knew their secret. Else she would have left Mom a Cupid too, right? Plus—she wears lipstick.

Oh, we were gonna nail her, Mom and I. We had the edge. Then the phone rang again.

"Hello?"

"Yes, good afternoon! This is Reverend Paula. Am I speaking to...Jocelyn?"

That nasal voice, like she was holding the receiver to her nose instead of her mouth. I froze. *Had she heard my thoughts? Felt a disturbance in the Force?* What did I know of the powers of Standers?

"Hello...?"

"Yes, hi, sorry," I muttered. "Dropped the phone. This is me. Jocelyn, I mean."

"Oh, wonderful! The very person I was hoping to reach. How is your brother doing?"

"He's fine," I said automatically. *How did she know...? Oh, shoot, everyone knows about Michael.* "He's asleep," I added, not like it was any of her business.

"Well, when he wakes up, you tell him we're all praying for him, okay?" *Yeah, I'll sure do that.* "Poor ol' guy. But listen, I have another reason for calling."

I shivered. What if she asked me directly about Mom? Tried to recruit me to ground her permanently? I had been ready to march right up to Mr. Howe and confront him, all those weeks ago. But Reverend Paula unnerved me. *That's the idea, dork. She's your enemy.*

My enemy must have assumed I was waiting respectfully, so she went on: "You know the Citizenship essay contest? What it Means to Be a Citizen? You're probably not aware of this, Jocelyn, but I'm one of the judges on the panel, so I got to read all the essays and help choose the ones that best address the question. And I have the honor of informing you..." she paused dramatically, "that your essay has won second place!"

Whoa. Major emotional mashup. I wanted to throw my arms around her for giving me the news. But...*eww*. She *read my essay? My innermost thoughts?* What if she could tell, just from reading...?

Revered Paula was still blabbing in my ear. "Now normally we only invite the first place winner to read his essay at the Citizenship Festival. But this year, the votes were so close, the panel decided we had to hear the runner-up's speech as well." Her voice went up another notch of cheerful. "And that's you!"

That was me. Through my swirling fog of feelings, I heard Reverend Paula explaining about a speakers' stage and our place in the program and sending me a schedule via email. I glommed onto that last word.

"Um, I don't have email. But you could send it to my dad. Or," I took a deep breath and stepped up to meet my Antagonist, "You could just give me the schedule at church tomorrow. I'm coming again."

Not sure what I expected—maybe a hiss of breath, like, *She knows I know. It's on.*

How idiotic am I? Reverend Paula laughed. "Oh, dear, bad timing. For me, I mean. Tomorrow's my off Sunday. I swap ministries with Reverend Styles on the mainland once a month, you know. Just to mix it up, keep our congregations on their toes. But I'll be there for the Fourth. I get to introduce you!" Then she asked for Dad's email and I mumbled it to her, and I think she told me to practice reading my essay in front of a mirror or something, and give her best to my family, and then we were done.

So I get to read "Live and Let Live" in front of the whole island. *Wow. Jeez. Yikes.*

No point going to church tomorrow. Citizenship Festival instead. Tuesday. Three more days.

But no way will they serve coffee at the Citizenship thing. Bottled water, though! They'd have that. I could pick it up when she's not looking… That would count as drinking from a cuppe, right?

Do we still have the edge, Mom and I? Reverend Paula couldn't really know about me. *Couldn't she?* The timing of that phone call was just coincidence.

In the tangle of all these thoughts, you'd think there'd have been room for this one: *Who won first place, anyway?*

I wanted to bust into the store and tell Dad all the crazy news: the Stander attack on Mom, our "epiphany" that the Stander had to be Reverend Paula. My prize-winning essay and my new idea of going after the Stander's water bottle at the Citizenship Festival. But the store stayed crowded—July is crazy on Dalby. So as soon as Lorraine got off work, I gave her the whole, breathless update. And I kind of apologized for not believing her before. She was nice about it, of course. Lorraine is nice about everything. Guess I'm going to have to live with that.

With Lorraine Michael-sitting, I rushed over to Mom's. The sun was high and bright, perfect flying weather, and the village was packed with tourists. Somebody's Labrador tried to tangle me up in its leash, and I nearly got run over by a guy taking a video of the Saturday Market out the window of his minivan. The whole busy scene made Mom's living room all the more shocking.

The walls were bare. She was sitting cross-legged in a sea of piles—her posters, her bird-clock, her string of paper Chinese lanterns—trying to pull the duct tape off without damaging anything. "Son of a bitch," she murmured as the Wicked Witch tore away from her "Wizard of Oz" poster.

"Here, Mom, lemme help," I said, shaking off my shock. I plopped myself down to hold the corner of the poster, and a giant ball of used duct tape tried to stick itself to my shorts. They were everywhere, those balls, like some kind of weird, rubbery-metallic alien. "Maybe use a soapy washcloth?"

"Tried that," Mom grunted, pushing her hair out of her eyes. It looked like she had been crying, which was a relief. I mean, I'd cry, if someone messed up all my stuff. It's the normal reaction. And normal is good, right?

Only if by "normal," you mean "healthy," we decided. Oh, what a great conversation we had sitting in her still-healthy kitchen! "My stuff is for s---," Mom declared after a frustrating twenty minutes, and we turned our backs on her ruined living room and ate mint chocolate-chip ice cream and plotted our revenge.

"Our normal is just to be ourselves," Mom said, sucking on her spoon. "That's all any healthy person wants. We're not hurting anybody. But the Standers' 'normal' means we have to be like them. Who died and made them king? They're not even faithful to real Christianity! Who said they could hurt us just to satisfy their rules?"

I love hearing my mom talk about healthy people. Plus she totally sounded like my essay, right? Live and Let Live is what the Flying Burgowskis stand for! Or fly for. So I told her about my essay, and she gave me a real, live hug. And more ice cream. And we planned our attack for the Fourth of July.

"So I'll hide under the stage, behind the bunting or whatever," Mom said as we turned to the nasty chore of stuffing all the giant alien tape-balls and wrecked posters into garbage bags. "If you don't get the chance to drink from her bottle yourself, you toss it down and I'll drink, then sneak it back up to you."

There was still duct tape across the front of the bookcase, but Mom said she couldn't deal with it now, so we draped her quilt over the whole thing. Nice to see it covering something besides a depressed mom for a change. "We need to be sure of the setup," she went on. "They're starting to put up the stage tomorrow, I hear. And your Mrs. Mac is one of the organizers, right? Why don't you go volunteer or something? Get the lay of the land."

"Yeah! I'll get Savannah to help me. And if there's no, like, flags or anything hanging down the back of the stage…"

"Then you suggest that, absolutely. Create some cover for your mom. Standers must love flags, right?" It was strange, but we'd both quit using Reverend Paula's name. The whole scene was beyond personal now, it was, I don't know…symbolic. Like we were getting ready to act out the parts of some ancient ritual. Which I guess we were. But with a cool modern twist—like when my mom narrowed her eyes and said, "Go ahead, Stander. Make our day."

I laughed, but the steely look in Mom's eyes made my stomach harden. This wasn't "research" any more. Dad was right. It was war.

CHAPTER EIGHTEEN

REALLY HAPPENING

It's for sure: Savannah's going to have her baby. BABY. She ran down the church steps next morning to meet me after the service, and we held hands and hugged like idiots. Savannah was wearing this wispy, pale-pink top over a soft lavender skirt, and I have to say, she looked beautiful. As we walked over to the community green she told me how Reverend Paula had talked with her parents till they agreed to support her; how her mom would help with daycare during school; how much baby stuff they had at the thrift shop; how Mr. Evans's stepdaughter would be her midwife.

I felt really young.

Just before we got to the Festival stage area, she said, "You'll be an auntie, Joss!"

Here's what Auntie Joss did not say: "Um. What if it's not as easy as you think it is? You're *fifteen!*" But I was about to ask about Tyler when Mrs. Mac stepped out from behind a stack of cardboard boxes to give us a hug.

Have I mentioned yet what a big deal Fourth of July is here? The Citizenship Festival is way more than speeches on a stage. There's a 10k race in the morning, a little kids parade with dressed-up dogs and bikes, a craft fair, face painting, all that stuff, and after the speeches there's a salmon barbeque and music that goes on all afternoon and evening, leading up to our monster fireworks display. Can't believe I missed it last year in stupid McClenton. People wait in ferry lines all day to get here, and you can practically walk across the boats crowding the harbor. It takes people like Mrs. Mac months and months to organize.

Mrs. Mac was happy to see us. Her hair's all grown back now, but she was still wearing a big straw hat with silk roses on it. "Who knew what a great fashion coach cancer is?" she told us when we complimented her. The stage builders weren't exactly ready for my advice about hanging flags; they were still laying out two-by-fours and looking at plans. But I was happy to see that the piles of boxes were full of water bottles. *Which one would Reverend Paula reach for on Wednesday? What if she sees us? What if bottles don't work?* Mrs. Mac brought me back to the moment. "Far be it from me to waste human resources," she said, and put Savannah and me to work folding programs.

"So you went to church even though Reverend Paula's not there?" I asked Savannah as we set up our little folding operation in the sunny grass.

"How'd you know that?" So I told her about my essay-conversation with the reverend, and she gave me another hug. Savannah's real affectionate these days. "Omigod, so your name must be in the program! Look, there it is!"

"Jocelyn Olivia Burgowski: Live and Let Live." My stomach clenched. I know I said I don't mind public speaking, but this was *seriously* public! Giving a speech suddenly felt a lot more like a sentence than a reward. What had I been so glad about yesterday? And look—my speech was first on the program, like a warm-up act for...

Oh, you have got to be kidding. First place: "Douglas Howe: All Pull Together in the Same Boat."

"Yeah, can't have anybody paddling off on their own," I muttered to myself. Mr. Howe–really? Dang, he was such a perfect

Stander. Maybe he and the reverend were in league? Would we have to drink out of both their cuppes? *I mean bottles.*

"What?" Savannah said. And then, "Oh, look, there's Zach's name! Did you know his band was called Standup?"

"Huh." *Hope Mom doesn't see that, she'll think it's a stupid sign.* "Like, stand up for your rights, I guess. Or stand-up comedy? Are they funny?" What was funny was what my heart started doing when it heard "Zach": a kind of bouncy jig in my chest.

"Oh, yeah, after church Zach was asking where you were."

My heart really did skip a beat then. Always thought that was just an expression. "That's nice," I said, folding programs.

Savannah stopped folding. "Get out, Joss. He. Is. *Awe*some, and you know it. So understanding! I told him about my…decision, and he—"

"You told Zach about your baby? How'd that come up in conversation?" *You told him before me?* "'Yeah, speaking of great sermons, did you know I was pregnant?'"

"Miss Mozart" did her piano-scale laugh. "Oh, you know how he is, Joss! Those eyes, right?" *Right.* "So we were talking about life paths, and all of a sudden I was just telling him, and he just kept nodding and saying stuff like how brave I was to take responsibility for my…you know, actions."

"Is that how Tyler reacted?" I demanded. Not sure why I felt kind of aggressive all of a sudden.

Savannah started folding again. "I haven't told Tyler yet," she said. "We have a date this afternoon, I'll tell him then."

"Jeez, Savannah! You don't tell the father of your baby, but you tell his cousin? That's messed up." It was harsh, I know. But, jeez. Why would she do that, unless she wanted Zach to pay attention to her? And when people—boys—pay attention to Savannah… Let's just say the only reason she hadn't swept up Nate as her boyfriend was because he wasn't as cool as he was hot. But Zach is both. And, I have to admit, so is Savannah.

Maybe it was a good thing Zach was leaving soon. But unlike me, Savannah did email and Facebook, and she had her own
phone. Maybe Zach had already given her his number, murmur-
ing, "Y'know, you can call me anytime, if you need someone to
talk to…" *Maybe he would even invite her to go for a walk somewhere!
I mean, she's so pretty, and she's obviously into sex, and maybe Tyler was
just, like, a kind of stepping-stone…!*

"Hello, Earth to Joss," Savannah snapped. "I *said*, Bite me. How
can we have a fight if you aren't even listening?"

I laughed, still feeling kind of jittery, and I let Savannah tell me
how Zach said she was redeeming herself, how his own mom
had him when she was sixteen, and how he would pray for her
to have strength in the weeks ahead. And my stabs of jealousy
turned into stabs of guilt for thinking Zach could be so nasty.
I'm as bad as Mom, looking for dark motives everywhere. Zach's
a better person than both of us.

"He did say something funny about his brother, though," Savannah continued, as our pile of folded programs grew. "Did you
know he has a gay brother? I'm like, 'Yeah, I hope I'm not a bad
role model for my baby,' and Zach goes, 'Well, you can't do worse
than me, with my homo-bro.'"

"'Homo-bro?' What's that supposed to mean?"

"Queer, fag. Bumboy. He called his brother all that too. Rory,
his name is."

A new stab this time: doubt. It felt more cold than painful.
This is what Michael had said about Zach, but Michael I did not
believe. Savannah, though—she had no reason to lie about this.

"Wasn't he just talking about what other people call Rory?"

Savannah shrugged. "Maybe. I mean he is Ty's cousin, right?
And I love Ty to death, but he does have this thing about gays."
She laughed again. "It's on my list of stuff to talk about with him,
but kinda far down, y'know? Hey, hand me that next pile."

Tyler's cousin, right. Zach must have been describing Rory

from Tyler's point of view, or people like Tyler who would make Rory suffer if he didn't tone down his lifestyle. I could understand that. He loved his bro, wanted to protect him so he could be himself but still find a way to survive in this mean world. Just like my mom. Sometimes you have to work a little harder to live and let live. Like stopping the people who are trying to stop you.

So by the time we were done with the programs, I was totally re-psyched for my speech and our battle plan. And when I told Mrs. Mac we should hang flags all the way around the stage platform, she loved my idea and sent me to Howe's to buy some more.

"When they're open," she added. "Doug's pretty old-fashioned, he never opens before noon on Sundays."

"Okay, I'll go later," I said. "I gotta get a new ink cartridge anyway, so I can print a clean copy of my essay."

This earned me another Mac-hug. "Yes, well done! I'm so proud of you!" Maybe cancer is like pregnancy: Mrs. Mac never used to be that mushy before. "Make an extra copy for me, will you? No, wait—make me a copy of your original. I want to read Norm's comments." *Norm?* Oh, Mr. Evans.

"Mr. Evans helped me a lot," I said. *And Zach. That's how I know he believes in my message.* "His comments were kinda harsh at first, but at the end he said my essay has legs."

"Well, read it proudly," my old teacher said. "We'll all be right there beside you."

Yeah, and underneath me, crouched behind a hanging flag. Ready to snag Reverend Paula's water bottle. *Oh, they better count as cuppes. They have to.*

I brought Savannah home with me for lunch, and found Lorraine and Mom in the kitchen quickly changing the subject when they saw I had a guest. One of these days, I really will tell Savannah…maybe. The longer I wait, the harder it's going to be.

When I become an auntie, I'll kind of owe it to her, won't I? If only I thought she could keep her mouth shut.

"Why not?" Michael called from his room, and Mom zipped in there to warn him. Savannah stayed for mac and cheese, but then excused herself to go home and take a nap. I saw Mom and Lorraine exchange glances, and wondered if they'd guessed Savannah's secret. Her boobs are bigger these days. But no one said anything. They must have known I was sworn to secrecy, and I felt a rush of gratitude to my "moms" for not pushing me.

Michael, it turns out, had been filled in on the entire plan by Mom: who we were after, and why, and how. And he wanted to be there.

"Are you kidding?" he said when Savannah was gone and I went to get his plate. His voice sounded almost normal now. "Drink out of her water bottle? I wanna kick her ass! Mom was gonna give me some of those posters."

I laughed. "That's why you want revenge on the Stander? For wrecking some posters?"

Michael's face settled. Mom, of all people, had given him a haircut, and he looked older and, I don't know, harder. Maybe it was the bruises. "Look," he said quietly. "I know now, all right? I got it. Lorraine told me all about…your research. The stuff you learned about Standers and all. I'm not surprised they exist. It's just cool we have a way to fight back."

We? "Michael—" I began hopelessly. Oh, I did not want to have this conversation. Talk about grounding. But he had to know…

"I *know*, Joss," he interrupted, fiddling with his blanket. "I told you, I got it. I'm never gonna fly. I'm a guy. Lorraine told me in all the millions of pages she read—no flying dudes. Or almost none."

"Yeah," I said hastily, "and that one boy they caught…"

"Yeah." Michael frowned. "Lorraine said. They ripped him

apart. And he was one in a million. And I'm not." More blanket-patting. "Thought it was gonna kill me if I couldn't fly. But I can't, and I guess that's just the way it is." Then he looked right at me. "But I KNOW it's gonna kill me if you and Mom can't. So. I'm in this too."

I nodded. "You are." I felt like saying a lot more, but I was choking up, and Michael gets bugged when I cry.

"So...hey, Savannah's gone, right?" I nodded again. "Mom! Lorraine!" They both appeared in the doorway looking anxious. "Here's what's up: after Joss's speech and all, when everyone's, like, mingling, I'll distract Reverend Paula, okay? Ministers can't resist a cripple."

Lorraine said, "Do you really think you should be out already...?" but Mom cut her off.

"That's my guy," she said. I felt the same way.

My heart started doing its little dance again as I stepped onto the deck of Howe's. It knew perfectly well that if Mom was in my kitchen, Zach must be at work.

Didn't see him, though. Or Mr. Howe. Aaron Robbins's mom waved at me from the cash register. I pushed past a group of tourists examining Dalby T-shirts and mugs with eagles and or-cas. So what if people wanted to buy cheap, cheesy stuff instead of handmade? They'd already paid all that ferry money just to get here, right? And didn't people in mug factories have to earn a living too? I remembered that beef between Mr. Howe and Mr. Evans back at school, and thought, *Live and Let Live*. Mr. Howe's only trying to give people choices, like he said.

The flag section was easy to find, but they only had two big ones left. Mrs. Mac had told me to buy five, and I was wondering if we could maybe attach a bunch of small ones together to hang down, when someone behind me started humming, "Three Cheers for the Red, White and Blue."

Wow, my heart took off. I stood up so fast I got dizzy, had to lean on the sparkler display.

"You win a contest, you gotta wrap yourself in a flag and take a victory lap?" Zach teased. He seemed even more tan than yesterday, had he been laying out? Maybe on a towel out behind Tyler's house…I felt myself blushing.

"How'd you know about that?" Probably sounded rude, but Zach only smiled brighter.

"Well, my uncle said he's gonna be sharing the stage with a certain famous local teen orator. And since I have a little stake in that essay of yours…"

"Oh, yeah. Thanks, right? I mean it's just second place, but it's a pretty good deal, and…you know." *I couldn't have done it without you,* but who really says stuff like that?

He nodded gravely. "It is a good deal. And thanks for letting me help. Hey, that's it there, right?" He picked up my essay from the carpet behind me. "Wow. An 'A,' extra credit, AND three hundred dollars. Looks like all those rewrites paid off."

"Oh! I didn't know there was money for second place." Reverend Paula never mentioned three hundred dollars! *Wow. I can give it to Dad, help pay for Michael's helicopter ride…then maybe quit feeling guilty for not stopping Michael in the first place.*

"Yeah, kid. Think I should get a share, don't you? Kidding." He handed my essay back. "So watcha need?"

"You got any more big flags? I need a bunch." My heart kind of cramped up, like, *Really? We're just gonna talk about merchandise?*

"Man, someone sure has the patriotic spirit," Zach said, and my heart expanded, sending a warm buzz through my chest. "We might have more in the back, lemme check."

"And I gotta make a copy of this too." I waved the essay, and Zach turned.

"Well, let's take care of that right now. Copy of that big, fat 'A,' huh? Don't blame ya. Tell you what," he said, as I followed him past the tourists to the back of the store. "I'm gonna copy this on primo stock paper, my treat. I'll just do it on our office copier, my uncle doesn't have to know." He winked at me, and I gave him my essay again, trying to think of something wittier to say than "thanks." "And I'll look for those flags while I'm back there, 'kay? Be right back."

You'd think I would have remembered to get the printer cartridge while I waited for him, but you'd be wrong. I stood in the first aid aisle staring at tubes of anti-itch cream. One thought briefly crossed my mind: *How weird is it to be collecting the weapons for our epic anti-Stander battle in a place where they sell Scooby-Doo Band-Aids?* But then it was back to: *He really did wink at me!* My chest-buzz started tingling into my limbs.

"Got five more, will that do?" Zach reappeared with his arms full of packaged flags, my essay balanced on top. "Oh, and your conclusion? I took a peek while it was copying. Nice." He proffered his armload.

I didn't need five more flags. But when they tumbled from Zach's arms into mine, our hands touched. And then he nudged my essay over with his chin. That *It's really happening* feeling hit me so strong my mouth went dry.

"'Live and Let Live,'" Zach continued thoughtfully. "If you don't mind my asking...you think your essay had any influence on your friend? Savannah, right? She told me this morning that she's, y'know, expecting, and I wondered...Live and Let Live? 'Cause that's what she's decided to do."

I swallowed to get some spit back in my mouth. "Umm," I said. My essay didn't have anything to do with choosing not to have an abortion. Zach must not have read it very carefully. But I was done with my shopping and he was still talking to me. So I made my face go thoughtful too. "Maybe."

"I told her I thought she was real brave," Zach went on. "Raising a kid at her age, in this small town where everyone's gonna judge her…that's pretty special. Don't tell him I said so, but I don't think Tyler deserves her." Now he was smiling again, but not for me. It was for my brave, special friend. And I'm a total idiot, but I felt those envy-knives again. *I'm special too.*

"Yeah, I'm gonna be there for her," I said stupidly. But those golden eyes focused on me again.

"Are you? Good for you, kid." It ought to bug me when he calls me that, but it doesn't. "You guys have that kind of friendship where you totally have each other's backs, huh. Right on. That's worth a lot."

"Well…" His gaze was making me kind of squirmy. "We don't totally…like, I do have this one thing I haven't shared with Savannah yet. 'Cause I'm not sure how she'd take it."

"Dude," Zach said, sounding nothing at all like Michael when he says it, or Nate. "You gotta be open with a friend like that! I mean, look what she's shared with you, right?"

It was crazy. Here we were, standing in front of the foot deodorizers, and everything inside me was yelling, *Hell with Savannah, I want to be open with* you*!* My whole body felt fizzy. And any second now some customer was going to yank him away to help them find the dental floss.

"But my thing…it's not like being pregnant or anything." Zach raised his eyebrows. "It's…hard to explain. I don't want her to think I'm crazy."

"But you don't mind if I do," Zach said, and he was right. *No, I don't! Because you won't think that. You'll understand. It's really happening.*

"Can I show you something?" I blurted. "Like, outside? If you see what I'm talking about, you can tell me if…I should go ahead and tell…" My courage began sinking backward like the end of a wave, slowing my crazy heartbeat.

"Outside? You mean right now?" But he looked serious. "Well, sure thing, if it's important." *Ohjeezohjeezohjeez.* He looked at his watch. "Got a break coming up, I could take it a little early. Will whatever it is take longer than ten minutes?"

I shook my head.

"Okay, go get your stuff rung up while I check in with the boss. Meet you outside in a few?"

I nodded. The wave crested again. My blood raced. *It's really happening.* As I accepted my receipt, I suddenly recognized my crazy heart-buzz: flying energy. *Of course I could fly for him!* Zach was like Dad's jumper cables, revving up my magic battery. Nate never jump-started my powers like that.

But when I stepped outside...*Oh.* I'd forgotten how bustle-y the village was. What was I thinking? People everywhere. Even if we went behind the store and I just hovered a few feet in the air, someone would See me. *Now what?* Zach was coming out, politely holding the door for a lady with a baby carriage. He only had ten minutes, no time to take him to the Toad. Not my house, either. I mean, Michael would probably be okay with Zach knowing about flying, but I'd have to prep him first. And Mom and Lorraine...no way. *Where? Where?*

Then Zach was beside me again. "So where we going, chief? Where you keeping this big, fat secret?"

The village looked like one of those old *Busy, Busy World* kid books, everybody doing a different job. The kayak shop guy was spraying a rack of boats with a hose. A tandem bike swerved to avoid a woman talking on her cell phone. In front of the craft store, Molly's mom was hanging fluttery batik clothing out in the sunshine. Over on the green, the carpenters must be starting to raise the Festival stage, I could hear them banging. No peace and quiet anywhere.

Peace and quiet. That's it—should have thought of it before. "This way," I said. And I led Zach across Howe's lawn toward the church.

"In there?" he asked, surprised.

"Nope," I said, resisting the urge to grab his hand and run, right into the perfect sanctuary: the Meditation Path. It's not marked, tourists never go in there. And this long after church services, I was pretty sure I'd find the secluded elbow of path I needed. The salmonberries were fully leafed out now, making a twisty green tunnel. "In here."

"Oh, nice." Zach nodded his appreciation, stroking the big cedar at the entrance. "I used to come in here a lot, when I first moved to Dalby. Good place to clear your mind." He looked at me. "Or share a secret, right? So what's up?"

"*I'm* what's up," I did not say. This was uncharted territory— nothing like telling Louis. In my dreams of Zach—okay, fantasies, whatever—there wasn't any conversation. We just flew. I knew that part backward and forward, the weight of his hands on my shoulders, his hair brushing my cheek. But the getting up in the air part? No script for that, just the wild swirling of my blood.

I walked us down the first bend of the path, peeked around the next. Nobody. The sunlight was so green it felt like being under tropical water. I laid my load of flags down on the bark with my essay on top, fingers vibrating with power. "Okay. First you have to promise you won't freak out."

"Whew! This is getting exciting! But yeah, I promise. Hurry up, okay? I only got five more minutes of break."

Deep breath. *Really happening.* "Okay then. Here we go." I aimed myself for an arch-shaped gap above the salmonberries, curtained by cedar boughs. Felt the energy flood down my limbs. Took my two powerful launch-strides, *step step*—

Boom! Ran straight into Louis, coming around the twist of the path.

CHAPTER NINETEEN

HOW A HEDGEHOG FEELS

I laid him out. My knees hit Louis's waist, just barely missing the most sensitive part of a guy. He thudded flat on his back on the bark. Me? I fell sideways, into a patch of nettles.

Ohhh, fire! Down my whole right side! But Louis, still lying on the bark, said, "Unhh," and I stifled the yells inside me and scrambled to help him sit up. "Sorry! I'm so sorry!"

Louis shook his head hard. Guess I really nailed him. "Louis, you okay? I'm sorry," I repeated until his eyes focused.

"What the hell, Joss?" he muttered.

Zach stepped up behind us. "He's your secret? I've met this guy before, right? Why'd you have to attack him like that?"

From the ground, Louis shot me a more piercing stare than I'd thought his eyes could manage.

"Uh, surprise," I stammered. My skin was burning, and not all from the nettles. "This is Louis…Louis, Zach."

Zach said, "Good to meet ya." Louis rested on his elbow and stared. I busied myself with spitting on my nettle-burns. Didn't help. A bumpy, red racing stripe was coming out on my right arm and leg.

"You okay?" Zach leaned over me, and I swear I could feel Louis's eyes narrowing. "Man, look at you. You are one crazy chick. Wanna come on back to the store, get some ointment on that? My break's over."

"No, I'm okay." *I'll just stand here and slowly burn away into nothingness.* "You go on."

"And you'll explain all this to me later, right?" Zach kept his tone light, but his eyes were serious. "Whenever you need to talk, kid. Dude," he nodded at Louis, and headed back to work.

The first words Louis spoke after Zach left were, "Are you kidding me?"

"What?" I said. "Oh jeez, it hurts. I gotta get home, get some first aid cream. You're okay now, right? Sorry again." But I couldn't meet his eyes.

"You were about to fly for him."

There was no point in denying it. Louis knows my launch-steps better than anyone. "Yeah, so?" He continued to glare. "Zach's ready to handle it, okay? And besides, it's my decision." *And none of your business*, I was luckily not mean enough to say.

Slowly Louis stood up, brushing the bark off his jeans. "I don't think he's someone who should See you," he said softly.

"Why not? Arrghh, dammit!" I stamped my feet, trying to shock the burn-pain away. "Look, I'm going home, you coming?"

"I just get a bad vibe from him," Louis said, and his eyes softened into their normal solemnness. I felt a rush of impatience. *Of course you do, you're jealous, dummy!*

Or did I say that aloud? Louis flushed and said, "Whatever, Joss," sounding like Savannah. I might have said it aloud.

"Aaaaaaarrghhh! I'm burning up, I'll talk to you later!" I scooped up my pile of flags and essay, and ran for home.

A hot shower helped, and pretty soon my nettle-burns were only itches. But I did not go back to Howe's. Zach must think I'm an absolute moron! The humiliation burned longer than the nettles.

I brought the flags out to Mrs. Mac, who promised me they'd be hung all the way around the stage when it was raised. And she thanked me for the copy of my essay, shooting a huge rush of adrenalin into me. *Yikes, only two more days, I have to practice!* Of course I didn't have time to talk to Zach now.

Still, he wants to talk. He wants to know. If I could get him alone again, somewhere further away, I could really fly for him. And in the middle of his amazement, I could explain the whole stupid Louis-crash, and we could laugh about it, and then…then I could take him flying. Maybe tomorrow on his lunch break! That had to be longer than ten minutes.

But Zach wasn't at work on Monday. Must have been off rehearsing with the Standups. I spent the morning practicing my essay with Michael till he got crabby, then Savannah and I helped decorate the Festival stage. She'd chickened out of telling Tyler again, and I was starting to see why. Tyler can be a real bastard when he doesn't get what he wants, and something told me what Tyler wanted was not to be a responsible daddy.

When Savannah and I walked through the village for ice cream I saw Louis going behind the Co-op with hay for their goats, but I did not go over. What would be the point? We couldn't talk about flying in front of Savannah. Plus I didn't feel like it, okay? It's not my fault if people get jealous.

Fourth of July burst open next day like a fireworks finale, hot and fast: breakfast as a family for once, with the store closed. Pushing Michael around the yard in his new wheelchair. Repeating "nonconformity" at the mirror so I wouldn't stumble on the word. Scouting the festival stage with Mom so we'd all know our parts for this little drama. And dodging the crowds of people who had transformed our quiet village into one giant party. There were people doing weird-looking leg-stretches before the 10k race; people helping their kids weave streamers through their bike wheels; people putting red-white-and-blue costumes on their dogs; people eating shave-ice and pretzels from the festival tents, and people taking pictures of each other doing all that.

I was a nervous wreck.

Nate Cowper tried to hang out with me and Michael when the parade started. He was wearing a red, white, and blue tuxedo he'd found at the thrift shop, and he looked pretty frickin' adorable, but the third time I answered "What?" to something he said, he shrugged, "What is with you, Burger?" and wandered off. I couldn't help it. My mind was bursting with its own little pops and flashes: Flying with Zach! Explaining to Louis—you're all wrong, but I'm sorry! Reading my essay so perfectly everyone— *Mrs. Mac-Mr. Evans-Mom-Dad-Lorraine-Michael-Zach Zach Zach*— would be totally blown away. I patted my stiff back pocket where I'd tucked my primo-paper speech.

And, oh yeah. Snagging the Stander's water bottle while my brother distracted her, so my mom could drinke knowingly from it, then putting it back unnoticed. All so my mom and I could fly on without worrying about someone trying to zap our power away from us. That little thing.

"Stand still, can'tcha?" Michael grumped at me as the happy mass of balloons and flags paraded past. He tried unsuccessfully to twist his neck. "What're you doing back there, dancing? To *this*?"

That's when I noticed the energy whooshing through me. It must have been there all morning, but caught up in my nerves, I hadn't recognized the signs. My body wasn't grooving to the random rhythms of the parade-drummers or the guy with the solo tuba. It wanted to *fly, fly, FLY!* Oh, I should have gone flying after the stupid thing with Zach on the path Sunday! Or the day after, just to get it out of my system. Now my energy was overflowing. My right foot, my takeoff foot, quivered so hard it kept raising itself off the grass.

"I gotta fly," I muttered to Michael through clenched teeth.

"Pee? Well, go home then. I'm not gonna die if you're gone for five minutes."

"No, not pee, fly," I whispered in his ear. "I'm practically hovering right here. Not sure I can stay down."

"You kidding?" He sounded more impressed than grouchy, and I felt another brief throb of, yeah, I guess you'd have to call it love, for my bro who'd finally decided to let me do the flying for both of us. "Well, sit down or something. There's way too many people."

"I've got, like, twenty more minutes, right?" I said. "Before the speech-thing starts? I'll tell Mom to come get you—be right back!"

"Joss, hold up!" Michael called, but I had already ditched him. Threading my way through the parade-watchers, it was all I could do not to launch myself. Where was Mom? She wouldn't be under the stage already, would she? Mom was never early. There was Savannah—oh! Talking to Tyler on a bench at the side of the green. *Good luck, Savannah. Oh shoot, there's Louis looking at me, can't deal with you right now…Mom, where are you?!*

Oof—I ran straight into Dad. "Jocelyn? Honey, where are you going? Your speech is in fifteen minutes!" And Lorraine added, "We need to take our positions, Joss. She's already over there." I didn't need her to say who *she* was.

"I know, but I gotta do something, okay? I just stranded Michael by the side of the road. Over there," I waved vaguely toward the tail end of the parade, which was literally that, all dog-tails. "Can you go get him? I'll be right back, I PROMISE," I gasped. I had never felt the flight-energy take hold of me this way. Did it somehow know it was about to confront its enemy? *Wow. Like Harry's scar burning in the presence of Voldemort! If I don't get airborne in the next sixty seconds, I really might explode.*

"Jocelyn! Now is NOT the time!" I heard Dad roar, but I was gone, running across the green toward our house. Past the stage, a blur of flags and bunting and people on fold-out chairs and blankets, and somewhere in there Mom was crouched—or was she?—to pop out like a weasel and drinke from—*whoa!*

I launched. Must have been the wild surge of energy from the thought of our triumph, but I was in the air, above our lawn where a young couple with a baby-pack was trespassing, and *oh jeez*, did their heads just turn? I dived, flying only feet above the ground to make it around the back corner of our house where the store was blessedly closed, so there should be no one—

—except the large group of tourists standing stupidly on the store's front step to read the Closed sign.

I should have landed—duh. The tourists, still in running clothes, weren't paying attention, discussing whether the store would open later, or would shave-ice make a good substitute for Gatorade? Maybe they wouldn't notice.

But I had too much gas. That's what it felt like: someone had their foot down on the gas pedal, and it wasn't me. I mean, *I* was the gas pedal—the foot was my crazy magic. I couldn't land.

Now what? I was trapped. *Can't fly over these people. Can't go back around the house. Can't come down.* So the only place to go is…up.

I'm sorry, Mom. I think I understand now why you ended up on the roof of Howe's. You couldn't control it either, huh? Silly me—assuming what I knew from my year of superpower was all there was to know. Assuming I could control my body's urges any better than Savannah and Tyler.

So I lay there. Flattened, just like Mom, with the roof ridge cutting into my breastbone and a foot on each side of the house. Our roof did not smell like lilies. Below me on the yard-side, I heard the woman saying, "Did you see that? Did you *see* that?" just like that old minister's video of my mom. And on the store-side, the group of runners continued to argue about hydration. I inched my way on my belly over to our chimney and crouched behind it, trying not to scrape the shingles with my sneakers. Oh jeez, there they were, a guy with a red beard wearing the baby, the woman using her handbag to shade her eyes. If they looked up right now we'd be staring at each other.

At least they hadn't seen me fly *up*; their gaze took them around the house.

Over by the green came a blob of microphone-sound, then a burst of applause. It was starting.

"The Star-Spangled Banner" saved me. When the notes of a trumpet wafted our way, both sets of people below me turned and headed for the green. Three cheers for the red, white and blue! I scrambled over to the back of the house, hung from the roof and dropped myself in a pile—couldn't risk allowing my magic energy to strand me in the air again. As I landed, my essay popped out of my back pocket and fell on the grass. *Holy shih tzu, if I hadn't noticed that...*

The regular kind of energy, plain old adrenalin, works just fine. I snatched up my essay and ran.

"...and the home...of the...brave," the crowd was singing along with the trumpeter. All the paraders and runners and shave-ice eaters had gathered into a mass behind the lawn chairs and blankets, and were now vaguely cheering while finding seats on the grass for themselves and their dogs. Up on the stage, the trumpet guy gave a little bow, and into his place at the microphone stepped our mayor. As she began a speech of welcome, I danced through the crowd, trying not to step on babies. There was Michael's wheelchair, right up front, Dad and Lorraine on either side. They were looking around like crazy, not seeing me.

But Savannah did. Grabbed me, in fact. "Jo-oss," she moaned.

I was about to shake her hand off—*I don't have time for this*! Then I saw the mascara running down her face. Savannah never cries, because she never gets into situations where she needs to. Until now. "Hey, what happened? Are you okay?"

"Nooo," she wailed. A gray-haired tourist couple glanced at us and moved away. "I told him, and he...he was so mad, Joss! He said it was totally my fault, and why didn't I just take care of things, and don't expect him to have anything to do with any stupid baby!"

"'Take care of things?'" Even in my rush, even with my low standards for Tyler, I was stopped cold. "You mean he's too chickens--- to say the word 'abortion,' but he still wants you to have one?"

"He said how's he know the baby's his. He called me a slut," Savannah choked, and then she was crying for real, hunched up. I know that feeling; it's like being a hedgehog without the spiky parts. You don't really have any defenses, you just hope the next kick won't hurt as much if you're curled up tight.

I haven't had much practice comforting people, since Michael and Mom have plenty of hedgehog spikes. But I put my arms around her and let her rub her makeup on me. Above us, Mayor Susan seemed to be telling a rambling story.

"It's all right," I muttered. "You don't need him, Savannah. You have your mom and dad and me and all your friends, remember? It's gonna be okay. Why'd you want to be with someone who calls your baby stupid before he's even born?"

Even holding her tight, I couldn't feel her belly. What I did feel surprised me: my tough, head-tossing friend felt vulnerable. *Her, too?* I thought, amazed. *Is that how it works?* Anyone flying high on their own courage can be brought down by anyone else mean enough to try. A wave of anger pulsed through me.

"Savannah." Her sobs were drying up. I took her hands and stood back. "I gotta go do my speech. But I'm with you, girlfriend. Okay? I'm here for you." I never talk like that, but it didn't feel fake. I wanted to protect all the vulnerable people. There's a ton of different ways to bring people down, a ton of duct tape out there. We Flyers have a lot of company.

Suddenly I heard a hissing sound: Dad had spotted me and was wildly jerking his head toward the stage: *Get up there!* I nodded, squeezed Savannah's hands, and trotted behind the stage where the steps were, trying to get control of my breathing. My brain whirled. Should I peek underneath, whisper something to Mom? No time! Mayor Susan was wrapping up, and I knew from all those programs who was next: Reverend Paula, to introduce Jocelyn Burgowski.

Up onto the stage—*whoa, that's a lot of people!*—and into the only empty chair. Deep breaths. *C'mon, heart, gimme a break.*

"Afternoon, young lady," Mr. Howe said in a low voice from the chair next to me. "They were worried you'd succumbed to cold feet, but I knew you'd be here."

"Thank you," I said, instead of screaming, "Do you know what a DIRTBAG your son is?" Then: *Cold feet? Hah, I'd had the opposite.* But thank goodness my feet were calm now. Lucky I got that little flight-burst out of my system! I was going to stay safely grounded on the stage. Grounded, but by my choice, no one else's. It was time. *Let's do this.*

There was the back of Reverend Paula, and her nasal voice on the mike. Next thing I knew she was turning to me and clapping and so was the whole crowd, all those vulnerable people looking up at me. How many of them had spikes of their own? How many were busy right now bringing someone else down? Maybe the world was full of Standers. *There's Savannah, still wiping her eyes. Oh, there's Zach!* Off to the left with his guitar, giving me a thumbs-up. I rose, feeling grateful that my knees were only shaky, not buzzing, and stepped to the microphone.

As soon as I started speaking, the familiar words took over and the "legs" of my essay carried me forward.

"What does it really mean to be a citizen? In a big city, it can be hard to tell. Everybody's so busy protecting themselves, finding their own little group, not getting in a car crash on the freeway. In the city, it's all about you, yourself." I thought of Mc-Clenton, the apartments where my Mom lived without knowing any of her neighbors. "But here on Dalby, we can do like Henry

243

David Thoreau said and 'Simplify, simplify.' We don't need to rush around talking on our cell phones, plus they don't even work on most of the island." Laughter. *Yay.* "So we have time to get to know each other, like in the old days. That's a huge part of being a citizen." I thought of the goat-pen work party, all those grown-ups and kids hanging out together. The library where Lorraine had made herself practically Mayor of Dalby by reading all those stories to us kids, year after year. My dad gabbing at his cash register.

"But that's not the only part. We also have to respect each other's differences. And there are a ton of nonconformists in this community." Laughter again, and I built on it, describing some of the more colorful "characters" everyone would recognize, including Molly's mom, who wore crazy hats way before Mrs. Mac started, and my own grandpa Al, who once painted his fishing boat bright purple and called everyone he met "Wally" or "Shirley," just to mess with them. But as I spoke, I thought of the real nonconformists in my life, and the obstacles they faced just being themselves: Louis's mom Shasta, figuring out who she was while the whole town watched. Louis himself, never needing to follow, to be cool, but always paying the price. "Thoreau said some people march to the beat of a different drummer, and that's another huge part of being a citizen: allowing those people to 'step to the music which they hear.' Not getting on their case for it, trying to make them all march the same way." *Like Rory. And my magic Mom.* "That's called 'live and let live.' But that's not all citizenship means either. Because it takes a ton of courage to actually live that way."

I'd written this speech a long time ago, right? And my examples of courage still worked: the American colonists who had to risk everything when they decided to listen to the revolutionaries and fight the British, and Martin Luther King's wife getting her house firebombed because of what her husband was saying.

But now I had my own examples of courage: Savannah, about to be the only teen mom on the island while her own boyfriend calls her a slut. Michael letting his ache for flight pass through him. And Mom, pulling herself out from the thorn bush of her physical cravings, getting herself back in the sky like it was a huge, scary horse that had thrown her. Facing down the enemy she had once agreed with.

"Ralph Waldo Emerson said this about courage: 'Do the thing we fear, and death of fear is certain,'" I said. "This means that to be a citizen, sometimes you have to face up to danger or things you don't like, but when you do, you get rewarded with even more courage, like all those revolutionary guys who fought the War of Independence, and Mrs. Coretta Scott King, who carried on the movement after her husband was killed." But I was thinking of Mom, crouched in the shadows under my feet. At least I sure hoped she was.

"So we also need courage to be citizens, courage to live and let live and deal with all the disruption people's nonconformity might cause to our lives. But where does that courage come from?" I asked the crowd. Somebody's baby cried, but no other sound, from all those people. They were right with me. "That's right," I improvised, as if we were conversing, "it comes from wisdom. As Emerson said, 'Before we acquire great power we must acquire wisdom to use it well.' This doesn't just mean the power of putting together a revolutionary army or a civil rights movement. This means the power of a community that really works well together, that looks out for everybody." I actually thought this part of my essay was pretty much b.s., even in the final draft when Mr. Evans liked it. But now as I read it, looking out over that spread of faces, I saw Dad nodding, and I thought, *You. You got wisdom, Dad.*

I had never thought of him that way—he was just my dad, kind of boring, sometimes jolly, sometimes really frickin' uptight.

But he has this amazing gift: he gets what he doesn't get. He lets it go, lets me spend summers in McClenton with my crazy mom, lets me read big books with Lorraine without interfering, lets us educate him about our magic beef with the Standers. Wisdom, yeah. He trusted himself enough to know when he needed to step away from his wrecked marriage, all those years ago, and now he knows it's time to look that scary magic stuff in the eye and deal with it. *Thanks, Dad.* I reached the part about "Trusting thyself" and the iron string, and my voice choked a little, thinking about how much I owed him. But I got through.

"So in the end, being a citizen means knowing each other, caring about our differences, being brave enough to deal with them, and having the wisdom that comes from trusting ourselves. That's what it takes to live and let live. It sounds like a lot, but it really isn't, when you think of how many ordinary people are doing it every day." That was the end of my speech, but I didn't feel done. I had all these people—my family, Louis, and now Zach—encouraging me to be my magic self. Savannah deserved the same help. "And just think of what a great world it would be if all those people who aren't letting others be themselves would just be nice and try it for a change. Thank you."

"Nice job," whispered Reverend Paula as she stepped up to introduce the next speaker. *Just you wait,* I thought.

"Well done," Mr. Howe said, smiling broadly. "You're a tough act to follow." I thought, *Yeah, I am.* But he managed to follow me. Boy, did he ever.

From the very first sentence it was clear that Mr. Howe was not delivering the speech that had won him first prize. "Ladies and gentlemen, before I begin, I'd like to ask someone to join me on stage." I saw the heads of Reverend Paula and Mayor Susan swivel sharply toward each other. "Miss Savannah Enderle? Would you be so kind?"

The crowd mumbled. Somebody laughed, another baby started

howling. And up the stage steps came Savannah, looking dazed. She'd only managed to un-smear half her face.

Mr. Howe put his arm around her and drew her toward the mike. She barely reached the stupid formal hankie in his suit pocket. "Folks, I was gonna give you a speech about how being a citizen depends on everybody pulling together. I had some nice quotes, too." Uncertain laughter. "But right here's the best example I could give you of what I'm talking about. Ladies and gentlemen, I have recently learned that, thanks to this brave young lady here, I'm going to be a grandpa."

The crowd made the same noise as my brain. *Wait, WHAT? He knows? Did Tyler just tell him? Or did Zach…? And he's cool with it? And he's using Savannah's pregnancy in his speech?*

The next part was a blur. The crowd kept muttering, plus the mayor and the minister were whispering furiously behind Mr. Howe's back, so I didn't catch everything he said. Something about going along with the power of nature, following the rules and accepting responsibility. Then very clearly he said, "As the previous speaker said, it takes great courage to live and let live, and my family *will* support this young lady's brave decision, helping her to meet all the obstacles of raising a child." I thought, *Wow, he's quoting me!* And: *Ha, take that, Tyler—your dad just called you out.* Finally, applause. Savannah stood stock-still, arms wrapped around herself.

But Mr. Howe held up his hand, waiting for quiet. "Folks, I have another reason for inviting this lovely young woman up here with me. I want to draw a contrast. I want to paint a picture for you. In every society, you have the people who pull together, following the rules, doing what nature and God intend for them to do. Like this." He pulled Savannah closer, as she seemed to be edging away. Behind him, Mayor Susan started to get out of her chair, but Reverend Paula stopped her. "Then you have the other people, the ones who think the rules don't apply to them." *Is he talking about Tyler?* "The ones who raise up chaos and selfishness under the name of nonconformity. Folks, they tell you they're celebrating freedom and self-expression, and we heard just now great praises heaped on the heads of those who dare to stand up and be different." My stomach turned icy. *No. He's talking about me.* "But ladies and gentlemen, there is a huge difference between fighting a war for independence or civil rights, and just doing what you want because you want to. When it comes to living your life as a citizen, there is such a thing as too much freedom. This young lady here found that out, but she's willing to pay the consequences, and I honor her for it."

The crowd sounded ugly now. I heard boos, and somebody shouted, "Get off the stage, you jerk!" *Was that Dad?* Both Reverend Paula and the mayor stood up. But Mr. Howe stepped forward, abandoning Savannah but not the microphone. "You want the proof of it?" he said, his voice rising. "The proof of the false promise of nonconformity? The proof that honoring freedom for its own sake can lead you down unrighteous paths? Folks, I have it right here in my hand. Ladies, let me finish." He held up papers, sidestepping the women who were coming to take the mike from him. *Why don't they just unplug it?* "You must have thought this was my speech, didn't you? But sadly, it is not. What I have here is the speech you just heard, the one praising nonconformity to the skies." *He has my speech? What? How?* My whole body got cold.

"And do you want to know the irony of it all?" Apparently the crowd did; in the sudden silence all I heard was a seagull. Even the mayor and the minister froze. "This speech, ladies and gentlemen, I downloaded this morning from the internet. Word for word. The whole thing is cribbed, plagiarized, stolen. All because the author thought she could. This is what you get when you think the rules don't apply."

Not even a seagull this time.

"I am sorry if my words are hurtful," Mr. Howe said quietly. "But they are true. Honor the rules, be a good citizen, and have a wonderful Independence Day. Thank you very much."

Pandemonium. Wish I could have enjoyed it.

Mayor Susan was in Mr. Howe's face: "How dare you do that to a child!" He came right back in hers, shouting that somebody should get him a computer, he'd show her right now, this festival shouldn't reward fraud, that's exactly what was wrong with this country today. The microphone dropped to the stage with a screech. More shouts from the crowd, drowning each other out in a rising wave of ugliness.

I sat frozen.

Savannah threw herself at my knees, her face white. "Joss, I swear I had no idea! He just called me up so I came, but I had no idea he was going to do that to you! Joss, whaddya think, is it true? Your speech?"

Think? Frozen people don't think. Mr. Howe and Mayor Susan continued to shout at each other. Someone seemed to be handing a smartphone up to the stage. Reverend Paula stood unmoving, her back to me.

Suddenly Dad was there, lifting me out of my chair in a whole-body hug, saying, "It's okay, hon, he won't get away with it, it's gonna be all right." His words thawed my thoughts: *Mr. Howe called me a fraud. He smiled at me, and humiliated me in front of the whole town.* My family. All my friends. His nephew.

Zach. Where was he? He knew my essay was real, he'd helped me write it! Maybe that was his voice I heard yelling. Calling his uncle a jerk. If he really cared about me, he'd be climbing onto the stage right now. It'd be his arms around me, not Dad's. Except no, he wouldn't do that in front of all these people, he'd find me alone, comfort me…

All these people. Staring at me, talking about me. I needed to curl into a ball, Dad's arms weren't spiky enough to protect me. Wriggling free, I bolted off the stage.

CHAPTER TWENTY

THE POWER OF CHEESY DREAMS

Back to the meditation path. That's where Zach would know to find me. To hold me and soothe my burning humiliation, let me cry and spill my secret at last. But as I reeled down the back-stage steps, I heard a sharp whisper coming from under the stage.

"Joss! Get ready!"

Mom. I froze again, in disbelief: *seriously?* After what just happened, we're still going along with the plan? Didn't she hear? What was I supposed to do, stand around chit-chatting with Reverend Paula about what a little plagiarist I was, just to grab her water bottle? *If you cared about me at all you'd be out here hugging on me too*, I thought savagely.

"Joss, you hear me? Ron's distracting Paula right now—you need to go get that water bottle!"

What I needed was to get out of there. But before I could move, Louis came barreling around the back of the stage. "Joss, it's Zach, I know it is! Told you I had a bad vibe."

I grabbed the stair railing, barely registering the stab of a splinter. The grass back here was trampled flat. I knew the feeling. "Go away."

"But your plan," he whispered urgently. "You guys have to do it knowingly! If you get it wrong and the real Stander sees you doing it, it's all over, right?"

"F--- the plan," I muttered. But Louis drew himself up.

"Joss. Look at me." I did. Louis's eyes weren't big and round like they get when he's excited. They were hard. "I saw him pump his fist."

"Mr. Howe? Great, Louis, thanks for reminding me what a jerk he is."

"Joss!" Mom hissed from beneath the stage. "She's drinking! Lorraine just told me. Get up there and grab her bottle!"

"No, not Mr. Howe," Louis went on breathlessly. "Zach. He pumped his fist, Joss, when Mr. Howe said that stuff about your essay. When the crowd got all shocked. He was *glad*. It's his bottle you have to drink from."

"You're crazy," I said. "Zach doesn't even have a bottle." But Louis had dragged me back to the moment. *No WAY am I climbing back up there.* Without another thought I flung myself through the hanging flags and under the stage.

The scent of fresh boards closed in with the darkness. Those flags were thick; only a few thin lines of sunlight striped my hiding place.

One sun-stripe fell across Mom's face, making her squint. "Joss, no. You're supposed to be up there! The plan—"

"Shh," Louis ordered from outside.

Above us, boards creaked with commotion. I heard Dad's voice: "You guys gonna do something about this?"

The mayor: "Paula, what do you think? Paula!"

Mr. Howe: "Look, look! Here's that essay on the internet, right here…"

Movement toward the backstage steps—were they coming down?

Fine, I'll stay put. Let Dad grab Reverend Paula's bottle and hand it down to me. Who cares if this isn't what we'd planned? Plan B: Jocelyn Burgowski defeats the stupid Stander without her mom's help. And then I could get the hell away from these people, off to the shelter of the meditation path.

That's when I heard Zach's voice, low but clear, coming from around the corner of the stage: "Now what, Uncle Doug?"

He didn't sound outraged, or shocked, or disappointed, or any of the ways he should have sounded. He sounded like Michael: sarcastic.

Louis, backstage: "I'm telling you, Joss!"

Mom, in the darkness with me: "Babe, you need to go!"

Reverend Paula, right above us: "What in the world is this all about?"

And Mr. Howe, at the top of the backstage steps. Whispering down to his nephew: "I think we achieved the desired result, don't you?"

"Psh," said Zach. Maybe twenty feet away, on the other side of those flags he'd sold me.

"I thought you said she had to be exposed." Mr. Howe was coming down the steps. Even whispering, he sounded pouty, like a scolded little kid.

"Not like that," said Zach's voice, with that same tired patience he used to talk about his brother. "Not publicly, man. All you've done is create sympathy for her. I meant exposed to *herself*. If you can't undermine 'em quietly, you might as well leave 'em alone."

I stopped breathing.

"Ohhh," Mom said into the darkness. "There's two of them."

Reverend Paula seemed to be pacing the stage, repeating shrilly, "Will someone please tell me what this is all about?"

"Well, excuse me for trying it my way," Mr. Howe blustered, stage-whisper. He was on the grass with Zach now. "What's wrong with a little publicity? You said you wouldn't have done the YouTube thing either, but look what results I got: flushed 'em right out of the woodwork!"

YouTube thing? The air forced its way back into my lungs with a gasp. Or maybe that was Mom: she clutched me and I hung on. I wanted to cover my ears like a little kid in a thunderstorm.

"And got exactly nowhere till I came along, Uncle Doug. Don't forget that. You had Number One zooming around up there, getting stronger by the day, and you didn't even know there was a Number Two!"

"Maybe someone should fetch the sheriff," the reverend's voice pierced the babble above.

"Well, guess we don't have to worry about her after all," Mom muttered into my ear. "Babe, I'm sorry. But we still have to do this. Mr. Howe had a water bottle too, right? What about—"

"No," I said automatically.

"I had her on my radar," Mr. Howe grumbled. "After we grounded Number One with the letters—"

"—another idea of mine, thanks," Zach interrupted. "Which is exactly the route I was trying to take with Number Two, the psychological approach. You don't want confrontation, man. Public denouncement, seriously? We've talked about this! Make 'em think about what they are, really *feel* it, then they ground themselves. If you'd stuck with the plan, sent that plagiarism charge to the newspaper next week, I could've taken it from there, no problem. Talked to Number Two, made her think the whole thing really was cribbed, that she never had an original idea in her life. She trusts me, man. I could've talked her down so easy! Now I'm gonna have to do it the old-fashioned way."

"Babe…" Mom said.

"No," I repeated. "Nuh-uh." *Not Zach. Not the one who understands me, who flies with me in my dreams. Who doesn't need to know I'm magic to know I'm special.*

But he does know. Why else would Zach show so much interest in me, my mom, my essay? *I tried to fly for him. He could have prayed me down right there.* The Flying Burgowski, grounded forever—and the whole disaster my fault. All my gut instincts! My iron string! How could it be so right about Mr. Howe and so wrong about Zach? Mom squeezed me harder; guess she felt me shaking.

"So now what? I have to deal with these people," Mr. Howe whispered grumpily. Above us, the microphone squawked as one of "these people" picked it up and said, "Uh, sorry about all this, folks..."

"I'll go find her," Zach said. "I know where she'll be. You really took her apart, man. Doubt she'll want to fly for me now, but I'll make it happen. Really hate doing it that way, but whatever. Gotta save who you can."

"You want me to take care of Number One while you're doing that?" Mr. Howe asked. That voice of authority, taking orders. From his nephew? *Maybe I was wrong—that wasn't Zach out there, it was some new Stander we hadn't foreseen, some towering man with fierce, black eyebrows...* My fingers quivered on Mom's shoulders, a current passing through. Above us, the mayor seemed to be making another speech.

"Yeah, right," Zach's voice mocked. *Yes, and maybe a dark little beard...* "You've done enough for one day, Uncle Doug. Go work in the store, let me take care of it." Then, sadly: "There's still a way to ground 'em both. Just...sure wish I could've done it my way."

Mr. Howe muttered, "Fine. I'll go work on inventory, then." The magic buzz was flowing backward, up my wrists, through my arms, coming from...

"Mom!" All of a sudden she pulled away. A flag flapped sunlight into my darkness as she ducked outside.

"Yeah, you do that, Uncle Doug," Mom snarled. "Number One can run the cash register."

"And Number Two can help," I said, and ducked out behind her to face them down in the brilliant sunlight.

"Go, Joss," I heard Louis murmur behind me. I was jangling like a puppet. My chest-engine roared, blasting the numbness of betrayal with the pure energy of flight.

"Oh, boy," Zach said. No bearded, evil man. Just Zach: hands on hips, face flushed. My heart gave a pathetic spasm that had nothing to do with flying.

I've never seen an old cowboy movie, okay. But I know what they're supposed to look like, black hats and white hats facing off across an empty dirt square. That was us. No more guesswork, no more research. Everything out in the open. Standers vs. Flyers. We hadn't expected two of them? Well, they hadn't expected two of us. Standoff.

Into this movie set blundered Savannah, pulling Reverend Paula with her down the backstage steps. She got right in Mr. Howe's face and threw the worst insult in the world there: "Now I know where Tyler gets it." Not letting go of the reverend's arm, she waved some marked-up papers at her. *My rough draft? Where did Savannah get that?* "Joss didn't plagiarize this, Reverend, and that a--hole knows it! Sorry, Rev. But I can prove it. I got this from Mr. Evans."

"What was that plan again?" Mr. Howe said pleasantly to Zach, who was looking at the ground. Not that I was trying to meet his eyes. My body was vibrating so hard, if Zach looked at me now I would go instantly vertical.

"Never mind. I got this." Zach turned to head back to the green, and found himself face to face with my teacher.

I had never seen Mr. Evans so angry. His round body quivered. "My student has been slandered," he told Reverend Paula. "That's her rough draft right there, with all my comments. Are you planning to confront this liar, or shall I?"

"I'm sorry," gasped Reverend Paula, still hovering on the bottom step. "I just don't know where..." She flapped her hands helplessly.

"Sir," Mr. Howe boomed, "when you see this work, as I did, plastered all over the internet, I think you'll feel differently. Even the rough draft is there, all she did was copy it." *Ohh...those copies Zach made for me. He must have scanned the whole thing, drafts and all, uploaded it...made it look like it was there all along. And I'd just thought he was proud of me...* A stain of nausea coursed through my energy-swell like pollution. "I'm sorry you got caught up in her lies, but as her teacher, you bear some responsibility for not detecting this fraud."

"Sir," Mr. Evans replied, "screw you."

"Yeah," put in Savannah, "and screw your family support. My baby's got nothing to do with you. You'd be a horrible grandpa."

Mom took a step forward then and Mr. Howe threw his hands up like he thought she was going to attack him. But she only said, "Pff," and shouldered past him, up the stage steps. I glimpsed Dad up there for a second, then they stepped out of my view.

"You're horrible too," I told Zach. My voice quavered.

Our clean little standoff got really messy after that, like a dust storm sweeping in. A wordstorm.

Zach said, "Look, kid."

Louis: "Joss."

Mr. Evans: "Reverend, what other evidence are you waiting for?"

Mr. Howe: "Young lady, I want you to know that—"

Savannah: "Stop calling me that, you pig!"

They swirled around me, the dusty words; they made it hard to see. The magic swelled through me and I grabbed at the stage— another splinter, same thumb. That spike of pain opened a window in the wordswirl, and through that window I saw Mom's hand reaching something down from the stage, a bottle, and I saw Louis take it from her. Calm, quiet Louis. I saw him step around the knot of angry people and proffer that water bottle innocently to Mr. Howe.

He took it automatically. "I beg your pardon, Savannah, but you're upset," Mr. Howe said, his face bright pink. He did look like a pig. "You don't know what you're saying right now. I understand. We all just need to take a moment and simmer down," he added, summoning that respectable authority of his, and he demonstrated with a nice, cool drink of water.

"HAH!" Mom swung back down the steps like a monkey. In all of our research, Lorraine never found any special incantation for defeating Standers, but Mom made up her own: "You are BUSTED, Stander."

Zach drew his breath in like a hiss.

Mr. Howe looked down at the plastic bottle in his hand. "Oh," he said softly.

Zach said, "Wow, man. Really?"

The books said nothing about how a Stander feels with "all his power forsaken." Maybe a little stab? Mr. Howe kind of deflated, his pink face turning gray.

"Guess bottles count as cuppes," Louis said cheerfully.

"Whoa!" I hung onto the edge of the stage for dear life as the power pounded through me. Mom did too, like we were riding the same wave. "Don't, don't, don't," she gasped. *Don't fly? I have to fly! I'll burst.* Triumph. Heartbreak. POWER. *How did I ever think I was in control of this?*

Zach looked at me then. His golden eyes bore into mine, not a lifeline any more. A fuse.

He can feel my energy. He's going to launch me right here. This is what those poor women in the sixteen-hundreds must have seen in the faces of their ministers. The light of absolute self-righteousness, kindling the town. *"And they did cast ye witches down."*

I turned and ran.

It was a horrible risk, letting go of that railing, but I wasn't weighing pros and cons. I moved my feet as fast as they could go, muttering "Stay down stay down stay down" as each step gave way to the next. No launching. No flying. Stay down. *Go.*

Meditation path. Launch there, out of sight of the crowds. Out of reach of Zach. Fly across the road, evade the tourists. Head for the Toad. Circle in safety till the power loses its hold.

And then what? If he can launch me just by looking...I'll have to avoid him forever. Till he leaves the island. Never see him again. Never visit at UW. *He doesn't care for you, stupid. He's been using you the whole time to attack your mom and your friends. Now he's going after you. What is it about the word "antagonist" that you don't get?*

My heartbreak caught up with me as I swung around the big cedar at the path entrance. *I was in love with you. You took my beautiful trust and turned it on me.* Forget launching—I staggered to my knees in the bark.

And that's where Zach found me, howling like a baby.

"Jocelyn," he said.

I clenched my eyes. "Go away."

"Kid," he murmured, "you've got it all wrong."

"I know what you are! I'm not flying for you! I hate you!"

"I know that's how you feel," Zach said. His voice came close. "I know you've been hurt." His hands on my shoulders, rubbing gently. "Joss, it's okay. I'm not like my uncle, all right?"

"You said you'd ground me. Break me down." My body heaved under his fingers.

"I'm trying, Joss," he sighed. "We can't help how we're born, right? I'm a Stander, you're a Flyer, that's just who we are. But we don't have to act on it, right? Who wants to spend their whole life on guard against magic? I want to be a regular guy, not a puffed-up cartoon like Uncle Doug." His voice felt soft. He stroked my hair.

So good. So sweet. "I know what you're trying to do!" I cried, clenching harder.

"Do you?" Zach murmured sadly. "Do you really, Joss? You know, I've been imagining this moment—totally cheesy, but it's true, this moment, this exact spot." He rested his chin on the top of my head. "When I realized what you were…I hated it at first. That's how I've been trained. But then I started to imagine what it would be like if you could…you know."

My flight-engine drowned out my heart. Zach's body tightened above me. *He can feel it!* "Let go of me," I said.

"Fly for me, Joss. I want to love the magic like you do. Get me out of this stupid Stander thing, it's not who I am anymore."

"Stop it."

"You've imagined this too, I know you have," he whispered. "You think I'm too old for you, right? Joss, I don't want what other guys want. You're special. I want you to share your power with me." His hands slid down my wet face. "Please."

No, no, no. He's your enemy.

Cupping my chin. His breath on my tears. "Jocelyn."

I squeezed my eyes tighter, but I did not turn away. And he kissed me.

Zach was right. I had dreamed this. Over and over. And it was cheesy. And it was so damn sweet.

"Look at me," he said.

Don't open your eyes! But he's there, it's real, it's really happening...he needs me...he wants to change...

Of course I opened them. Can't blame the pulsing magic for that. I just wanted to see his face against mine. And I did, too.

Yup. Zach Howe may be only eighteen, but his power is a thousand years older, and it blazed into me from a distance of two inches. I launched right there.

Straight up like a helicopter. My back hit a cedar branch so hard I should have crashed, but our combined powers kept me in the air, flailing madly.

Below me, Zach brought his hands together. "Dear Lord," he shouted, "let those who stand their ground defeat—"

A pinprick in the ribs. An arrow hole. *Cupid?* I thought crazily. My power hissing out like air... "*...powers forsaken...*"

"NO!"

Midflail, I saw someone hurtle into Zach, knocking him sideways in a churning of arms and legs.

"Joss, I got him! Come down!" Mom yelled. I grabbed at a higher branch, my body fighting for the sky.

Below me, from the grunting tussle, Mom's voice: "Joss, I know it's hard! Doesn't...get any easier."

"—all enemies of Thy grace..." *Arrow-hole tearing larger...power bleeding away...*

"You just...have to...own it."

"—by this holy...prayer... Aah!" cried Zach. I think she bit him.

"Leave us alone!" I shrieked, and thrust with all my puny strength against that branch.

I came down, all right. On top of them.

Someone kicked me. I rolled off Mom, looking up into the tree. The stinging hole in my ribcage closed. *Too late.* My back throbbed. *I'm down. I'm grounded.*

Coughing, Mom squirmed to the side of the path, leaving Zach face-up, hands still together, eyes closed, chest heaving. He looked so beautiful.

"Sonuvabitch," he said.

My own chest jittered, caught. Hummed weakly. *So I'm still... me?* "You're right," I whispered to Mom. "It is hard."

She gave a sad little nod, trying to repair her ponytail. "Hate to say it, but the next few years are probably gonna be the worst. Something about that mix of magic and sexual maturity, I guess. Sorry I let you in for this, kiddo."

"I'm not," I said. *I'm still me.* I sat up, feeling the engine-hum deepen. "We did it, Mom! We got Mr. Howe, and..." I looked down at Zach. *You didn't ground me. We won.* So why did my heart feel so flattened?

With a slithery wrestling movement, Zach rolled to his feet. His eyes were on low-beam now, but I still shivered as they flicked over me. "Sorry, kid, I tried," he said. "You have no idea what I could've kept you from..." He turned, shaking his head, and headed down the meditation path. At the bend he stopped. "Just ask yourself this, okay? Why d'you think I care so much about your soul?" And he was gone behind the cedars.

"Zach Howe." Mom shook her head. "Never felt anything like that, did you feel it? Almost launched us both back there! Babe, I am so proud of you, I can't even—unhhh!"

Another flying tackle, but this time it was my little mom on the bottom, and on top of her, Mr. Howe, his hands around her throat.

"Bitch! Heathen! Disempower me? I'll take you out!"

"Stop it, stop it!" I screamed, kicking Mr. Howe's back. He seemed to swell, blocking out my mother. "Mom! Help! Somebody!"

Zach could not have been far. Must have heard us. Just kept walking.

It was Dad who rode in to our rescue.

"Take your hands off her, you piece of s---!"

He hasn't hauled in a fishing net for sixteen years, but my dad is plenty strong. He got Mr. Howe in a headlock of his own.

"You see that, Sheriff?" *Michael?* There was my brother's wheelchair, Lorraine behind him, at the grassy opening of the path, finger pointed like he was about to yell "Charge!"

Must've been the word "sheriff"—Mr. Howe let go. Dad released him and shoved the big pig aside to help Mom lie gently back on the bark. She gave a gasping cough, clutching her neck. "Thanks," her lips said.

Lorraine was making herself into a seatbelt to keep Michael in his wheelchair. "Told you, Sheriff!" he yelled. "I told you he was after my mom! Get 'im!"

And Sheriff Gil did just that. "Hands on your head, Doug," he snapped. "You're under arrest, you gawdalmighty fool."

One thing you can say for Standers—or ex-Standers—they respect authority. Mr. Howe shrunk under the power of the law, and I felt my own flight-power subside back into the core of me. Guess that's where it lives.

As Dad helped Mom to her feet, Lorraine left Michael and knelt beside me on the bark path. "Joss, are you okay? Did Zach…?"

"No," I said. "He didn't. We beat him." Suddenly I was exhausted. "But he got away."

"Oh, honey." She smoothed my hair. "He's out of your life now. Don't think of him. I'm so sorry. I missed him completely. And Reverend Paula…oh, I was so wrong. What a disaster."

Out of my life? "Yeah. But no. Not your fault." I closed my eyes again. "I missed him too."

CHAPTER TWENTY-ONE

DEDICATION

"Chapter Thirteen: The Muggle-Born Registration Commission," reads Greta dramatically. She's the best reader of all of us, but everyone gets a turn: that's the second rule of the Last Harry Potter Book Club. The first rule is, no one reads ahead. We all signed a pledge—me, Louis, Savannah, Greta, Molly, Heather, Erin, seven of us, like Book Seven, right?—and we got Lorraine to collect all our books so no one cheats. It's the last Harry Potter book that will ever be, and we want it to go slow. We only read five chapters a day, and we make ourselves stop after every chapter and talk about it, like savoring a piece of fudge.

We are sitting on our picnic table, leaning back-to-back in pairs, us girls in tank tops since it finally turned into real summer, nearly two weeks after the Fourth of July.

"Hold up, won't Professor Umbridge recognize their voices even though they're disguised?" Louis asks. He doesn't do tank tops, but he's wearing a new T-shirt, sitting back-to-back with Erin, which I guess is cool. Of course it is.

"Yeah, that's part of the risk they're taking, they have to fake their voices too," Savannah says. Through my shoulders I can feel her patting her belly, which she does all the time now that it's pooched out a little. Since that whole crazy thing with Mr. Howe, Savannah's family and just about everybody on the island has come out and declared that her baby girl—yup, it's a girl— will be the most loved kid that ever got born. Reverend Paula's practically adopted her. The old Savannah would have gotten horribly stuck-up with all the attention, but this amazing new one looks down and smiles, and glows, just like they say. I'm feeling guiltier than ever for not sharing my secret with her.

The Howes moved off-island last week. Just closed up the drugstore and the house and took off. I have no idea where, and I couldn't care less. Standerville. No, Ex-Standerville! When I think of Mr. Howe, I still feel that wave of triumph that Mom and I shared—well, and Louis and Dad and Lorraine. They all helped get his water bottle, in fact pretty much everyone *but* me got Mr. Howe to "forsake his power." Still, I knew it was him all along. But I can't think about that without thinking of the whole Fourth of July disaster, and I'm not exactly there yet. Still kinda raw.

"You guys're giving me a headache," grumbles Michael from over by the wheelchair ramp. Dad set him up there with his own little table and a beach umbrella. "Just shut up and read, okay?"

Savannah giggles and pinches my arm. Michael is way too cool to join our club, but he says he's bored out of his mind, sitting around all day, so he might as well hear the story. I could point out he could read it himself if he felt like it, nothing wrong with his eyes. But I prefer feeling smug every time he has to admit he's as hooked as we are on the slow drama of Harry's story. And it's fun watching him try not to flirt with Savannah. She's so good at it, he doesn't even realize how easily she can make him blush.

My brother and my best friend? Yeah, I don't know. I'll get back to you on that one. Might take his mind off not being able to play guitar, anyhow. Me, I'll be okay if I don't hear anyone play guitar for a while.

Greta launches back into the story and Harry, Ron, and Hermione try to blend themselves in with their own antagonists. Somehow anti-Muggle wizards seem much more real than Standers. I stretch my arms out, feeling the sun soak in. Some kind of warbly bird makes background music for us all, a bunch of happy, sunny, normal teenagers. Savannah rubs her belly, and I think, *Yeah, it's time to tell her.*

"Hey, guess what?" calls my mom's voice from the driveway. Greta stops in midsentence. "The big bastard's going to pay."

"Who, Voldemort?" Molly asks. You gotta love her.

"You got the settlement deal?" I jump off the table.

Most of the Last Book Club look annoyed at the interruption, but Savannah high-fives me: "Woo-hooo!"

"You rock, Mom! How much?"

"Not sure yet," Mom says, strutting up to the table with her arms raised like a winning boxer. "Have to see what he counter-offers. But my lawyer's asking for a hundred thousand. For pain and suffering. Ow," she adds, bringing her arms down and clutching the brace on her neck. She's been wearing that thing since Mr. Howe attacked her, and I'm sure it really hurt in the beginning. But I also happen to know it hasn't damaged her flying one bit. "Actually kinda improved my range of motion," Mom admitted last night as we flew back from Seal Rocks under a full moon. "Must've loosened up my vertebrae or something." But in public, she still complains of neck pain and no one, not even Lorraine, argues with her. We all want to see Mr. Howe pay for the damage he caused.

"How come you guys decided not to, like, press charges?" Erin asks. It's a good question, one I asked Mom myself in those crazy moments after Sheriff Gil popped Mr. Howe in the back of his car like some punk kid.

Mom gives Erin the same answer she gave me: "No need to see him in jail. I wanna hit him where it hurts: his wallet."

"Right on, Beth," says Louis. "That's awesome." It still startles me to hear him sounding so...mature, I guess. *Like Zach.* No, nothing like Zach. Louis is a good friend, even if he is starting to hang out with Erin. He's still the only one I'll take flying. Well, till Michael recovers. And till I tell Savannah. It's just…I'm not really feeling like talking about my power with anyone right now. Flying, sure—talking, not so much.

Pain and suffering, hah. I'm the one who needs a brace, but I need it for inside of me. Too bad I can't sue for that.

"Can't believe he attacked you like that, just 'cause you stuck up for Joss and called him some names," Heather says. That's our story. "What will you use the money for?"

"Well, if we get it, which who knows," Mom says slowly, "I got some medical bills, of course. And then there are Michael's bills—yeah, you're an expensive little cliff-climber," she adds, ruffling his hair since she knows he hates it.

"A hundred thousand? Wow," Savannah breathes. "I knew the Howes were rich, but I didn't think they were *that* rich. Well, good. That piglet's gonna send my baby to college." She's taken to calling Tyler "piglet," since Mr. Howe is "that pig," and I know it's her own form of neck brace.

"Why would Mr. Howe go along with that?" Erin asks. "I mean, why give you all that money instead of fighting you in court?"

Louis and I look at each other: we know why. Since he's put his house and store up for sale, Mr. Howe can't risk a trial. Even if flying and standing and praying never got brought up, he'd still come out looking like a huge jerk, which he is. "He needs to protect his reputation," I explain.

"Seems like you'll have some money left over," Heather says dreamily. "Even after all the bills? A hundred thousand, wow."

"A hundred thousand plus three hundred," I put in. "Don't forget my essay money!"

Reverend Paula stopped by on July fifth to deliver the check I had won. "The committee wanted to give you the first prize check as well, seeing what happened, dear. But rules are rules, so Mr. Howe will get his too." Narrowing her eyes: "Much good may it do. I'll be praying for that man!"

Lorraine apologized to her then, "for misjudging you." Reverend Paula had no idea what Lorraine was talking about, but she nodded till her curls bounced like crazy, and said she hoped she'd see us all back in church soon. Lorraine and I smiled politely. But when the reverend left, we looked at each other and shook our heads.

Lorraine said, "I think kindness is enough religion for me." I'm totally stealing that.

"Yeah, well, IF there's any money left over," Mom says, "I'm gonna use it to help your dad get another boat."

Silence. Most of my friends don't even know my dad ever had a boat, ever spent his days out on the water, thinking of weather and fish and nets instead of canned soup and dish soap. Even I forget sometimes. It's not like he talks about it.

"Oh, wow," Louis says finally. "That'll mean, like, the whole world to him, getting back out to sea." *Wait, how does Louis know how my dad feels?* It's like his own kind of magic or something.

"That's the idea," Mom nods. "I'm kinda tired of watching folks be prevented from living the lives they want."

"Hey, like Joss's essay," Savannah says proudly, and Mom winks at me like we're in a sitcom.

"That would be amazing, Mom," I tell her. "Does Dad know yet? Will he sell the store?"

"Oh goodness, no, this is only my little dream," she says. "So don't say anything, okay?" I have to smile—just like Mom to expect eight teenagers to keep their mouths shut. "Anyway, it's not such a great time to be selling stores right now," she adds.

"Yeah, not until that pig sells his," Savannah says. "See ya, pig."

"Sure wish his nephew would've stuck around," Greta sighs. "*Dang*, that guy—! I mean, you know?"

Yeah. That guy. I know.

"He had to go get ready for college," Mom says firmly, which is the official story going around since Zach disappeared with the rest of the Howes. And maybe it's true, maybe he's in summer school. "All those college-student Flyers better watch out," Mom joked with me last week, trying to get me to smile. I told her I didn't care where he was, as long as it wasn't Dalby.

"Yeah, so Michael, maybe you could, like, visit Zach at University of Washington next year, right? Don't you want to go to U-Dub?" Greta urges.

"U-Dub sucks," Michael says. *Wow, he's being loyal to me!* I mean, he's wearing a Washington Huskies T-shirt. I feel like hugging my bro.

"Dude, college? You still kinda need to graduate first," says Erin. "And you guys all have three more years, y'know."

"Well, at least we're done with Mr. Evans," Savannah says. "He's all yours now, Erin."

"Nuh-uh, didn't you hear?" Molly cuts in. "Mr. Evans is teaching tenth grade next year! He told my mom yesterday at the market." She glows with superior information.

Savannah and Greta groan. But I think, *Huh. Another year of Mr. Evans?* A couple months ago I would've hated that news. Now… it gives me an idea.

Then Greta clears her throat. "Getting back to Harry…"

So I'll keep thinking.

"I have something to tell you," I say to Savannah, then take a sip of my milkshake for courage. "But you might get mad."

It's two weeks later, the end of July, and we are lounging on a sunny bench on the edge of the village marsh. It smells like salty mud and roots. From here you can see tall grass and briar bushes, and the little channels where the low-tide muck meets the clear water of the harbor. That's about it. Oh, a few houses over on the Spit, like Nate's, and a blackbird who keeps flashing his bright red wing-patches at us. Maybe he wants our milkshakes. But the thing is, nobody can see us. That's why I steered us here. Time to